Trashy Romance Novel

JACQUELINE E. SMITH

To: Sohya
Lots of love!
♡ Jacque E Smit

Wind Trail Publishing

Trashy Romance Novel

Wind Trail Publishing
PO Box 830851
Richardson, TX 75083-0851
www.WindTrailPublishing.com

First Paperback Edition, October 2017

ISBN-13: 978-0-9972450-4-2
ISBN-10: 0997245042

Library of Congress Cataloguing-in-Publication Data
Smith, Jacqueline E.
Trashy Romance Novel / Jacqueline E. Smith
Library of Congress Control Number: 2017915849

Cover Design: Wind Trail Publishing

This is a work of fiction. Names, characters, and
incidents are either products of the author's imagination
or used fictitiously. Any resemblance to actual events
or persons, living or deceased, is entirely coincidental.

Printed in the United States of America.

This book is a love letter to the land of my dreams, Scotland.
Dedicated also to all of my celebrity crushes. Here's hoping that none of them ever read it.

Prologue of *The Queen's Surrogate*

Queen Annette had been a disappointment from the moment she was born.

"A daughter, my lord," Therese, her mother's midwife, had announced as she handed the new baby over to her father.

"Another daughter," the wealthy landowner grumbled. He already had a daughter. An ugly daughter, at that. There was no way he could hope to advance his family's stature by marrying off his first-born, Jane. He'd be lucky to find a pauper desperate enough to marry her. "Well, I hope this one is pretty."

Annette did grow to be pretty; tall and graceful with long ebony hair and amber eyes that glowed with the sunset. In that, she was not a disappointment. However, she was not nearly as clever as her older sister, nor as strong, nor as fine a singer. It was not that she didn't try. Her parents found her the finest tutors in the land, but when they tried to teach her words on a page, she simply could not see the words as her tutor described them.

"It's a good thing she has that face," they all remarked to her father. "Without it, she would amount to nothing at all."

Although not as witty, Annette was a kind and gentle girl who showed great compassion to everyone around her. That, along with her resplendent beauty, had been why King William had selected her for his son, Prince Malcolm. In the King's mind, she was just the sort of lady that his rebellious, stubborn, thick-headed son needed.

Now, she had disappointed him as well.

"Your Majesty, the Queen is barren," the royal surgeon announced after an extensive evaluation of Annette's body.

Deep down, it was nothing she hadn't known. In the ten years she'd been married to Malcolm, she'd suffered seven miscarriages and delivered two stillborns. It had been four years since she'd managed to conceive at all.

The King's advisor, a sleazy, rat-faced man named Rigsley (though Annette had never been quite sure whether that was his first or last name; to her, it sounded like something she might call a dog) tried to appear distraught, but Annette knew he was secretly delighted. Rigsley adored conflict and despised the Queen. Her failure had presented him with the opportunity to step up. The only thing Rigsley loved more than conflict was proving that he was smarter than everyone around him.

"How can this be?" Malcolm asked, staring down at his Queen.

"I am sorry, my lord." And she was. The one thing she was supposed to be able to do, not only as Queen, but as a woman, and she couldn't even get that right.

The King's steely blue eyes were cold. He was a good man and he'd never given her a reason to fear him, but in that moment, Annette felt a sliver of uncertainty. What would become of her now that she could not produce an heir? Would he get rid of her? Send her to a nunnery? What if he locked her up? Or worse?

No. Malcolm would never do that to her. Even if she couldn't give him the son he needed, he would never hurt her.

But he still needed a son.

"So, what do we do?" Samuel, the old Viscount who had been Malcolm's father's friend, advisor, and confidante asked. "We need an heir. The Kingdom must have an heir. Unless you want it to go to your no-good cousin in Glenbury."

"If your Majesties would permit me," Rigsley intervened with an oily tone that made Annette's skin crawl. "I believe I might have a suggestion..."

Chapter One

It all started with a crush.

How cliché is that? I mean, of all the things to motivate a person to do something, how often does it go back to a silly infatuation? More often than most of us would probably care to admit.

Of course, this wasn't an ordinary crush on a cute coworker or a charming friend of a friend I hooked up with at a party. No, I've never met the man who inspired my books. But I'm about to.

That's right. At this very moment, I am en route to the Scottish Highlands, where a production crew is preparing to film the long-awaited television adaptation of *The Surrogate* series by Lorelei DuBois.

That's me, by the way. I'm Lorelei DuBois.

My real name is Delaney Brooks, but when I first decided to try my hand at trashy romance, I also decided I didn't want anyone I actually knew to know that I was writing. Well, that's not entirely accurate. Everyone knows I love to write. I just didn't want them to know that I was writing sixteenth-century smutty fanfiction featuring a character who happens to bear a striking resemblance to British heartthrob and the not-so-secret object of my desire, Matthew Kent. Who, wouldn't you know it, was cast as said character in the upcoming drama series, which, I'm told, is guaranteed to be equally trashy, but much less smutty. Thank God.

I never intended for anyone to actually read *The Queen's Surrogate* or any of its sequels. It started out as a fun side project for me to enjoy while I tried to finish up my Ph.D. in English at the University of North Texas. I say "tried" because I didn't actually finish. Writing a terrible romance series that somehow became an international bestseller kind of got in the way of me graduating.

Perhaps calling my own books terrible is a little harsh. But if I'm being totally honest with you, they're not good.

The idea for the story came to me one night as I was cruising my secret Tumblr account for new pictures of Matthew Kent. I found a still of him from one of his movies in which he plays a sexy nineteenth-century vampire hunter. In the picture, he's crouching in a graveyard behind the vampire's tombstone and he's wearing one of those flowing white shirts that you usually see on Disney Princes. He's covered in dirt and blood, his wavy, light brown hair is falling down and around his face, and he's sporting a really rugged beard. It was pretty much the hottest picture of anyone in the history of ever.

I've never been very good at dating. Most of the men I know exist as words on the pages of books I can't seem to stay away from. You know the old saying, "Those who can't do, teach?" Well, I have a little saying of my own: "Those who can't date, write."

That's how Matthew Kent became the inspiration behind the girlish fantasy that eventually evolved into the ultimate guilty-pleasure romance series, *The Queen's Surrogate*, *The Surrogate's Princess*, *The Surrogate's Tutor*, and *The Surrogate's Affair*.

The story goes something like this. The King and Queen of the fictional kingdom of Edin need an heir, but the Queen has just been declared barren. So, as per the evil advisor Rigsley's suggestion, King Malcolm (inspired by Matthew Kent) decides to hire a young maiden from the village to become the Queen's surrogate. After a series of competitions and challenges, Corrine Fletcher, a farmer's daughter, is chosen to bed the King and bear his child.

Like I said, it's a *really* dumb story. Admittedly, it was a lot of fun to write. I mean, a *lot* of fun. But still...

Of course, in the end, Malcolm and Corrine don't end up together. He does fall in love with her, in the beginning anyway, and she enjoys her task of making love to him a lot more than she was supposed to, but as the story evolved, she actually began to fall in love with her tutor, a brilliant young man who also happens to be Queen Annette's cousin. I honestly never intended for that to happen and I find it so interesting how characters and stories often go off on their own, in spite of whatever the author has to say.

When the producers first contacted me about filming a television series based on the books, I thought they were joking. Then I thought that even if they were serious, there was no way that it would ever actually happen. I've met several writers who've penned screenplays and signed over rights to movies that were never made. There was always a hitch, some dispute over the contract or perhaps a scene that the producers hated but the writer refused to change. But for *The Surrogate* series, there were no such hitches. The contracts were signed. The actors were cast. And the day after tomorrow, production officially begins.

I'm not going to sugarcoat this. I'm terrified. How can they expect me to act like a normal human being when real live people are going to be acting out my trashy romance novel?

My best friend, Gemma, on the other hand, is thrilled. She's traveling with me and gets to act as my "personal assistant." Of course, what that really means is that I didn't want to go by myself and I figured it might be less awkward if I had her there for emotional support. There is no way she'd ever fetch me coffee (unless I paid for it and offered to buy her one as well).

"I still can't believe this is actually happening," Gemma just whispered. We're somewhere over the Atlantic Ocean. It's the middle of the night and most of our fellow passengers are sleeping, or at least attempting to sleep. Gemma and I, however, are both wide awake. "Flying first class to Scotland and meeting Matthew Kent! Not to mention Genevieve Browne, Rose Cervantes, Colin Ward, Benjamin Wyndham... Did you ever imagine even once that one day all those famous names would be playing your characters on television?"

"Never in my wildest dreams," I admit. And it's the truth. Not just because I never dared to dream that anyone would ever create a television series based on my work, but because most of those actors are not what I envisioned for my characters at all. With the exception of Matthew Kent, of course. But Genevieve Browne is far too young to play Queen Annette. Rose Cervantes is incredibly thin and petite, quite the opposite of the curvy and voluptuous Corrine Fletcher. Notorious Hollywood rebel Colin Ward is way too hot to play the scheming, greasy Rigsley. And don't even get me started on Benjamin Wyndham who will portray Tristan, Corrine's tutor. Tristan is supposed to be handsome in a subtle, scholarly way. Benjamin Wyndham is all those things, but he's also known

5

around the world as Great Britain's Greater Playboy.

But you know, for the amount of money they paid me to turn my books into a television series, they can cast whoever they want. I'm sure all the actors will do an amazing job. Besides, it's not like these books are my pride and joy. Not by any means.

"So, while we're there, am I allowed to call you Delaney? Or is everyone on set supposed to know you as Lorelei?"

That's a very good question, actually. One to which I hadn't really given any thought. I've been too busy planning out exactly what I'm going to say to Matthew Kent when I meet him for the first time. So far, all I've come up with is, "Hi. I love you. Can I have your babies?"

That's probably not going to fly.

"Call me Lorelei. I don't need my real name getting back to anyone." There really aren't too many people out there who know that Delaney Brooks is secretly Lorelei DuBois. My parents know, of course. A few close friends. But everyone else is totally in the dark. Let's face it, penning a novel that the *New York Times* calls "sinfully satisfactory" isn't exactly something you brag about at family reunions.

"You've got it," she says. Then, she closes her eyes. For a brief moment, I think she's drifted off to sleep. But then she says, "You know the only thing that sucks, though?"

"What's that?"

She opens her eyes and looks at me.

"No one knows."

"What do you mean?"

"I mean, we're about to have this amazing adventure with some of the hottest celebrities on the planet... and we can't tell anyone without totally blowing your cover. That means no pictures with Matthew Kent, no updates from all the tourist traps we'll be visiting on our days off, no bragging about all the hot Scotsmen we get to hook up with..."

"You know, we *can* tell people that we're in Scotland. We just can't tell them why," I remind her. "Besides, we can share pictures on my author sites."

"You're missing the point, Delaney."

"What is the point?"

"The point is that we have direct access to Tommy Riggs, Gabe Abrams, Jillian Seabury, and all of our other high school nemeses through social media. We could be rubbing all of this right into their cyber faces. And yet... We can't."

"That is unfortunate," I quip.

"Oh, come on. Tell me you haven't fantasized about all of those jerks finding out who you really are. Who you've become."

"Gem, high school was more than ten years ago," I remind her.

"Yeah, and may I remind you that you skipped the reunion because of them. Don't even pretend like you're over it because I know you're not."

I really don't want to talk about the *it* to which she's referring. I'd rather sit back, turn on a movie, and try to get some rest before we land in Edinburgh. But Gemma likes to talk, especially when she's convinced she's right about something.

"I am over it. My therapist says I'm over it. Even my horoscope says I'm over it. I know you worry about me - "

"I do."

" - and I appreciate it. But right now, all I need you to worry about is making sure I don't make a complete and total fool out of myself tomorrow."

Finally, Gemma laughs.

"Sweetie, I'm your best friend, not a miracle worker."

Chapter Two

Our first glimpse of Scotland is a lovely one. The skies are gray and a glittering, silvery mist dances on fields of lush green. I've seen gray skies and green meadows back home in Texas, but nothing quite so whimsical as Edinburgh's real-life fairy tale setting. As my eyes seek to take in as much of the magic as they can through the tiny airplane window, I have to remind myself that I'll be spending the next two months here. I'll have plenty of time to gaze and wander.

A young man and woman are waiting inside the airport, holding a sign that reads *Lorelei DuBois*. I don't know why, but seeing that sign sends a nasty shock through my already jet-lagged system. As Gemma and I approach them, I struggle to calm my frazzled nerves.

You've done this before, I remind myself. *You've met people from all over as Lorelei DuBois. This time is no different. You're going to be fine.*

"Hi." I pause to clear my throat. "I'm Lorelei. And this is my friend, Gemma Price."

"I'm her assistant," Gemma clarifies.

"It's a pleasure," the young man smiles. It's a sweet smile, warm and comforting. "I'm Andrew Campbell. This is Louise Thomson. We're Mr. Reynard's assistants." Carl Reynard is *The Surrogate*'s executive producer.

"It's nice to meet you," I tell them. Meanwhile, Gemma is all but wiping the drool from her chin over Andrew and his curly golden locks.

"Oh my God, I love your accent," she gushes. I hesitate to remind her that Andrew is probably at least five or six years younger than we are. Then again, I doubt she'd care. She's been crushing on that one kid from The Kind of September for years now.

"Thank you," Andrew smiles politely. He's probably used to American women fawning over him.

"We're to ask you if there's anything you need. Coffee? Food? You're probably starving," Louise says.

"I could go for some breakfast," Gemma says. "De - Lorelei?"

Nice save, Gem.

We travel in a sleek black car to the heart of Edinburgh, passing meadows of yellow flowers and purple thistles, buildings that look like churches, churches that look like castles, and even a Starbucks. But when I catch my first glimpse of Edinburgh Castle atop a grassy green hill, overlooking the road into the city, my heart leaps into my throat. What must it be like to live here? To pass this grand, elegant, enchanting castle every day, like it isn't a scene straight out of your wildest dreams? Or your favorite romance novel? I don't think I could stand it. I think it would truly be too overwhelming. A fleeting glimpse is enough to take my breath away.

It's only then that I notice Gemma digging through my backpack.

"Where's your camera?" she asks frantically.

"It should be in there somewhere," I answer. Probably buried beneath the laptop, the power cord, the fancy UK adaptor so that I can actually plug my computer in over here, my notebook, my day planner, my water bottle, and the five different books that I brought to read on the plane but of course, I didn't read even one of them because the plane had little individual televisions for each passenger. "Why do you need it?"

"Because I'm your assistant. I need to document our trip. And because my camera broke last month and I've been too lazy to buy a new one."

"You know you can order one off of Amazon, right?" I ask her. "I'd have even let you use my Prime account. You could have had it in like, two days."

Gemma glares at me, the same way she always does when I go out of my way to explain the obvious.

"Don't worry about the camera now," Louise advises from the front passenger seat. "We'll make sure you don't miss out on anything."

"And we *can* take you to buy a new camera if you'd like." Andrew grins and catches Gemma's eye in the rearview mirror. I guess he did enjoy her flirting after all. We haven't even been here an hour and she's already scoring with the Scottish guys.

I guess I'm not really surprised, though. Gemma is blonde and gorgeous and curvy with a killer sense of style and the confidence to match. Men gravitate not only to her bombshell good looks, but her energetic and outgoing personality. She once explained to me that the only thing that men love more than a girl with nice boobs is attention from a girl with nice boobs. Not exactly Shakespeare, but she may be on to something. Guys have never flocked to me the way they flock to her. And my boobs are nothing to sneeze at if I do say so myself.

But then, I don't put myself out there the way that she does. I don't normally go out of my way to talk to guys unless they talk to me first. I don't want to say that I'm your stereotypical writer with the mousy brown hair and Manic Pixie Dream Girl quirky personality, but I'm definitely an introverted brunette who spends most of her time reading books or writing books. Or reading fanfiction that people have written about my books. By the way, can I just tell you how shocked I was to discover that those readers have taken my smutty books and made them even smuttier? I've read stories about my characters that make my own work seem mild, boring even. I honestly don't understand why anyone would bother paying for *The Queen's Surrogate* when they can read all that glorious trash online for free.

And of course, when I say trash, I mean it in the best sense of the word.

After a traditional Scottish breakfast at a small diner called Coat of Arms, we step back out onto the busy street, and I find myself glancing around the city.

"Looking for something in particular?" Andrew asks.

"Where's the Elephant House?" I ask.

Gemma closes her eyes and sighs.

"You don't need to pay homage at the birthplace of *Harry Potter*."

"Actually, yes, I do. This is very important to me."

Louise laughs. Andrew checks his watch.

"Unfortunately, we're supposed to have you back for the final read-through by two o'clock. Since it's about a three-hour drive to location, we're going to be cutting it close as it is. But don't worry. You will be able to come back."

"And you can build your shrine to the Boy Who Lived then," Gemma assures me.

"You know, you're awfully sassy for a personal assistant," I remark.

"I keep you humble."

Oh yeah, right.

Within ten minutes of our journey to the Highlands, Gemma has passed out. I guess those three cups of Scottish coffee didn't do her very much good. I should probably try and get some rest too, but how can I when this extraordinary new country is passing by before my very eyes? If I fall asleep, I might miss something.

Growing up, I always dreamed of traveling, but my family never had the money. We'd take the occasional trip to the beach or drive down to San Antonio for a weekend at the Alamo. But I wanted more. I wanted to see things that no one had ever seen before, climb the tallest mountains, and dive into the deepest seas. The older I got, however, the more I came to realize that those were pretty lofty goals, especially for a girl who couldn't run more than a few meters without having an asthma attack and who had a crippling fear of water deeper than an inflatable kiddie pool.

That's when I turned to writing. Writing, in a way, provided me with a whole new way to see the world. In fact, it did me one better. It allowed me to create my own world. One without limits. My stories became my own personal getaway, my secret escape from anything the real world could throw at me, from unpaid student loans to bad city traffic to memories of the *it* that happened back in high school.

"Oh," Louise says, breaking me out of my trance. "I thought you were both asleep back there."

"Can't sleep. There's too much to see."

"Is this your first trip to Scotland?"

"First trip anywhere, really." I know it sounds weird, but after my books hit all the bestsellers lists, I didn't go on any crazy spending sprees. I paid off my student loans, paid my parents back for all the financial support they've given me since I became a legal adult, and bought myself a house. True, I did quite a bit of traveling around the United States for book signings, but this is my first time overseas. And I'm determined to savor every millisecond.

"And what do you think?" Andrew asks me.

"It's captivating."

"I bet it's beautiful back where you come from," Louise says.

"Not like this," I tell them.

I'm not sure if anything can compare to this.

"So, are you looking forward to filming?" Louise asks me.

"I am. I think I'm also a little nervous, though. I've never been a part of anything like this before, so I really don't know what to expect," I explain.

"It's a lot of work, but a lot of fun," Andrew says. "Everyone on set is just great. We've been working with the actors a few weeks now, read-throughs and rehearsals and such, and they all seem to really be enjoying themselves."

"Really?" That's good to know. I'd hate for any of them to take one look at the script that I helped to write and instantly regret... you know... *everything*. Especially Matthew Kent because, let's face it, we're probably going to get married.

Okay, that is not even remotely true. I'll be lucky if he gives me more than two minutes of his beautiful British time. But it's the way a fangirl's mind works. Speaking of fangirling, I hope he doesn't actually read his Twitter mentions because I've tagged him in more embarrassing posts than I can even count.

"Oh yes. It's a wonderful script. Very scandalous," Louise grins. "And you know, I think it's actually going to be a very beautiful series. Aesthetically speaking. The costumes, the actors, the setting..."

She's right. I can't imagine a place more beautiful than Scotland. Or a man more beautiful than Matthew Kent. But I'll just keep that to myself.

God, maybe I need to get drunk before I meet him. I've been trying to come up with some sort of sure-fire plan to prevent me from embarrassing myself in front of him, but every scenario I imagine ends with either humiliation, heartbreak, or his withdrawal from the series. And then everyone would be royally pissed at me because then they would have to recast the part and viewers around the world would have to settle for a King Malcolm who is significantly less hot than Matthew Kent. It would probably go to someone really generic-looking and then the show would suck because, let's face it, Corrine bedding King Malcolm is kind of the point of the entire series.

Maybe I just shouldn't speak to Matthew Kent at all. Then I can remain a mystery. Men like women who are mysteries, right? And if I don't speak, then I don't have to worry about embarrassing myself and ruining the whole production.

As the hours pass, we draw ever closer to our destination and our primary film site, Dunadhar Castle. Due to its obscure location and modest size, Dunadhar Castle is often passed over by tourists seeking more famous landmarks such as Loch Ness and Eilean Donan. Because it brings in so little revenue, the owners have barely been able to afford to keep up the castle's maintenance. That's why, when the producers of *The Surrogate* series reached out with an offer to restore the castle to its former glory and use it as the set for the show, the owners happily accepted.

Now, as we drive straight through the heart of the Scottish Highlands, I feel my breath once again catching in my throat, my heart fluttering in my chest. Not because of our impending arrival at Dunadhar, but because I can't bring myself to believe that the world outside my window is real.

I've seen images of the Highlands, of course, but nothing could have prepared me for their emerald majesty, for the absolute sense of awe and wonder that I now feel, beholding them with my own eyes. For the first time in my life, words actually fail me. How can I presume to describe these beckoning mountains, these hidden rivers, these misty gray skies with mere words when even a photograph can't do them justice?

I don't realize that I'm crying until Louise reaches back with a tissue in her hand.

"Thank you," I whisper and wipe my eyes.

"It's somethin' to behold, isn't it?" she asks.

"I don't know how I've lived my whole life without this place." And I mean it. With absolute sincerity. I mean it.

Excerpt from *The Queen's Surrogate*

In the country, every day is pretty much the same. My brothers and I rise with the sun to tend to our duties around the farm.

My eldest brother, Barton, is in charge of any task that requires strength. He repairs the roof, collects firewood, and, occasionally, he escapes into the nearby woods to hunt. He's a tall, handsome man with brown hair and kind blue eyes. He will make any woman a fine husband, and there are more than a few in the village hoping to catch his eye.

My second brother, Farley, handles the family resources and finances. He is neither strong nor tall, but he is crafty. He resembles our mother in the sense that they share the same golden hair color and pointed features. Farley, in a way, has always reminded me of a fox: sly and cunning with clever eyes. When we were children, he would tease me constantly, hiding my possessions and tricking me into believing silly things that a little common sense would instantly disprove.

And then there's Hugo. Poor Hugo isn't very skilled at anything in particular, but he has a good heart and has endured far more than his share of jaunts and jeers in his time. He is only ten months my senior, and we are responsible for the simple everyday tasks that keep the household running smoothly: cooking, cleaning, tending the horses. Hugo is not handsome, but he is soft in a way that neither Barton nor Farley is, both in body and in spirit, and our parents have always been proud of him. They have always been proud of all of us, even me, their youngest child and only daughter.

Today begins like any other spring day. I wake at dawn as I always do. I feed and water the chickens, the pigs, and the horses. I collect the fresh eggs. Then I wash my hands and my face before joining my mother and Hugo in the kitchen.

After breakfast, I clean the dishes and then, before the sun rises too high in the sky, Hugo and I head out to the gardens.

We've only just begun our work when we are approached by one of His Majesty's royal messengers. He rides up on the back of a silky brown horse, far stronger and handsomer than any of our meager steeds. The man himself is tall, strong, and has the look of a knight. For all I know, he may very well be. I rarely venture beyond the boundaries of our farm. I have almost no exposure to townsmen, let alone messengers of the King himself.

"Good day, my lady," he greets me. To Hugo, he simply nods.

"Good day, Sir," I answer breathlessly, taken by his very presence. He is an older gentleman, not extraordinarily handsome by any means, but he is striking.

"Is this your property?"

"No, Sir. Our father's. Shall I fetch him for you?"

But that isn't necessary. Our father, who'd been working in the fields, saw the stranger ride up and has come to see for himself what business he brings.

"Are you the master?" the rider addresses our father.

"I am. John Fletcher. This my son, Hugo, and my daughter, Corrine."

"A real beauty to be sure. And it is of that matter that I have been sent to speak. There is to be a Tournament. In two weeks' time, every maiden of eligible age is invited to participate in the event, the winner of which will be vastly rewarded..."

Chapter Three

I've never been very good at keeping my cool around famous people.

Once, when I was in college, I got to meet my favorite band. I was so star-struck, I blabbered on and on about how their music helped me through some of the worst periods of my life. Long periods. Emotional periods. Painful periods. Of course, when I said periods, I meant periods of time. It wasn't until I stepped away that I realized how they, their security team, and all the other fans within earshot probably interpreted it. Needless to say, I wanted to bury myself in a hole and die.

Now, whenever I get the chance to meet celebrities I admire, I make a very deliberate point not to talk. Unfortunately, I'm probably not going to be able to get away with that here on location.

"This is it?" Gemma asks, gazing around at the silver trailers, the golf carts, and the portable buildings that definitely wouldn't withstand the harsh summer storms we left back in Texas.

"This is Lot B," Andrew explains. "We won't actually visit the set itself until we begin filming tomorrow."

"Yeah, don't worry. This isn't the castle," I add.

Gemma shoots me another glare.

"Smart-ass."

"Sorry, I make bad jokes when I'm nervous."

"You must get nervous a lot," she remarks.

Okay, I probably deserved that.

Andrew and Louise escort us through one of the buildings back to a deceptively large room. At the far end of the room sits a small table with a coffee pot and several barren platters of leftover fruit, bread, and one single, solitary biscuit. There are two bulletin boards hanging on the walls, one on either side of the room, and they're both covered with sketches, typed-out lists, and hand-written notes. A long conference style-desk takes up most of the room, however, and it isn't until I take a second glance that I realize that most of the people sitting around it are very famous.

Rose Cervantes, a young fresh face from America, occupies the chair closest to the door. She's only twenty-two, which, granted, is four years older than Corrine Fletcher is in the book, but still! She looks so young! She is exceptionally beautiful, however, with her petite features, honey-golden hair, and big brown eyes that give her an innocent, almost elfin appearance.

Seated next to her is British actress Genevieve Browne, who will be playing Queen Annette. The Queen is supposed to be in her mid-thirties, but Genevieve is younger than I am, only twenty-five or twenty-six. Although I would be lying to you if I said she didn't look exactly like my vision of Queen Annette with her jet-black hair and gorgeous tawny eyes.

I can't name or place the three guys on the other side of Genevieve. They may be playing Corrine's brothers or other minor roles. But I definitely recognize the man at the far end of the table. Colin Ward was the stereotypical Hollywood bad boy when I was in high school. All my friends thought he was just so dreamy and rebellious with his dark hair that fell into his gorgeous brown eyes and his motorcycle and his tattoos and every other cliché you can possibly imagine. Unbeknownst to his fans, however, he had also fallen prey to a destructive drug and alcohol addiction. He was only twenty-six years old when he almost overdosed on heroin. I remember that day vividly. It was the same day I took the S.A.T. for the first time.

I'm just going to go ahead and make a mental note *not* to mention that to him.

Thankfully, he recovered, and after he was released from the hospital, he checked himself into rehab and dedicated himself to cleaning up his life. As far as I know, he's been clean and sober for almost twelve years now. I'm glad he was able to overcome his demons. He really is a phenomenal actor and I've enjoyed a lot of his movies.

But I still don't see him as Rigsley.

Sitting across from Colin is another renowned though not quite as notorious heartbreaker, Benjamin Wyndham. Benjamin's rise to fame is a bit of a unique one. Like so many British stars before him, he actually trained to be a theatre actor. He caught his big break a few years ago when he was cast as a young Dr. Frankenstein in a modern-day remake of Mary Shelley's classic. Tall, lanky, and very ginger, I don't think anyone really expected him to become a heartthrob. But there was something about his soft-spoken nature and boyish charms that made him *very* popular with the ladies. And it didn't take him long to embrace his newfound popularity. What's funny is that he still gets type-cast as the sweet, brainy, awkward characters who rarely get the girls.

Go figure.

Carl Reynard, the executive producer, and Elizabeth Cook, the series' director, sit next to Benjamin, but there... next to Elizabeth... oh my God...

It's him.
It's really him.
Matthew Kent.

And he's looking right at me with those eyes... those intense blue eyes.

Oh God, I don't think I can move. He is *so* much hotter in person than on the silver screen. Or any screen, for that matter. To play King Malcolm, he's let his golden-brown hair grow out again. Not quite as long as it was in that vampire movie, but long enough to give him that wavy, renaissance look. His beard is also much fuller than I've ever seen it. Very regal. Very sexy. But seriously, everything about him is sexy. Even the plain blue t-shirt that he may have bought from Target for all I know is sexy, probably because it's hugging those broad, sturdy shoulders.

Lucky t-shirt.

"Ah, just in time!" Carl Reynard stands to greet Gemma and me. "Welcome, ladies. I'm assuming one of you is Lorelei DuBois?"

"That would be her," Gemma answers because I've temporarily forgotten how to breathe.

"Yeah, um... Hi." I wave like an idiot.

"It is a pleasure, Ms. DuBois," Carl says, shaking my hand. Then he turns to Gemma. "And you are?"

"Oh, this is my friend - my assistant! My... friendly assistant?" Okay, this is why no one should let me talk. Thankfully, Benjamin Wyndham chuckles, like maybe he thinks I'm cute or something. Or maybe he just feels sorry for me. It's probably the latter.

"I'm Gemma Price," Gem introduces herself.

You know, maybe we've been doing this all wrong. Maybe I should have let her stand in for me and pretend to be Lorelei. She is far more confident and charismatic than I'll ever be. She could definitely pass for a sultry romance author. Besides, it's not like Lorelei DuBois is a real person.

"Ms. Price, welcome. We're delighted to have you."

"And we are delighted to be here," Gemma says.

"As we were just discussing, this is the final read-through before we begin filming tomorrow," Elizabeth fills us in. "Now, since most of the season will be filmed inside and around the castle, we're going to begin by getting the studio scenes out of the way. The farm scene, the tournament scene, and so on. So there will be a few days this week that we won't be needing our principles quite so bright and early."

"But that's not to say you get the day off," Carl remarks, casting a sidelong glance toward Benjamin.

"Why are you looking at me?" he asks, feigning innocence. Wow, he is so aware of how cute he is.

Carl doesn't answer. Instead, he sits back down and motions for Gemma and me to sit down as well. Gemma deliberately takes the empty chair at the close end of the table, leaving the only seat available for me right next to Matthew Kent.

I'm going to strangle her.

Heart beating erratically, hands and knees trembling like I just downed ten espresso shots, I make my way over to my spot. Thankfully, I don't trip or knock anything over.

Matthew watches me the entire time.

"It's nice to meet you," he murmurs, his voice low, rough, and oh, so sexy.

"Likewise," I somehow manage to squeak. *Don't be embarrassing. Don't be embarrassing. Don't be embarrassing.* "I'm uh... really happy you're here."

I'm really happy you're here?! I mean, I guess it wasn't as embarrassing as it could have been, but I still sound like a bumbling idiot. *I'm really happy you're here?* This is his job! Where else would he be?

Mercifully, he smiles.

"I'm happy I'm here, too. I think your books are wonderful."

"You're kidding," I remark before I can stop myself. I'm instantly mortified. "I'm sorry. That was so rude. What I meant was thank you. And I think your films are wonderful."

"You're too kind. They're not even my films."

"Sure they are. What are you talking about?"

28

"Well, I didn't write them or anything. I just read the lines they tell me to read."

"I don't think you're giving yourself enough credit. You're an amazing actor."

"Well, thank you, Ms. DuBois. That's very sweet."

"Oh, D - Lorelei. Please."

"All right, Lorelei," he smiles.

I think I smile back. My face is feeling sort of numb. Probably because I just got smacked really hard with the fact that I'm sitting here talking to Matthew Kent like he isn't an actual god of hotness among mere mortal men.

"Let's begin, shall we?" Elizabeth asks. "It is worth noting that this series will be eight episodes long. Each episode will last fifty-five minutes with the exception of the pilot episode which will last eighty minutes. Now, without further ado..." She picks up her copy of the script and begins to read. "*The Queen's Surrogate*, episode one. *The Tournament*..."

I actually co-wrote the script with two other writers, Cody Wagner and Sarah MacTavish, who helped me condense all four books into an eight-episode series. Although I've never met either in person (most of our collaboration was done via Skype), I thoroughly enjoyed working with them, which sort of surprised me. Growing up, I was never one for group projects. Probably because I was usually the only one who cared to get the work done.

Like I said, I was a bit of a nerd. And an overachiever. And a goody-two-shoes who would never, ever in a million years read a trashy romance novel, let alone write one.

Unlike my moocher classmates, however, Cody and Sarah are wonderful, hard-working, and nothing short of brilliant. If this show is a success, it will be because of them, not me.

The read-through itself is actually a lot of fun, which surprises me. Normally I hate hearing my own words read back to me, but when they're recited by professional actors, it's not only bearable, it's enjoyable. I can't wait to see it brought to life on set.

It's especially thrilling to hear King Malcolm's lines spoken by Matthew Kent in his sexy, gravelly baritone voice. After all the times I tried to conjure up the sound of his voice in my head, it's surreal to actually hear it with my own ears.

"I trust him," Matthew reads.

"Well, I don't," Genevieve Browne, as Queen Annette, insists. "He is cruel, manipulative. Why else would he suggest such a thing?"

"Because the kingdom needs an heir!" Matthew spits. "And you have failed to provide one."

"I am sorry, my lord..." Genevieve sounds like she's weeping, so much so that I glance over to make sure she's okay and to see if she needs a tissue.

"You are not to blame," Matthew concedes with a sigh. "But don't you see, my love? This is the only way."

"I know," Genevieve whispers. "But to bed another woman... To parade her around in front of me while she carries your child… I don't know if I will be able to bear it..."

"The child will be *ours*. Not mine. He will belong to you as much as me. The girl... She will simply be a vessel. A mere object. Nothing more."

Of course, they're discussing Colin Ward's character, Rigsley in this scene. Rigsley is King Malcolm's evil advisor. Part of what makes him such a douchebag is the way he acts like he has the best intentions at heart while in reality, he knows precisely how hurtful he's being. The problem with Colin Ward playing him is that no one is supposed to find Rigsley even remotely attractive. I abhor Rigsley. I wrote him to be abhorred. And yet I guarantee you now, thanks to whoever decided to cast Colin Ward, fans are going to start fawning over Rigsley and writing trashy romance fanfiction about *him*. And that's just... ugh. Gross.

After Colin reads the final line in the episode, "Welcome to His Majesty's service, Mistress Fletcher," Gemma leaps up out of her seat and applauds. I'm guessing that's not something that's often done after table reads, because everyone turns to stare at her. She sits back down. Benjamin Wyndham chuckles.

"Right," Elizabeth Cook announces, "Thank you so much, everyone. Well done. I will see you all tomorrow! Except for you, Rose. Kara from the costume department needs to see you..."

"So, how have you enjoyed your time in Scotland so far?" Matthew Kent asks me as we all prepare to leave.

"Oh, I love it here," I answer. "We haven't seen very much yet, but I'd love to go back and explore Edinburgh. Maybe visit the castle."

"You definitely should," he tells me.

Then he gathers up his script and jacket and walks straight out the door without so much of a "goodbye" or "it was nice to meet you." I hate it when guys do that.

"Lorelei!" Gemma exclaims, rushing to my side. She's in such a hurry that she almost collides with Benjamin Wyndham as he tries to slip past me. "Oh! Oh, I'm so sorry, Benjamin!"

"No, don't worry. No harm done," he assures her as he flashes one of his million-dollar smiles.

"I just want you to know that I'm a huge fan. I've seen practically everything you've ever been in," Gemma sighs.

"Thank you. You're very sweet."

As Gemma attempts to work her charms on one of the world's most eligible bachelors, I can't help but notice Colin Ward maneuvering his way around his fellow cast members on the other side of the room. He slings a black backpack over his shoulder and runs a hand through his dark locks as he strides toward the door. He must sense me watching because before I can look away, his dark brown eyes lock with mine. I blush, embarrassed to have been caught staring, but, to be fair, he's probably used to it. Sure enough, he gives a swift nod, a casual acknowledgment, before disappearing out the door.

Crisis averted.

"...Well, maybe I can show you around the country sometime."

And just like that, my attention snaps back to Benjamin Wyndham, who, unless my ears are deceiving me, just offered to be Gemma's own personal tour guide.

"Oh my God, I'd love that!" Gemma squeals.

"Wait, what?" I ask.

"You'd be welcome to come along as well, Lorelei," Benjamin says.

"Well, *if* she has the time," Gemma declares. "Her schedule is going to be pretty hectic. And I should know, being her personal assistant and everything."

I'd love to point out that if my schedule is hectic, then so is that of my personal assistant. But Gem, of course, isn't really my assistant, and even if she was, I know she wouldn't let that stop her from running off to some small Scottish town with Benjamin Wyndham.

"Oh, of course," Benjamin winks at her.

"Ms. Dubois?   Ms. Price?" Louise approaches us.   "Pardon the interruption, but we're scheduled to get you checked into the hostel at four so you'll have to time to unpack and relax before dinner."

"Oh, okay. Thank you, Louise," I tell her.

"I guess I won't keep you," Benjamin says. "See you both tomorrow?"

Before I can answer, Gemma flashes him her brightest smile.

"We'll be here."

Chapter Four

"Oh, my *God*," Gemma cries out once we're locked securely in the back seat. "I can't believe this. I can't believe this. I met Benjamin Wyndham. *And* he wants to show me the country."

Judging by the look that Andrew and Louise just exchanged, this isn't the first time Benjamin has invited a girl to go exploring with him. But I'm not about to crush Gemma's hopes and dreams. Besides, it's not like I'd turn down a date with Benjamin Wyndham either.

"You wouldn't mind, would you?" Gemma asks me.

"Mind what?"

"If I took a day off to go exploring with Benjamin."

"Are you kidding? Of course not!"

"You're the best boss ever, you know that?" She smiles at me. "Speaking of hot British guys, you looked like you were getting pretty cozy with Matthew Kent..."

Oh, she did *not* just say that in front of our two new co-workers. Who know Matthew Kent.

Who work with him. Who don't know I'm totally in love with him but will probably figure it out if Gemma doesn't shut her big fat mouth.

"We were talking, that's all. He was being polite."

"I don't know. He seemed pretty interested if you ask me."

"He did just break up with his girlfriend," Louise chimes in.

"Guys, we talked for a grand total of thirty seconds, if that," I remind them. Though it is good to know that he's one hundred percent single. You never can be certain when it comes to celebrities.

"De - Lorelei, why do you always do this?" Gemma asks.

"What am I doing?"

"You're *resisting*. You have this bizarre notion in your head that it is impossible for men to find you attractive and for the life of me, I have no idea why. Well, actually, yes I do. But it's time you got over it. You're beautiful. You're smart. You're hilarious in your own special little way. It's not a crime to let yourself be desired."

God, Andrew and Louise are going to think we're insane.

"I'm not *resisting*. I'm being realistic. And the reality is we exchanged pleasantries. That's it," I insist.

"But you do fancy him?" Louise asks.

You've got to be kidding me.

I think Gemma can tell that I'm beginning to feel flustered, so without missing a beat, she grins and asks, "Doesn't everybody?"

Louise shrugs in acknowledgment as we pull into a long, circular driveway leading up to a two-story building that resembles a cabin. But not an idyllic log cabin that you'd find on the edge of an enchanted forest. This looks more like the kind of cabin you'd stay in at your first sleep-away summer camp.

"Wait a minute, where are we?" Gemma asks.

"We're here!" Andrew announces. "Welcome to the Dunadhar Highland Lodge, your new home for the next two months."

Thankfully, the Dunadhar Highland Lodge is much nicer inside than its outward appearance might suggest. Granted, it's not all that big or fancy, but it's very clean, and the air smells like fresh pine. Inside the main entry hall, there's a reception desk, just like a hotel.

"Yes, of course, welcome Ms. DuBois, Ms. Price." The girl working the desk smiles once Andrew and Louise introduce us. "Your room is on the second floor, as are the women's showers and toilets. We do serve a continental breakfast every morning and supper every evening. There is no curfew, but we do ask that you do not bring any unregistered guests into the hostel with you.

If you have any questions, someone is always here to answer them."

Once Gemma and I each have a key to our room, Andrew and Louise bid us a good evening and promise to be there first thing in the morning to pick us up.

"Call is 7 AM. But don't worry! There will be breakfast. And plenty of coffee," Louise assures us.

And then they're gone, leaving Gemma and me alone with our luggage in the lobby of the Dunadhar Highland Lodge. Thankfully, the girl who checked us in calls for two employees to help carry our bags up to our room.

Our room, it turns out, is little more than just that: a room. It's very small and almost completely empty except for a single set of bunk beds and two three-drawer dressers.

"Delaney?" Gemma says, glancing around at our meager accommodations. "We need to talk."

Yeah, I had a feeling this was coming.

"Oh?" I feign innocence.

"You told me we were staying in a four-star hotel."

"Actually, I told you we were staying in a four-star *hostel*."

"What's a hostel?"

"Well... this is," I answer.

"This is certainly about to *make* me hostile."

38

"Come on, Gem, it's not that bad."

"Delaney, we're sleeping in bunk beds."

"Yeah, so?"

"I haven't slept in a bunk bed since I was eight!"

"I'll let you have the top bunk if you'd like."

"How am I supposed to seduce Benjamin Wyndham in a *bunk bed*?"

"Well, technically since we're not allowed to have guests, you probably can't."

Not to burst her bubble or anything.

"Oh, this is *so* not how I imagined this day ending," she moans and rubs her eyes like she's trying to fight off a headache.

"Look at it this way. Chances are, we won't be here all that much. We'll just be sleeping here."

"And bathing in the community showers!"

Okay, that part does kind of suck.

"It's kind of like a dormitory."

"Delaney, I am almost thirty years old. I am well past the age of dorm living."

"So, we'll revisit our youth for a while."

"I don't want to revisit my youth. I want to make passionate love to Benjamin Wyndham while he whispers sweet British nothings in my ear."

"Well, he probably has a cot or something in his trailer. I'm sure he'd be happy to shag you there."

"Oh yeah, that'll be sexy. 'Hey Ben, you're looking hot today. Let's go hook up in your *trailer.*'"

"Better than hooking up in a bunk bed," I shrug.

Gemma narrows her eyes and glares at me.

"You think this is funny, don't you? Well, we'll see who's laughing when Matthew Kent wants to spend the night with you and you have to explain to him that he can't come back to your place because your place is *this* place."

"First of all, no, I don't think this is funny. This isn't exactly what I was expecting either. But I also don't think it's worth getting upset over something that isn't going to happen."

"And exactly *what* isn't going to happen, Delaney?"

"I wasn't talking about you and Benjamin," I assure her. And honestly, I wasn't. When Gemma decides she wants something, she usually gets it. Especially when that something is a man. "I meant Matthew and me."

"And why wouldn't that happen?" she demands.

"Because I'm just trying to be realistic, okay? Being here is a dream come true, I know. But the fact of the matter is that Matthew and I both here to do a job. The chances of him actually being interested in me are about slim to none."

"Wow, way to write him off before you've even spent any time with him at all," Gemma remarks. "Or maybe it has nothing to do with him. Maybe you're just writing yourself off before you give him the chance to prove you wrong."

I open my mouth to argue, but deep down, I know there's no point. We have this same discussion every time I meet someone. She thinks I fear rejection, so I go out of my way to sabotage my relationships. And okay, fine, maybe I do have a minor fear of being rejected, but this is different. This isn't just some guy I met at a bar or through one of those godawful dating apps. This is *Matthew Kent*. He's a movie star. He's rich. He's gorgeous. He could literally have any woman he wants. He's not going to be interested in me.

"I just don't think it's going to happen, Gem."

"Delaney," Gemma sighs. "I wish, just for five minutes, you could see yourself the way that I see you. The way that everyone around you sees you. Because if you could, believe me, you wouldn't need all these walls. You wouldn't resort to constant self-deprecation because you can't get it through your head that someone might actually find you attractive. You would be able to let yourself be loved the way you deserve to be loved."

See, this is why Gemma Price my best friend. She's picky and loud and high maintenance as hell, but she's always been

41

protective of me. She's always stood up for me, even when I'm the one putting myself down. She loves fiercely and shamelessly, and that's something that I both admire and envy.

"I love you, Gemma," I tell her.

"I love you too. Even if I do have to share this cold, crappy, not-luxurious-in-any-way room with you for the next two months."

"I appreciate that."

"You'd better," she grumbles. "So do you think the food here is better or worse than the accommodations?"

I check the time on my smart phone as my stomach begins to growl. Dinner should be served by now.

"I guess there's only one way to find out."

The dining room of Dunadhar Highland Lodge is something of a mess hall. Fitting, considering the food tastes exactly like my elementary school cafeteria food. Except instead of pizza or burgers, the hostel serves a dinner roll, overcooked green beans, roasted potatoes with no seasoning whatsoever, boiled chicken, and something that looks like brown, grainy fish eggs.

"What is this?" Gemma asks me.

Of course, our server overhears her.

"That's haggis, ma'am."

Gemma pulls back and stares at her plate, horrified.

"You mean that gross stuff that they cook in a sheep's stomach?"

"We are in Scotland," I remind her, scooping a small sampling onto my fork.

"Delaney, if you eat that, I swear to God..."

But it's too late. I bring the fork to my mouth and take a bite. It's an interesting texture, not one that I particularly like. But it doesn't taste *bad*. It's sort of like a seasoning, which surprises me. Maybe that's why the rest of the food is so bland.

"Well?" Gemma asks.

"It's not bad, actually."

"Are you kidding?"

"No." And then I take another bite, this time with the chicken.

"You do realize what you're eating right now, right? You're eating sheep guts."

"It's kind of tasty."

"Ugh, that's disgusting," Gemma shudders.

It's funny because Gemma is usually so open-minded about everything... except when it comes to food. She's the pickiest eater I've ever met. That was something that neither of us considered before embarking on this international voyage. Hopefully, she won't starve to death while she's here. True, she enjoyed breakfast this morning, but we were in an actual restaurant. Here in the hostel, our menu is rather limited.

After dinner, we retreat back to our bedroom, where Gemma climbs into the top bunk and falls asleep almost immediately. I, on the other hand, am somehow still wide awake. Grabbing a towel and my pajamas, I wander down the hall until I reach the bathroom. Inside, there are a grand total of four toilets, two sinks, and three showers.

This could be interesting.

There aren't many people staying here at the moment, but seeing as it's summer, that's likely to change. Of course, it doesn't feel like summer at all. It's the middle of June, but here in the Highlands, it feels like it could be late October.

Well, late October in Texas, anyway.

Because it's so cold and because today has been so wonderfully yet excruciatingly long, just to be able to stand here beneath the soothing, steaming water is nothing short of genuine bliss. There are few things in life that I appreciate more than a hot shower after a busy day. God, what a day. I flew across the ocean for the first time. I set foot in a new country, a new continent, for the first time. And I met Matthew Kent.

Oh my God, I met Matthew Kent. We were in the same room, breathing the same air. I could have touched him if I wanted to.

And in spite of everything I said to Gemma and everything that I still mostly believe, now that I'm alone, I allow my mind and my heart to drift, to fantasize, to imagine scenarios that might, in fact, lead to me falling into Matthew's arms, not as a starry-eyed fangirl, but as a strong, confident person, an equal… a lover.

As I daydream about what it might be like to run my hands through his golden curls, to feel his kiss on my mouth, his hands on the small of my back, a quiet voice in the back of my mind reminds me that it could never happen.

But then, something strange occurs. I remember the way Matthew smiled at me when I sat down next to him. How he told me that he'd enjoyed my book and actually seemed to mean it. He had spoken to me as though I already were a strong, confident person, an equal. And true, now I'm just a colleague. But for the first time, a new voice, even softer than the first, begins to whisper in the back of my mind.

"You know, maybe it could *happen…"*

Chapter Five

I feel like I've only just fallen into bed when my alarm goes off the next morning. I'm in the process of fumbling around for the snooze button when Gemma leaps down from the top bunk.

"Morning, Glory!" she greets me with a bright, sunny smile.

"Ugh, I forgot you were a morning person," I mumble.

"Come on, Delaney Bird! Up and at-em! First day of filming!"

As much as I am *not* a fan of loud, chipper blondes before I've downed at least two cups of coffee, I'm grateful that Gemma seems to have forgiven me for the misunderstanding about the four-star-hotel that she's not staying in.

"Okay, so how are you going to dress?" she continues as though I'm actually responsive. "I'm thinking that since we'll be outside most of the day, we should probably go comfy. And it's kind of chilly here so we'll definitely need a jacket or something. But then, we don't want to look *too* casual because, let's be honest, I'm trying to get into Benjamin's pants and you're trying to get into Matthew's pants..."

I roll my eyes and attempt to laugh off her girlish eagerness, but of course, I fell asleep last night trying to figure out exactly how to style my hair so that it says *I am a professional but I'm also totally single and open to romantic advances*.

While Gemma steps out to shower, I finally drag myself out of bed and change into my most flattering pair of jeans (you know, that one pair that fits just right, that's worn but not faded, that hug your hips just enough to flaunt your figure but not tight enough to make you or anyone around you uncomfortable), a form-fitting white shirt, and a charcoal-colored cardigan. I complete my ensemble with a pair of comfortable black riding boots and silver jewelry. Finally, I pull my dark brown hair back into a tight, preppy ponytail and apply just a touch of smoky shadow around my eyes, making them appear more gray than blue. It's so cloudy here, I imagine that will be happening a lot.

Mere minutes before Andrew and Louise are scheduled to arrive, Gemma returns, looking like a total bombshell. She's wearing black pants, a tight knee-length black sweater, and a gossamer white scarf. She also somehow found time to curl and blow-dry her long blonde hair and she's wearing large designer sunglasses even though the sun is nowhere to be seen.

"Wow," I comment.

"What do you think? Too much?" she asks.

"I think you look more like a movie star than any of the actual actors in this project," I answer honestly.

"Perfect," she smiles.

"You know, no one is going to believe you're actually my assistant," I tell her.

"Nonsense. This is how all the personal assistants are dressing these days," she teases.

"Of course it is," I comment as my phone buzzes. "Come on. Andrew and Louise are here."

Once we're in the car and both Andrew and Louise have complimented Gemma on her fabulous outfit, Andrew asks, "So how was your first night in the hostel?"

I'm afraid that Gemma is going to make some sort of snide remark about the drafty bathrooms or the bunk beds, but instead, she smiles and answers, "Oh, I slept like a rock."

"Same," I agree. "I also tried haggis."

"How'd you like it?" Louise asks.

"It was actually pretty good."

"Gross," Gemma groans.

"You're in Scotland. You have to try haggis at least once," I argue.

"The hell I do."

"Aw, come on. Haggis is great," Andrew grins. "Heart, liver, lungs..."

"Blegh," Gemma shudders.

"So, are we going to the castle?" I ask.

"Not today," Louise answers. "Today, we'll be at the studio. They're filming parts of the tournament scene, which will involve a bit of green screen. But the set itself is still pretty incredible."

Listening to Louise describe what the day has in store, I realize that I know next to nothing about what actually goes into filming a television series. I mean, sure, I've watched a few behind-the-scenes featurettes, production diaries, and cast interviews from my favorite movies and TV shows. But somehow, I don't think a fifteen-minute-long documentary on the flip side of a Blu-Ray disc is really enough to prepare me for what I'm about to experience.

At 6:55 AM, we pull into our designated parking spot and make our way into an already bustling studio. I'm a little overwhelmed by everything that's going on around me. Everywhere I turn, I see lights, cameras, workers with headsets and clipboards... It's a dizzying spiral of color and movement and I'm struggling to not lose myself in the whirlwind.

It's not until I catch sight of the buffet table, packed with fruit, beans, eggs, bacon, biscuits, and the most beautiful coffee maker that I've ever seen that I find my footing again. Without hesitation, I grab a plate and help myself to a feast that actually might be fit for a king.

Speaking of kings, I wonder if Matthew is here yet...

As though summoned by my thoughts, an actor does come strolling up to greet us. But it isn't Matthew.

"Don't you two look stunning," Benjamin Wyndham grins at Gemma and me.

"Thank you." Gemma returns his smile. "You don't look half bad yourself."

This is not even remotely true. Benjamin literally looks like he just rolled out of bed. He's wearing plaid pajama pants and an old hoodie with some sports team logo that I don't recognize.

"Well, you know," he shrugs. Then he turns his attention to me. "You ready for this, Love?"

"Um... maybe," I answer honestly.

"Don't worry. It's going to be incredible. Just enjoy the process. And the free food."

As Benjamin winks, Colin Ward appears behind him, looking a lot rougher around the edges than he did yesterday. His dark hair is still dripping wet from his morning shower and he's dressed in black athletic pants and a white tank top. He also doesn't appear to have shaved, but maybe the hair and makeup department called for a bit of stubble.

"Morning," he murmurs gruffly, filling his fancy steel thermos up with coffee. I guess he's not an early bird either.

"Aren't you cold?" I blurt out before I can stop myself. He looks up and stares at me like I'm a total idiot. I can't say I blame him. That's probably not what most girls say to him when he shows up with bare biceps. Which are actually really nice, by the way.

"Hey, Colin. Did you get to meet the girls yesterday?" Benjamin asks in a chivalrous attempt to diffuse the awkward in the air.

"No," he replies, holding out a large hand for me to shake. "It's a pleasure."

"Yeah, same." His fingers are actually quite warm. Maybe he's not that cold after all.

"Oh, my God, I love all of your movies," Gemma gushes once it's her turn. "When I was in high school, I actually had a poster of you hanging up in my bedroom. It was one of the ones from *Teen Beat Magazine*. You know, the fold-outs?"

I can tell by the look on his face that Colin Ward actually has no idea what she's talking about and honestly, why would he? By the time Gemma and I were reading *Teen Beat Magazine*, he was well into his twenties.

But you know, for someone who seems not at all thrilled to be awake or in the presence of cheerful people so early in the morning, Colin is actually very polite.

"That's sweet of you. Thank you," he says.

As other members of the cast and crew begin to file over to the breakfast table, I keep a sharp eye out for Matthew. Suddenly, I feel like I'm back in high school, waiting for my crush to come strolling through the door and worried, for some unexplainable and totally irrelevant reason, that he won't show up.

I'm trying so hard not to be *that* girl. The one who becomes so focused on the next time she's going to see the guy that she likes or what she's going to say to him that she completely loses sight of her true purpose. I like to think that I'm a fairly well-rounded individual. I have my own interests, my own hobbies. Granted, most of those interests and hobbies revolve around collecting books and reading books and writing books. But there are far worse things than fiction out there. Obsession, for example. And that's what I'm feeling now. I'm completely obsessing over Matthew Kent and his gorgeous golden locks and sky-blue eyes...

... And the fact that he just walked in. And he's the only guy in the main cast who bothered to put on nice jeans and a button-down shirt.

Breathe. Breathe. Don't act like you're waiting for him to come over and talk to you. Do something else. Talk to Gemma.

Of course, Gemma is still talking to Benjamin and Colin. Well, mostly just Benjamin. Colin doesn't seem to be paying all that much attention. I think he was just looking for somewhere to stand until he needs to be in hair and makeup.

"... Then we get to our room and... bunk beds," Gemma is telling him.

"Bunk beds?" Benjamin laughs.

"I am not even kidding you."

"How are you supposed to sleep in bunk beds?"

"That's what I wanted to know!"

"Talking about our glamourous accommodations?" I ask.

"Oh, and get this. She ate haggis," Gemma points to me. Like she's sharing some scandalous secret.

"Good, isn't it?" Benjamin asks.

"Eugh, not you too!" Gemma exclaims.

"Maybe *you* can get her to try some, Benjamin," I say.

"Challenge accepted," he flashes Gemma his cheekiest of grins.

"What's challenging?" A new voice joins the conversations, sending my heart into a regular tizzy.

I glance over my shoulder to see Matthew Kent, holding a plate heaped with eggs, bacon, and sausage. Genevieve Browne is beside him.

"These two *think* they're going to talk me into trying haggis," Gemma explains.

"It's part of the experience!" I argue once again.

"So are bagpipes, but I bet you're not going to go out and buy a set," Gemma counters.

"No, but I could buy a CD. I hear the Red Hot Chili Pipers are pretty good."

"My God, you are such a nerd," Gemma sighs.

Benjamin and Matthew laugh.

"At least she's a cute nerd," Benjamin says.

I blush.

"Aw. Thank you."

I can't believe I'm saying this, but Great Britain's Greater Playboy is quickly turning out to be one of the sweetest guys I've ever met. Of course, it could be that he knows just what to say and, being an actor, he probably does. Still, being around Benjamin Wyndham is doing wonders for my self-esteem.

"So, what do you think of all this?" Matthew asks me.

Don't fawn. Don't fawn. Remember you're his equal. And Benjamin Wyndham thinks you're cute.

"It's... unreal. In fact, unreal doesn't even do it justice."

"Is this your first time on a set?" Genevieve asks.

"Yeah. I mean, I did a few television interviews back home, but it was nothing like this."

"Wait until you see the castle. It will take your breath away," Matthew says.

I'm tempted to comment that I'm already breathless, and it has nothing to do with my surroundings, but thankfully, Elizabeth Cook calls for everybody's attention before I can make a driveling, fangirling fool out of myself.

"Well, everyone," she announces. "We made it!" The entire room bursts into thunderous applause, cheers, and catcalls. "This is going to be an amazing series, and I'm so excited to be here with all of you. Actors, my amazing crew, writers..." She nods in my direction, and I can't help but smile. I also can't help but notice Matthew glancing down at me out of the corner of my eye. I hope I'm not blushing too hard. Elizabeth continues, "It's only the first day of filming and already, I can honestly say that this team is one of the best I've ever worked with. Everyone, everyone in this room is so immensely talented, passionate, and above all, dedicated to making this project a steaming success. I can't thank you all enough for being here and for being a part of something of which I think we will all be very, very proud."

"That's typical of the director to make a welcome speech," Matthew murmurs in my ear. "Next, the AD will stand up and remind everyone to be on their best behavior, to be on time, to keep the set tidy, etcetera."

"The AD?" I ask.

"Assistant director."

And sure enough, a man I've yet to meet but whom I know to be David Moseley steps forward and says exactly that.

I look up at Matthew.

"So, I take it you've done this before." I hope he can tell that I'm flirting. I'm not very good at it.

"Once or twice," he winks.

Or maybe I'm better than I thought.

It doesn't take me very long to learn that there is very little downtime on set once things get rolling, and especially once the actors have all been to hair and makeup.

Let me tell you, they all look *incredible*.

Rose, as Corrine, is dressed in a simple but beautiful tan-colored gown, a leather corset, and leather arm cuffs to match. Her golden hair is tied back in an elegant braid and her fresh, lovely face bears little make-up. She looks just as I imagined Corrine might, preparing for the grand tournament that will change her life.

Genevieve looks stunning in Queen Annette's spectacular red gown and pearl-beaded headdress. She probably won't have very much to do today since Annette and Malcolm are mainly spectators throughout the three tournament chapters of the book.

Speaking of Malcolm... Oh my God, Matthew looks so *unbelievably* handsome as His Majesty, King Malcolm Frederick William Saxe of Edin. I'm not even going to say he looks hot because that word is so cheap and overused and shallow. It's easy for guys to pull off hot. Very few men, nowadays anyway, can be described as genuinely handsome. But wow, is he one of them.

The costume department has given Matthew a very regal yet still very masculine look which probably isn't at all historically accurate. His burgundy tunic is trimmed with faux fur and gold and the golden crown that he wears fits more like a wrap-around headband. With his wavy golden locks and those bright blue eyes, he looks exactly like he just stepped out of a fantasy tale.

Or at least my fantasy.

Standing a few steps behind Matthew are Colin and Benjamin. I can't hear what Benjamin is saying, but whatever it is has Colin chuckling under his breath. Seeing the two of them together, I suddenly remember that this isn't the first time they've worked with each other. Colin played The Creature to Benjamin's Victor Frankenstein in the modern-day adaptation. He looked so monstrous, so deformed, he was virtually unrecognizable as Hollywood's hottest reformed rebel. I guess that's why it took me so long to make the connection.

I definitely recognize him now. Our costume and makeup department have made no effort to make Rigsley any less attractive than the actor portraying him. In fact, I'm almost tempted to say that he looks even better in his charcoal gray tunic and with his hair styled back off his face. Then again, this is also the first time that I've seen Colin smile in person. That smile brightens every one of his striking features, transforming him into someone entirely new.

I guess his eighteen ounces of coffee finally kicked in.

Then there's Benjamin. He looks so adorable as Tristan I can barely stand it. He's wearing a floppy brown cap atop his messy ginger locks that gives him that sweet, scholarly look. Of course, the cheeky, flirtatious British boy toy is still there in his sparkling hazel eyes.

The scene they're filming today was actually one of my favorites to write and I guarantee you it's going to look so much cooler on screen than it did as words on a page.

The whole point of the tournament is to select the maiden who is most likely to provide the King with a healthy, intelligent, and of course, male heir. Ergo, she herself needs to be strong, quick-witted, and skilled. In the book, beauty and age also played a factor, but Cody, Sarah, and I decided to cut that since Corrine's abilities are far more important than her looks. And there's only so much we can cram into an eighty-minute pilot.

What I love about this scene is how it will go on to show Corrine's relationship with her three older brothers and how they helped her to become resourceful and intelligent and strong. From Barton, she learned her skills. From Farley, her wit. And from Hugo, her strength and endurance. This will all be shown in a series of flashbacks as Corrine learns of each task and prepares for them. I can't wait to see the final cut.

The set itself, I hate to say it, is a little underwhelming. I'd been anticipating taking my first steps back in time to the country of Edin for months now, ever since I signed the contract. But so far, my imaginary kingdom looks a lot like a renaissance faire set against a green screen backdrop.

"It will look better in post-production," Matthew assures me with a knowing smile.

Oh, great. Do I really look *that* unimpressed?

"Is it difficult?" I ask him. "Acting in a place that's not really... you know... there?"

"No more difficult than crafting an entire world from nothing," he replies. It takes me a moment to realize he's referring to my books.

"Not quite nothing. I had... inspiration," I confess with what I hope is a sultry glance.

But before he can respond, he and the rest of the cast are called to set and he walks off, once again, without any sort of parting sentiments.

Benjamin, however, pats me on the shoulder as he passes.

"Here's to you, Love," he grins.

"No," I tell him. "Here's to all of you."

Excerpt from *The Queen's Surrogate*

I don't know what to think.

I fought my hardest in the tournament, all for the promise of a better life for my family. I withstood judgment and physical exertion, puzzles and excruciating riddles, truly believing that if I could just see these games through to the end, my parents, my brothers, and I would never want for anything.

I expected honor, glory, wealth.

I hadn't been expecting this.

"Your task is a simple one," the dark man named Rigsley has just informed me. "You are to bed the King and bear him a son. Once you are with child, you will not be permitted to leave the castle grounds. You may write to your family, but no one is to know of your condition. For although you may carry the young Prince in your womb, he will not be yours. He will be the son of Their Majesties, King Malcolm and Queen Annette."

Rigsley goes on to promise compensation for my services to the crown. Wealth, education, a match with an eligible and wealthy man of His

Majesty's court, a title... This was all contingent, however, on whether or not I could provide the Kingdom with a male heir.

"Do you accept these conditions?" Rigsley asks.

For what may very well be the first time in my life, I find myself unable to speak. I have, of course, dreamed of the act of love. Of warm embraces, gentle kisses, passionate whispers exchanged in the dark of night. But in those dreams, the man with whom I shared this love was my husband, a man with whom I had exchanged vows. I have never imagined lying with a man whom I had not wed. It simply was not done.

Yet, I am being instructed to do just that. To bed a man to whom I am not married. And not just any man. The King. The King himself. A man chosen by God to be my lord. My sovereign. And now, my lover.

How am I to stand in his presence? How am I to meet his eye?

... How am I to refuse?

"Yes," I finally answer. "I accept your conditions."

Rigsley smiles, a twisted, curling grin that chills me straight to the bone.

"Then let it be so. Welcome to His Majesty's service, Mistress Fletcher."

Chapter Six

Four days into filming and I'm finally beginning to adapt to waking up at 5:30 in the morning. I'm a night owl by nature. I've always had trouble falling asleep before 1 AM. In fact, my normal bedtime is usually closer to 3 or 4 AM. And adjusting to a time-zone six hours ahead of my own nocturnal clock has been quite the challenge, especially considering the sun doesn't set here until past 10 PM.

Our first night here, I was so tired I fell into bed without realizing that it was still light outside. But the painted blue and orange skies got the better of me after that first day of filming. Upon returning to the hostel, I showered, changed into my pajamas, snuggled into the bottom bunk that I eventually plan on converting into a blanket fort, and buried my nose in a book, *The Wall Outside* by James William Peercy. Lost in the mystical world of Elves and Pixies, and deceived by the warm glow of daylight outside my window, I didn't realize how late it had gotten until I checked the time on my phone. Of course, when I poked my head out to express my surprise to Gemma, she was already asleep.

Now, as we prepare to head downstairs to meet Andrew and Louise for our morning commute, I notice Gemma throwing her toothbrush, travel deodorant, and a tiny bottle of shampoo into her purse.

"Running away?" I ask her.

"Planning ahead," she corrects me.

"In case Andrew and Louise forget about us and we're forced to camp out on set?"

"Oh sweetie, you're so innocent. Are you sure you wrote all those steamy sex scenes?" she asks, tossing out her blonde hair with perfectly manicured fingers. "I'm packing a just-in-case bag."

"A what?"

She sighs.

"A bag containing my bare essentials just in case someone - like Benjamin - asks me out tonight."

Ah. I get it. I've never done that. But I get it.

"Okay, but what makes today so special? Did he say something to you?"

"No, but tomorrow is our first day off so I'm thinking that if something is going to happen, it will happen tonight."

God, what I would give to have even a fraction of Gemma's confidence. Even if only for an hour. I just want to know what it's like.

"I forgot about our day off," I comment.

"And that's why you have an assistant," Gemma grins. "So, what are going to do tomorrow?"

"Sleep."

"*What*?!" Her yelp is so high-pitched, it actually startles me. "Delaney, you are in *Scotland*. The land of kings and queens and witches and all that other crap you love. You need to get out! Explore! Have adventures! Get Matthew Kent into a kilt and then get him out of it! And then, after you've had your way with him, go see if you can catch a glimpse of the Loch Ness Monster!"

She has a point. I'd love to get out and play tourist. And see Matthew Kent rocking a kilt. I knew a group of frat guys back in college who would wear kilts to beer festivals and they just looked ridiculous. But here in Scotland? I'd totally go for a guy in a kilt.

"Okay, I promise I'll go out and have an adventure."

"That's my girl. Now, as your assistant, I feel it is my responsibility to let you know it is officially time to go downstairs."

As usual, Andrew and Louise are already waiting outside the hostel. Punctuality, I've learned, is a big thing in the film industry.

"We have a surprise for you," Louise announces as soon as Gemma and I have shut the door.

"Is it chocolate?" Gemma asks. Our dessert options are rather limited at the Lodge and we're both beginning to go into chocolate withdrawal.

"Not exactly," Andrew answers. "We're going to the castle today."

I can't help it. I gasp.

"Wait, really?"

"Really," Louise grins.

The drive into the rolling hills of the Highlands is dizzying, but not because of the ride itself or the breathtaking scenery. My head is literally spinning with excitement and anticipation over the thought of finally seeing the castle for the first time. I want to savor it. I need to savor it. Every decision I've made, every step I've taken, every word of every page I've read and written has led to this moment. Seeing my characters brought to life before my very eyes has been a dream come true. But there's something about Dunadhar Castle that keeps calling me. As if it knows me. As if it's been waiting for me.

Of course, like so many things, I know this is all in my mind. This castle isn't alive, nor does it possess any sort of real significance to my life. But it stands to remind me of every wondrous thing that exists, everything we tend to overlook or forget about.

This is a moment I don't want to forget.

And as soon as the castle comes into view for the first time, I am quite certain that I won't.

It first appears as little to behold, a fleeting glimpse of a mossy, gray structure through the early morning mist. But as we draw closer, it begins to take shape. Nestled against the backdrop of the majestic Highland mountains, Dunadhar Castle seems to have been frozen in time. For surely a building so beautiful, a fortress so grand, cannot exist in our modern day. And yet, here it is, before my very eyes. Its stone walls topped with turrets, its towers barely visible through the haze.

This land has a long memory, and I can almost feel the ghosts of centuries past watching as I climb out of the car and gaze up at a structure that has seen and endured more than I can even begin to fathom.

"Now *this* is cool," Gemma breathes.

I can only nod in agreement. For once, I have no words.

Breakfast is served in a large portable building set up in the parking lot, or the car park as the Brits may say. It's strange, I know, to imagine a seven-hundred-year-old castle with a parking lot. But since Dunadhar Castle now serves primarily to attract tourists, it makes sense that those tourists would need a place to park their vehicles.

"We've finally made it," Benjamin exclaims, joining Gemma and me at the breakfast table. "God, the castle is amazing. You know, I wanted to be an archeologist as a boy."

"Did you? I don't think I knew that," Gemma smiles. That's a total lie, by the way. She's just as big a celebrity stalker as I am. She could probably tell Benjamin the name of his maternal grandmother's childhood poodle.

"So, what changed your mind?" I ask him.

"Turns out archaeologists spend a lot of time outside and I've got very fair skin." His response is so prim and British that I actually find myself sputtering with laughter into my morning coffee. Very dignified.

"Please don't choke," Gemma begs me. "It may reflect badly on me as your personal assistant if I let you die."

"I'm not going to die," I assure her.

"You'd better not. I'd hate for you to kick it before you get to watch Matthew Kent act out all your dirty fantasies."

And that's when I almost choke for real. Thankfully, she worded it in a way that doesn't entirely betray the best friend code of honor. It's true, Matthew Kent is going to be acting out my fantasies. But still. Was that really necessary to blurt out *right in front of Benjamin*?

"Yeah, about that..." Benjamin begins and I swear to God, my heart almost stops. My mind is racing down every horrible path to which this particular conversation could easily lead. *Are you keen on Matthew? Did you write King Malcolm for*

67

him? Why are you always checking out his arse? "You wrote four whole books about Corrine shagging Malcolm, but you really couldn't throw Tristan a little love?"

"Hey, Tristan gets her in the end," I remind him.

"Well yeah, but he doesn't get to have any fun. Why doesn't Corrine tear *his* clothes off for a change?" he asks as Colin arrives to fill his thermos with his usual eighteen ounces of black coffee. Colin catches the last part of that and looks slightly alarmed.

"I'm not going to ask," he remarks.

"Wise decision," Gemma smirks.

"I'm sorry, Benjamin," I apologize. "If I had known while I was writing it that one day, you would be cast as Tristan, of course, I would have written you steamier material."

"Yes, well, remember that when you sit down to write your next book," he instructs me. Then he asks, "So do you lovely ladies have plans for tonight?"

"No - " I begin to answer, but Gemma elbows me in the ribs.

"We were thinking we might go out to dinner, then maybe go for a hike," she smiles.

Wait. What is she doing? I thought she wanted a date with Benjamin.

"Well, you know, Colin here and I were talking about driving into Inverness tonight. It's about an hour away, but it's got a few good pubs.

You know, if you'd like to join us," Benjamin says. "So, what do you say?"

"Yeah, what do you say, Lorelei?" Gemma asks me. Then she turns to Benjamin. "It's really up to her."

It's up to me? Since when? I think it's pretty obvious that of the two of us, Gemma is the one who wears the pants.

And yet, she's still waiting for me to make a decision.

Oh, right. I'm supposed to be her boss.

"Uh... I think it sounds like fun." I think that's the right answer. With Gemma acting so strange, it's difficult to know for sure. But I'm pretty sure she'll actually strangle me in my sleep if I deny her the chance to spend a night out on the town with Benjamin Wyndham *and* Colin Ward.

"Then it's settled!" Gemma announces. "We're in."

Colin looks up from his coffee but doesn't say anything. I can't tell if he's okay with Benjamin inviting us along or secretly wishing that we'd politely declined. Oh well. I guess it's too late to back out without making things really awkward.

"Great," Benjamin smiles. "I'll tell Andrew and Louise not to worry about picking you up this evening."

It isn't until Benjamin and Colin are called back to hair and make-up and Gemma grabs my wrist with a poorly suppressed squeal that I fully realize what I just agreed to.

"Did that really just happen?" I ask her.

"You bet it did! And you were marvelous!" she says. "But a friendly word of advice. Never tell a guy you don't have plans. It makes you sound like a loser."

"Gem, in case you haven't noticed, I'm a *huge* loser."

"But you're a loser going on a double date with two of the hottest guys in Hollywood tonight! Suck on that, Tommy Riggs!"

Okay, I truly don't think this is a *date* date. I think this is more of a friendly outing with colleagues. Granted, they *are* two of the hottest guys in Hollywood, and I'm definitely looking forward to getting out of the hostel for the evening, but still. It's not a date.

While assistant director David Moseley breaks down the scenes that the actors will be filming today, Andrew and Louise offer to take Gemma and me on a quick tour of the castle before they begin shooting the first scene. Of course, we have to weave our way through cameras, lights, and the entirety of the production crew that isn't still back in the main trailer, but I can still get a pretty good idea of how the castle might look on an ordinary day.

It's darker inside than I'd thought it'd be, and there are halls and passageways with ceilings so low, I could reach up and touch them without even standing on the tips of my toes.

"Back when these castles and abbeys were built, people were shorter, smaller," Andrew explains. "There're a few winding staircases here that'll have you feeling like you're crawling."

For the first time since finding out we were sleeping in bunk beds, Gemma's enthusiasm waivers. She doesn't have many downfalls, but claustrophobia is one of them.

Thankfully, the stairs that lead up to the bedrooms where all my dirty fantasies will be acted out are all quite open. And beautiful. The walls are lined with colorful tapestries, gold-plated lanterns, and stone carvings of lions and unicorns.

"The lion represents the royal banner of Scotland and the unicorn is Scotland's national animal," Andrew says.

"Wait, seriously?" Gemma exclaims. "Your national animal is the *unicorn*? I'm so jealous. That's so magical."

"Everything about Scotland is magical," I say. "Speaking of magic, do you know where I feel like we are right now?"

"Don't say it," Gemma warns me.

"You know what I'm thinking."

"Yes, I do, and I'm begging you not to say it."

"I feel like we're at Hogwarts!"

"And you said it," she sighs.

"Oh please. Stop acting like you don't love *Harry Potter* just as much as I do."

"*No one* loves *Harry Potter* as much as you do."

"I don't know. I think Benjamin Wyndham could give her a run for her money," Louise remarks.

"Wait. Benjamin is a Potterhead too?" I gasp. "Oh, I am so bringing this up tonight."

"Noooo," Gemma groans.

"What's tonight?" Andrew asks.

"Oh, I guess he hasn't talked to you yet. Benjamin and Colin are taking Gemma and me out to a pub tonight," I inform them. "That means you get the evening off."

"Going out with Benjamin and Colin, eh?" Louise asks with a mischievous grin.

"It's not like that," I insist.

"Speak for yourself," Gemma remarks.

"Okay, it's like that for *her*. But I just want to go out and have fun."

"Well, you couldn't have picked two nicer guys," Louise tells us. "Benjamin is a sweetheart. Such a charmer. And Colin is just a real gentleman. A genuinely kind person if ever I met one."

"He doesn't talk very much," I comment.

"Oh, no, he does. He just also happens to be a very good listener," Louise says.

"*That* is a very sexy quality," Gemma says.

"And uh... what about Matthew?" I ask, trying and failing to sound like I'm asking out of innocent curiosity. Aside from a few passing pleasantries, we haven't spoken very much since those first few days.

"Oh, he's friendly to be sure. But he's a bit aloof. He doesn't seem to connect very well with people. But he is *very* easy on the eyes and a splendid actor," Louise says.

Before I can figure out what she means by all of that, Andrew's phone buzzes.

"It's time to head back downstairs," he tells us. "They're ready."

Chapter Seven

In case you were wondering, no, they didn't film any of the fun stuff (i.e. the naughty stuff) today. That doesn't start up until the second episode and today was the last day of shooting the pilot. However, I did get to see Matthew Kent in his sexy medieval nightshirt so you know, today wasn't a total loss. Too bad when I mentioned that I was going to Inverness with Benjamin and Colin, all he said was, "That sounds like fun," and not, "Your eyes sparkle like moonlight glistening over the Atlantic Ocean on a clear summer's eve. Go out with me instead."

Okay, I doubt anyone has ever actually said that, but I'm a writer. I embellish.

Now, Gemma and I are waiting around outside the castle for Benjamin and Colin to change out of their costumes. It's a lovely evening, though of course, with the delayed sunset, it could very well be the middle of the afternoon instead of 5:30 PM.

"Are you nervous?" Gemma asks me.

"No. Why?"

"You're quiet."

"I'm savoring."

"It is beautiful, isn't it?" she sighs. "Next week, be sure to bring your camera."

"Yes, ma'am," I say as Benjamin strolls up, looking cute and relaxed in jeans, a long-sleeved t-shirt, and scarf. He's so British, it's adorable.

"So, when you're off the clock, you're the boss?" he asks Gemma.

"Something like that," Gemma grins.

"She's actually my best friend," I confess.

"Oh, I had that figured from day one," Benjamin says.

"Really? What gave us away?" Gemma asks.

"Well, for one thing, you are *far* too beautiful and headstrong to be anyone's assistant." Okay, if he hadn't already made her day by inviting us out tonight, that comment alone would have done the trick. "For another thing, I've never once seen you bring her coffee."

"See, I told you that would be a giveaway," I tease.

"I'm more of the emotional support kind of assistant," Gemma explains.

"Is she good at what she does?" Benjamin asks me.

"The best," I smile.

Colin appears moments later, dressed in well-worn jeans, an old concert t-shirt, and a black blazer. His hair is still styled back, but he can pull it off. I have a feeling Colin Ward can pull off anything. He also smells good. Like, *really* good. Very clean and masculine. And once again, he's carrying his backpack slung over one broad shoulder.

"I didn't keep you waiting long, did I?" he asks. I remember what Louise said about him being a gentleman.

"You've just always got to be the prettiest one in the lot, don't you?" Benjamin asks.

Colin shrugs.

"Guilty."

The weirdest thing about driving into town with Benjamin and Colin is that it really isn't weird at all. It feels like going out for drinks with two colleagues after a long day of work. And technically, that's what it is. Granted, they're rather famous colleagues, but after spending the whole week with them, I'm actually very comfortable around them.

Well, okay, I'm comfortable around Benjamin. Colin is still a bit of an enigma. He is a very nice person, but it's difficult to tell what he's really thinking. Unlike Benjamin, who is a precious and very chatty open book.

"... and then - and this is where it gets embarrassing - I ask her if she's seen the movie. She was *in* it. And I'm standing there like a bloody idiot rambling on about how much I love it and I didn't even recognize her. So if you happen to sense a little tension between

Genevieve and me, please know it's because I probably offended her."

"I'm sure she'll get over it," Gemma assures him. "Everyone has those moments."

"It's true. I had one the other day. I'd forgotten that you were both in *Frankenstein*, but when I saw you together, I realized," I tell Benjamin and Colin.

"That, I think, was actually one of my favorite roles," Colin says.

"Me too. It's the only time I can look at the two of us standing side by side and honestly say that I'm the better-looking of the pair," Benjamin remarks.

"Sounds like someone has a bit of a man-crush," Gemma teases Benjamin.

"A bit? It's a full-on man-crush," Benjamin admits. "Colin'll never admit it, but we've got a nice little bromance going on."

"What are you talking about? I fully acknowledge it," Colin insists.

"All right, then tell me something you love about me," Benjamin says.

"Your eyes," Colin answers automatically.

"Cop out. Everyone loves my eyes."

"Your sense of humor."

"That's a little better."

"Your ability to see the good in everyone."

"See? Now we're getting somewhere. Go on."

Colin turns around in the front seat and glances back at Gemma and me.

"Anyone else want to take a shot at it?" he asks.

"What? You can't have run out of things already!" Benjamin exclaims.

"I've always been an underachiever." So says the man who overcame drug addiction and alcohol abuse and went on to resume his career as one of the biggest movie stars of his generation. Yeah, he's a real slacker.

By the time we finally arrive in Inverness, we're all famished. We park and head straight to the first pub we see, The River Tavern. Like most pubs, the lighting is dim and the majority of patrons are seated around the bar, swigging beer out of crystal mugs. The tavern's color scheme is red, brown, and gold and the air smells of delicious food that is sure to enrich my soul and clog my arteries. We settle into a booth near the back, where our server appears almost immediately with laminated menus.

"So what'll it be? Drinks all around?" he asks. He barely looks old enough to drink himself. Then I remember we're in Scotland where the drinking age is eighteen, not twenty-one.

"Not for me, thanks," Colin says. "I'll take an Irn Bru."

Benjamin and Gemma each order a beer and a shot of whiskey, but I simply ask for water.

78

"What's this? A writer who doesn't drink?" Benjamin asks.

"I do drink, just not on an empty stomach."

"Yeah, do you think she could have written some of those scandal-icious scenes sober?" Gemma teases.

"Since you brought it up, I've got to ask. What actually inspired you to write those books? Have you got your own undercover lover back home?"

Gemma lets out a shrill and mildly insulting shriek of laughter.

"Lorelei? Please," she snickers.

"Thanks, Gem."

"So that's a no, then?" Benjamin asks.

"No. No secret boyfriends. No love affairs with kings or princes."

"Okay. So, what *did* inspire you?"

I'm definitely not about to admit to Benjamin and Colin that I wrote *The Surrogate* series exclusively as an homage to their fellow cast member, Matthew Kent, and all his heart-stopping glory. So instead, I tell them, "I watch a lot of *Masterpiece Classic*."

"And lust after all the sexy British men?" Benjamin winks.

"Exactly."

"Makes sense." Then, he turns to Gemma. "And what about you, Darling? What do you do when you're not pretending to be a personal assistant?"

"I'm still trying to figure that out, actually," Gemma confesses. "I've worked every odd job you can imagine. I've been a lifeguard, a bank teller, a salesgirl, an office assistant, a bartender... I've even thought about going to school to become a court stenographer."

"That is quite the impressive resume," Benjamin remarks. "Colin, you worked a few odd jobs, didn't you? Back in the day?"

"I was a busboy in L.A. for a while. That's actually where I made a few of my early connections."

It's Hollywood lore that Colin Ward was sleeping with famous actresses before he was an actor himself. *That's* how handsome and charismatic he is. Whether or not that's actually true, I have no idea. But I wouldn't be surprised if it were.

Our server returns with a tray of drinks and a notepad to jot down our orders. When I ask for fish and chips, Gemma laughs at me and asks, "Could you be more basic?"

"What? Fried fish is delicious," I argue. "Besides, I've been here almost a week and I haven't had genuine Scottish fish and chips yet. It's time to remedy that."

"In case you haven't noticed, boys, Lorelei is all about the experience," Gemma explains to Benjamin and Colin.

"That's not a bad thing," Colin says.

"Thank you."

"So what other experiences are you hoping for while you're here?" he asks.

"Oh God, that's a long list," I answer truthfully. "I want the chance to *really* explore Edinburgh. I'd love to see Eilean Donan. Then there's Isle of Skye and the Fairy Pools..."

"I want to find Braveheart," Gemma adds.

"You'll have to drive down to Stirling for him," Benjamin tells her. "Nessie, on the other hand, is right down the road."

"Wait, really?" I ask. Geography was never my best subject. If you handed me a blank map of Scotland, I couldn't point to Inverness. I probably couldn't even point to the Highlands, and that's a little sad since it's basically the northern half the country.

"Yep. Only about a twenty-five-minute drive," Benjamin says. "The name Inverness actually means Mouth of the River Ness. The river itself connects to Loch Ness and runs from Loch Ness to the sea."

Wow. Having Benjamin around is like having a tour guide. Even better because he's really cute and he and Colin have offered to pay for our food.

"That's what we should do tomorrow!" Gemma exclaims. "We should spend the day at Loch Ness. See if we can't catch a glimpse of Nessie!"

"Why, what a delightful proposition," Benjamin smiles.

My first thought is that while I'd love to see Loch Ness, it seems like a bit of a hassle to drive all the way back to our respective lodgings only to drive right back in the morning. But of course, everyone else is about five steps ahead of me.

"Is there anywhere we can stay for the night?" Gemma asks.

"Oh, for certain. In fact, I've already found a nice inn," Benjamin says, scrolling through his phone. "So, what say the bard and the Ward?"

"Sounds good to me," Colin says.

Although I'm sorely regretting not taking Gemma's advice and packing a just-in-case bag, I certainly don't want to be the only dweeb who declines because she forgot her toothbrush and jammies.

"I'm in," I agree.

Gemma gasps and leans in to hug me.

Since it's still light out after we finish eating, we decide to get out and wander around the city until we find another pub. Of all the people still out and about this evening, I notice at least one or two craning their necks to see if it really is Benjamin Wyndham and Colin Ward casually strolling down the street with one gorgeous blonde and a brunette who kind of looks like that girl who wrote that stupid trashy romance novel.

You'd be surprised how often I get that. I don't get recognized in public very often. That's one of the perks (or downfalls, depending on your perspective) of being an author. Unless you're J.K. Rowling or Stephen King, it's pretty easy to fly under the radar. But there have been several times, especially in bookstores, that someone has come up to me and said, "You know, you look a lot like the girl who wrote *The Queen's Surrogate*."

Yes. Yes, I do.

The second pub we happen upon is a music bar. Now, being the basic American tourist that I am, I expect to step into a rowdy scene of drunken Scottish men jigging along to bagpipes, fiddles, and drums. That, my friends, is what all the intellectuals out there refer to as a stereotype. And it's not what I find at all inside the pub simply known as Murray's. The atmosphere is mellow, very relaxed and laid back. Most of the patrons are gathered around the small stage at the center of the room, where a young man with long auburn hair strums out a slow contemporary tune on an acoustic guitar. He's accompanied by a girl playing an old-fashioned piano and another young man keeping time with a bodhrán.

"All right DuBois, your stomach isn't empty anymore. I'm buying you a drink," Benjamin insists.

"Okay, fine," I laugh. "Get me whatever the house recommends."

"And for you, my darling?" he asks Gemma. I can tell she's fighting the urge to squeal.

"I'll take a dark ale."

"Another Irn Bru for you, mate?" Benjamin asks Colin.

"No, thanks. I'm good," Colin says.

Once Benjamin returns with our drinks, we find another table near the back of the pub. It doesn't take very long at all for Gemma to scoot her chair over to Benjamin. Or for him to wrap his arm around her shoulders. Or for her to start leaning in and whispering to him and him alone. I try my best to ignore them, to keep my attention on the musicians on stage, but I keep stealing glances of my best friend wrapped in the embrace of her favorite celebrity crush. In this moment, she is simultaneously my inspiration, my hero, and the person I envy most in the entire world.

Then, out of the corner of my wandering eye, I notice Colin rise up out of his chair, weave his way through the crowd and out the door. It's probably the alcohol lowering my inhibitions, but I suddenly find myself standing up to follow him.

I peak my head outside the door to see he hasn't gone far. He's leaning against the wall next door, staring down at his phone. He looks up when he realizes he's being watched.

"Hey," I greet him before fully committing to stepping outside and letting the door close behind me. "You okay?"

It only then dawns on me that I may have made a mistake. Maybe he wanted to be alone.

But instead of sending me away, he runs his spare hand through his hair and says, "Oh yeah. I was just getting lousy reception in there."

"Oh."

Before things can get awkward, he beckons me with a wave of his hand. "Come here." Curious, I walk over to him. He holds out his phone. "Look at this. My nephew took his first steps this morning."

I don't know why, but I'm surprised. This is absolutely the last thing I expected him to show me. The little boy in the video is adorable, with wide, curious eyes and a headful of dark hair, just like his uncle.

"He's so cute. What's his name?"

"Brayden Kyle. He's a character, let me tell you."

"I don't think I knew you had a nephew."

"Oh yeah. Three. And two nieces. Brayden's the youngest of the bunch."

"I don't have any brothers or sisters," I tell him. "I guess the closest I'll get to being an aunt is if Gemma has kids. And somehow... I just don't see that."

"Is she not the settling down type?"

"Not exactly."

"She and Benjamin should get along then," he grins.

"I think they already are." Colin nods in acknowledgment. And then, for reasons beyond my mortal comprehension, I say, "You know, I really didn't think you'd make a good Rigsley."

Thankfully, Colin laughs.

"Since he's so despicable, I'm going to take that as a compliment." Oh, thank God. Then he asks, "So what do you think now?"

"Well, don't take this the wrong way, but I think you're great," I smile.

"Proved you wrong, did I?"

"No, it's not that. I always knew you were a good actor. You just don't look like Rigsley," I say.

"Oh yeah? What's he supposed to look like?"

"He's supposed to be gross. Not... you know... you."

"Not me?"

"You know. Hot."

"You think I'm hot?" Colin grins.

"You don't?"

This time, he actually throws his head back when he laughs.

"I'm not sure there's an entirely appropriate way to answer that."

A week ago, if someone had told me that I'd be standing on the streets of Inverness with Colin Ward, laughing like we were old friends, there's no way I would have believed them. I realize now that's because the idea of Colin Ward that I've been carrying in my mind is the one that all my friends were fawning over back in high school: the young, devil-may-care, Hollywood bad boy. This Colin Ward is older, more mature, and far more down-to-Earth. For the first time, I notice the crow's feet around his eyes, the silver strands of hair mixed in with his dark locks. Somehow, these small signs of age only add to his appeal.

I also realize that if I stare at him much longer, I'm going to start blushing, and that would not be good.

"So, uh... I guess I'll head back inside," I say.

"I'll be along in a minute," he tells me. Then, with a charming grin, he adds, "Save my seat."

I can't help but return his smile.

"I will."

Chapter Eight

The sun still hasn't set when we check into our hotel at ten o'clock in the evening. We end up with three rooms: one for Benjamin, one for Colin, and one for Gemma and me. Of course, we all know that's just a formality. Gemma isn't spending the night in my room tonight. I probably won't even see her. But you know what? That's fine by me. I haven't had one moment just to myself in the week that I've been here. A solitary night in a nice hotel room with a bathtub and a king-sized bed actually sounds like Heaven.

The room itself is a little plain, but warm and welcoming nevertheless. The large bed, with its plush tan comforter and red plaid throw blanket, is exceptionally inviting. But as tempting as the bed may be, my body is yearning for long, hot soak in a real bathtub, especially after a week of shivering in the Dunadhar Highland Lodge's community showers.

I've just begun drawing my bath when someone knocks on the door.

"Room service!" Gemma sings.

I open the door to find her grinning ear-to-ear and holding out a pile of clothes and a ziplock bag.

"What's this?" I ask.

"What do you think? I'm your personal assistant, remember?"

"Is that - Did you pack me a just-in-case bag?" I ask. I can't believe it. I'm so touched. Gemma is the best.

"You may not believe in yourself, but I am always holding out hope for you," Gemma says.

"But I'm totally alone tonight," I remind her.

"Be that as it may, you are still spending a night in a hotel room on a whim. If you ask me, that means you're halfway there. And I am very proud of you."

I guess I'm a much bigger square than I thought.

"Oh," she adds, "and Benjamin wanted you to have these." She holds out the clothes she's holding in her other hand.

"What is it?"

"A t-shirt and a pair of boxer shorts. Don't worry, they're clean. Turns out he likes to carry around a just-in-case suitcase," she explains. "Anyway, I told him that you're not very accustomed to spontaneous hotel stays and so he told me to take you his spare pajamas."

"Oh my God, that's so sweet of him. He really doesn't mind?"

"He's not going to be wearing them," Gemma winks.

Fair enough.

Once I bid Gemma a good night, which she is bound to have, I brush my teeth, climb out of my jeans that are way too tight and stiff to have worn for as long as I did, and step into the steaming oasis that is my hotel bathtub. I decide to take full advantage of the soaps and shampoos and the razor that Gemma packed in my just-in-case bag. Who knows when I'll get the chance to pamper myself like this again?

For the next thirty minutes, I wash and condition my hair, I lather my skin, and I even shave my legs. If only I had a bottle of nail polish to complete my at-home spa experience. My toes could definitely do with a new color. Alas, I guess you can't have everything.

As I dry off and change into Benjamin's t-shirt and boxers, I have to giggle. I am literally getting into Benjamin Wyndham's knickers.

And on the same night as Gemma.

I'm tempted to text her, but I doubt she'd appreciate the interruption. Besides, she never thinks I'm as funny as I think I am. I'll just tell her tomorrow when we get a moment to ourselves. I'm sure I'll still think it's hilarious.

After I finally emerge from the bathroom, I check the closet to see if the hotel provides complimentary bathrobes and, lo and behold, it does. I am particularly grateful because I'm freezing.

No sooner have I slipped into the robe than someone knocks on my door once again.

It must be Gemma, though I can't imagine why she'd come back to my room. Maybe she needs to borrow something? Or maybe she wants to stay here with me after all. I hope everything is all right and that she and Benjamin didn't have some sort of falling out.

But when I open the door, it isn't Gemma standing in the hallway.

It's Colin.

"Oh. Uh..." I'm so stunned that I'm actually at a loss for words. "Hi."

"Bad time?" he asks.

"No! No, not at all. I just... I wasn't expecting you. Um... Come in."

Colin has also showered and changed out of his day clothes and into gray sweatpants and a black t-shirt. I guess that backpack he carries around is his just-in-case bag. Apparently, I'm the only person in the world who doesn't think to plan ahead. I'm too busy living inside my own mind.

"Just so you know, I'm not here to take advantage of you or anything," he assures me. "I've never been very good at falling asleep in hotels. Or at all."

"I guess that's an artist stereotype that I kind of defy. I can usually fall asleep anywhere.

Except airplanes. Or cars. Moving vehicles in general." And now I'm rambling.

"Well, I don't have to stay. I just thought I'd stop by and see how you were faring. I figured you'd be alone tonight," he grins.

"Yeah, I guess I'm not as dreamy as Benjamin," I joke. "But please, you don't have to rush off. Stay." It's not like I'll be sleeping anytime soon. Now that he's here, I'm wide awake. "Are you hungry? Thirsty? I could call room service."

"I'm fine, thanks," he says. "You know I didn't notice it until now..."

"Notice what?"

"You've got a little bit of a southern drawl, don't you?"

"Do I?" I ask. People don't notice my accent very often. I guess here, it stands out a little.

"You do. Where are you from?"

"Dallas."

"Interesting," he says, making himself comfortable on my bed. "So, is your next series going to be about a sexy cowboy and a southern belle, riding their horses on the range and making love by the campfire?"

"God, I wish that was what Dallas was really like," I laugh.

"You mean you don't own your own horse?" he teases.

"Ha ha. You're funny. Have you ever even *been* to Texas?"

"Yes, actually. Several times."

"South by Southwest doesn't count."

"I'll have you know that I've filmed movies in El Paso, Houston, and Fort Worth. Thank you very much." He crosses his arms and for the first time, I catch a glimpse of one of his tattoos: a Celtic eagle. "Granted, I was younger and stupider and I don't necessarily remember a lot of El Paso or Houston."

I shrug.

"That's okay."

Colin grins.

"So tell me something about yourself. Apart from the obvious," he says.

"What's the obvious?" I ask, sitting down cross-legged next to him.

"Where you're from, what you do for a living. I already know those things. Tell me something about you."

"Um... I'm not sure there's all that much to tell..."

"All right, let me help you out a bit. What do you like to do? And it can't be anything to do with books. No writing, no reading, no Friday night trips to the bookstore."

"Wow, you're no fun at all," I quip. "I like traveling. I like seeing new places and trying new things. Like Gemma said, I really like to experience."

"What's your favorite thing you've experienced so far?" he asks.

I stop to think for a moment. I'm lucky enough to have made several memories that I will always cherish and to have met so many people whom I will always hold dear. But what's been my absolute favorite thing?

Finally, I have an answer.

"At my very first book signing, a girl came up to me and said, 'I've never been all that into reading, but I loved your book so much. Now I read all the time.' I almost started crying. It was the coolest thing that anyone has ever said to me. Even though those books are just so stupid."

"Why do you say that?" Colin asks.

"Have you read them? They're awful."

Colin looks at me like he's trying to understand how or why I might feel that way. Then he asks, "Do you know why I signed on to be a part of this series?"

"No." But I'll admit I was wondering.

"A few years back, my mother was diagnosed with cancer. Pancreatic. Very aggressive. The treatment was horrible. It made her violently sick. She lost all her hair. I truly didn't think she was going to make it. I don't think the doctors did either," he confesses. "Then my oldest sister bought her a copy of your first book. A close friend of our mother's recommended it. My mother was too weak to read it herself, so my sister read it aloud to her."

"Oh no..." I can feel myself blushing. No daughter should ever, ever read the words I wrote aloud to her mother.

Colin just grins.

"As you can probably imagine, my sister was scandalized. But my mother loved it. Even after it got to be too much for my sister, my mother requested for a hospital volunteer to come sit by her bedside and read. And then, after she got strong enough, she read the rest of the series herself. She's been in remission almost two years now," Colin says. "Your books helped get my mom through the roughest year of her life. And you'll never hear me speak ill of them for that reason."

"Colin..." Again, I don't know what to say. His story is breaking my heart... but in a good way. I had no idea my books had affected anyone's life... Not like that. "I take it back," I whisper through the tears I'm trying desperately not to shed. "*That* is the coolest thing anyone has ever said to me."

"Hey now, I didn't mean to make you cry. Come on, no tears." He flashes me a heart-stopping grin and hands me a tissue. I take it and wipe the moisture away from my eyes.

"Thank you." Then, with one final sniffle, I say, "Okay, we've talked about me enough. Tell me one of your stories. One that I can't find on Tumblr."

"Oh boy, you're getting personal," Colin feigns concern, casting me a sidelong glance. "I'm not sure there's a whole lot out there that you can't find online. I haven't exactly lived my life in obscurity."

"There's got to be something that someone got wrong. Or maybe something you wish more people knew," I press.

"I've had a lot of ex-girlfriends try to take revenge on me. Does that count?" he asks with a nervous chuckle.

"If it makes a good story, by all means, tell."

"Okay. Now, please keep in mind that all this happened years ago. I like to think that I'm not the scoundrel I was in my twenties. Or early thirties."

"Noted. Go on."

It turns out that Colin has a lot more angry ex-girlfriends than I'd originally given him credit for. Or would have. I really never spent all that much time wondering about Colin Ward's former conquests. But I think his younger playboy self could probably give Benjamin a run for his money. The only difference is that Benjamin is known for ending flings on good terms. And I think that's because the girls he dates know that they're going to be just that: Flings. One-night stands. Hook-ups. There's no promise of a commitment. Just pure pleasure.

Colin, on the other hand, makes it sound like he was once a dirty, lying womanizer. He'd mastered the art of telling a woman exactly what she wanted to hear, exactly what he knew would get her into his bed. He filled their heads and their hearts with empty promises and beautiful lies that anyone would want to believe. Especially coming from him. And then he'd leave them without a word, and without a second thought.

"The worst part," he says, leaning back on his elbows, "is that I really didn't feel bad about it at all. Or I guess, I tried to pretend I didn't. There was definitely a part of me that knew what I was doing was wrong. But I usually muted that part with drugs, alcohol... anything I could get my hands on, really. After I got sober, it became harder and harder to not care that I was hurting people." When he catches a glance at the look on my face, he smiles sheepishly. "I'm sorry. This isn't exactly a fun story, is it?"

"I didn't ask for a fun story. I asked for a good one."

"I'm not sure I'd call this a good story, either. Feels more like a confession."

"You'd be surprised how often our deeper truths reveal themselves in stories," I tell him.

"So which of your deeper truths did you reveal in your stories?" he asks, his dark brown eyes suddenly sparkling with mischief.

Oh, God. I can't think of a conversation I'd rather *not* have with him.

"There is nothing true about those stories," I laugh.

"Are you sure? From what I've heard they're written with quite a bit of passion."

"You've heard of living vicariously? Those stories are a result of late-night internet surfing and having absolutely nothing better to do. So I created a life for Corrine. And Malcolm. And Tristan."

"But not Rigsley."

"Well, he's kind of an asshole," I remind him.

"Point taken," he grins, running his hand through his dark locks. He does that a lot. And it's actually quite distracting. "Can I ask you something else?"

"Sure."

"Why did Gemma laugh? When Benjamin asked if you had a boyfriend back home?"

"Because she's rude," I answer semi-jokingly.

Colin chuckles.

"Okay, I'll give you that," he says. "But seriously. What's the story there?"

"No story. And that's exactly why she laughed. She thinks I'm a little hermit. And I guess, to be fair, she's not completely wrong," I acknowledge.

"Well, that's a shame," Colin says.

"A shame?"

"Yeah. For all the men who've missed out on their chance to be with you."

Oh wow, that was smooth.

"Was that a line? Because it was very corny."

"And what if it was?" he laughs.

"I wouldn't buy it."

"All right, fine. How about this?" He sits up and looks me directly in the eye. "I think you're beautiful. And clever. And charming. And you deserve to have someone notice you every once in a while."

And that's when I lose the feeling in all of my extremities. Seriously, who says stuff like that? Furthermore, how does one *respond* to something like that? I feel like laughing. I *am* laughing. Because I honestly, truly can't remember the last time someone made me feel this way. I feel... *light.* Confident. Uninhibited. How can he make me feel all of those things at once?

"Okay, that was pretty good," I breathe.

Then, without speaking, he slips my bathrobe off of my shoulders and tucks my still-damp hair back behind my ear. He takes my waist in his hands and pulls me closer and closer until my hands are pressed against his sturdy chest. Then, without a trace of uncertainty or reservation, he leans in and presses his mouth to my neck. Lost in everything about this moment -

his touch, his smell, his warmth, his rough stubble against my skin - I close my eyes and allow his lips to explore. I feel my own fingers grasping at his collar, fumbling around his neck, clutching his hair. I want to sink into him. I want to give into him. I want *him*.

But then, as quickly as it all began, he abruptly pulls away and looks down at my body, his eyebrows furrowing with confusion.

"What... what are you wearing?" he asks.

Oh, right. I forgot my nighttime attire isn't exactly sexy.

"Benjamin's undergarments," I answer matter-of-factly.

Colin stares at me for half a moment longer before succumbing to a fit of ridiculous laughter. His mirth is contagious, and I collapse back onto my pillows, laughing so hard I can barely breathe.

When my laughter finally subsides, I sit up again, taking deep breaths and trying to regain my composure. Colin is watching me, still amused. The smile on his face is the same one that has beguiled and broken so many hearts.

And I have a feeling my heart will be no exception.

Then again, maybe it won't be. Because I have no preconceived notions about where this may lead. He's not promising me anything, and that's fine by me. I don't need anything from him.

But that certainly doesn't mean I'm through with him.

Without even thinking about it, I rise up onto my knees, take his face in my hands, and kiss him. There's nothing sweet or tender about this kiss. It isn't shy or gentle or anything like the kisses I've shared with guys in the past. That's probably because those guys weren't Colin Ward, who I know must be very used to women throwing themselves at him.

Not that he seems to mind at all. I've no sooner begun to run my fingers through his hair than I feel his strong arms wrapping around the small of my back. He pulls me toward him once again as he returns my kiss, teasing my tongue with his and nipping at my lower lip. *That* sends my body into a regular frenzy and I'm certain he can feel my heart racing against his chest.

"You know something?" I breathe, tearing myself away from his intoxicating mouth.

"What's that?" he asks.

"I've never had a crush on you."

And of course, he starts laughing again.

"I have heard a lot of strange things after kissing a woman, but never that." And since he said the word, I decide to kiss him again. And again. Then he asks, "So what would you be doing if you *did* have a crush on me?"

"Probably sleeping, since I'd be too intimidated to even speak to you."

"Oh. Well then, thank God you don't find me attractive," he grins.

"I didn't say I didn't find you attractive. I just said I'd never - " But Colin cuts me off by pulling me into another exceptionally good kiss. I guess he doesn't care all that much about technicalities. And I must admit, I'm glad he doesn't.

After the kiss finally ends, he rests his forehead against mine and whispers, "I should probably let you get some sleep."

"Already trying to get rid of me, huh?" I tease.

"Hey, you're the one who doesn't have a crush on me," he teases right back. "Besides, I meant what I said earlier. I didn't come here tonight to take advantage of you." Even though it would be so easy for him to do so. And as tempting as it would be to have him right here, right now, I appreciate the standards to which he's holding himself.

That or he really is just trying to ditch me. But for the first time, I honestly don't think that's the case.

"I guess I'll walk you to the door, then."

"How kind of you," Colin grins.

"Not really. I need to deadbolt it once you leave."

He laughs again. I love his laugh. I could listen to it all night.

"You are something else, aren't you?" he asks.

"I hope that's a compliment."

"It is," he smiles. Then, he trails one warm finger down my cheek and tips my chin up toward him. "Good night, Miss DuBois."

I almost, *almost* ask him to call me Delaney. But something holds me back.

"Good night, Mr. Ward."

And then he pulls me into one last unapologetically pleasurable kiss.

And then he's gone.

Chapter Nine

Surreal.

That's the only way to describe what I'm feeling right now. Surreal.

The dull glow of hazy morning sunlight is shimmering in through my window. Seagulls are crying and cackling in the city streets below. I can smell coffee brewing from one of the neighboring rooms here in the hotel. And I totally made out with Colin Ward last night.

How the hell did that even happen? Is this one of those bizarre instances where someone stepped on a bug and accidentally rewove the tapestry of fate? Because I'm pretty sure if the universe were in any sort of proper alignment, I would not have ended up in Colin Ward's arms in a hotel room in Inverness.

But before I can further ponder the workings of destiny or the way that Colin's mouth tasted of fresh winter mint, my phone chimes with a text from Gemma letting me know that she and Benjamin are on their way down to breakfast and that I'm welcome to join them. Accompanying her message are a string of heart-shaped emojis and one winking smiley face. I guess that tells me everything I need to know about her evening. I can't wait to see her reaction when I tell her about mine.

After changing back into my clothes from yesterday and freshening up as much as I can with what little I have to work with, I make my way down to breakfast, very consciously trying to act as natural as possible. I spot Gemma and Benjamin almost immediately. Her radiant morning-person energy coupled with his messy auburn hair is pretty difficult to miss.

"Good morning, Lovely," Gemma grins and rises to greet me. "How are you today?"

"I am fantastic, thank you. And Benjamin, thank *you* for letting me borrow your pajamas," I say.

"Think nothing of it. I wasn't using them," he says, exchanging a smirk with Gemma.

"So how did you sleep?" Gemma asks me.

"I slept fine."

"Was the bed comfortable? Did you like your room?"

See, this is why no one should ever have to be the third wheel at a morning-after breakfast. You're either ignored by the happy couple or worse, they try to engage you in awkward small talk to make sure you feel loved and included even though everyone is well aware that no, you did not have as good a time as they did last night.

Let's be real here. No one cares if my bed was comfortable.

Alas, I play along.

"Everything was great," I reply, casually glancing back toward the hallway, hoping to see Colin sauntering in.

I don't.

"I particularly enjoyed the not-sleeping-in-a-bunk-bed part," Gemma quips.

Oh, right. *That's* the part she enjoyed.

"I still can't believe they're making you sleep in bunk beds," Benjamin giggles.

"Writers don't get trailers," I remind him.

"Speaking of writers, Gemma and I were talking last night," Benjamin says. "You know, we've got some great ideas for your next nov - "

"Hold it right there," I lift up my hand. "No."

"You don't even know what I'm going to say yet!"

"And I don't care. My mind is already littered with my own unfinished narratives and I have no room left for someone else's story. If you have an idea for a book, write it yourself."

"Told you she wouldn't appreciate it," Gemma murmurs.

I'm almost tempted to ask why on Earth I even came up as a topic of conversation last night when Colin finally walks in, looking refreshed and far too handsome for his own good. And mine, for that matter.

"Colin, my friend, thank you," Benjamin declares as Colin sits down. Colin looks to me for some sort of explanation. I shrug. I've got nothing. So wordlessly, he turns back to Benjamin who says, "You're supposed to ask what for."

"Why?"

"That's close enough," Benjamin clears his throat. "I want to thank you for finally deeming to grace us with your resplendent presence. Please know that every minute not spent in your company is a minute wasted."

"I was wrong, Benjamin," I remark. "Maybe I should let you write my next novel."

"I do have a way with words," he insists.

"Is that what they call it?" Colin quips. Gemma and I both laugh. That's when Colin looks at me again. This time, he raises one eyebrow, a playful smirk of an acknowledgment. I hope that neither Gemma nor Benjamin notices me blushing.

For only the second time since arriving here in Scotland, I order a traditional Scottish breakfast complete with eggs, thinly sliced bacon, sautéed mushrooms, baked beans, sausage, potato scones, and half a tomato which I know I won't eat, but it does add a nice touch. Besides, I'm so delighted to not be eating hostel food or set food that they could decorate my entire plate with tomatoes and I wouldn't complain.

After breakfast, we check out of the hotel and load ourselves and our few belongings back into Benjamin's car.

"Wish we could stay another night," he laments. "But we've got a call tomorrow at what? Two?"

"Think so," Colin answers.

"We'd better make the most of today then," Gemma smiles.

"Right you are, Love," Benjamin declares. "Let's go find Nessie!"

The drive to Loch Ness is a short one, only about thirty minutes. Even so, by the time we arrive, the sun has broken through the morning clouds, painting the hills a lush, vibrant green, sparkling atop the profoundly blue surface of the water, and illuminating the remains of a castle overlooking the Loch.

"That's Urquhart Castle," Benjamin informs us. "What's left of it, anyway. We can go visit it if you'd like."

"I'm in!" Gemma exclaims. "Lorelei?"

As if I'm going to turn down a chance to explore a castle. Especially on a beautiful summer's day like this one.

And I'm not the only one. The grounds are already crawling with tourists posing for pictures, examining the ancient architecture, and chasing their kids around the grassy knolls. There are a few families sitting down for picnics.

It's an idyllic setting to be sure, a beautiful juxtaposition of past and present.

"I wonder what the original owners would have thought," I muse aloud.

"Of what?" Colin asks.

"If someone had told them that one day, their fortresses and royal residences would become the background for someone's Facebook profile. A place to stop for chips and a soda."

"Or the film set of a television series," he adds.

"Touché."

We've just reached the gatehouse when it happens. A young girl, probably in her early twenties, gasps and grabs her friend.

"I think that's Benjamin Wyndham!" she exclaims.

"No! Where?"

"Over there!"

Benjamin, who is well aware of the scene he is about to cause, grins and waves at the girls. Before I can even think to react, Colin takes my hand and casually yet steadily escorts me away from the gathering crowd, through a crumbling archway, and down a long pathway to a secluded strip of beach outside the castle walls, leaving Benjamin and Gemma to fend for themselves.

"Should we have just left them like that?" I ask Colin.

"It's too late for them now. We can't look back," Colin declares dramatically. Okay, maybe Benjamin isn't the only ham in our little quartet.

"So, I take it this isn't a first for you. You evaded that crowd with the skill and precision of a master ditcher."

"I may have had to disappear once or twice in my day. Fortunately for me, I'm not as famous as I used to be. You, on the other hand..."

"Me?"

"Yeah. What, you don't think any of those girls would recognize you?"

"Not unless I was standing in the middle of a bookstore beneath a giant banner that read *Lorelei DuBois*."

"Oh, come on."

"It's true. Books are recognized so much more than authors are. Last year, I went to a book festival down in Corpus Christi. I rode up seven stories in an elevator with a lady who'd written one of my favorite books of all time and I didn't even realize it until I saw her again the next morning."

"I find that very hard to believe."

"Well, what I find hard to believe is that you don't think *you're* all that famous."

"I didn't say I'm not all that famous. I said I'm not as famous as I used to be."

"How does one become not as famous as he used to be?" I ask.

"There are newer, hotter stars on the horizon; younger and far more interesting than boring old duds like me."

"Oh *please*," I roll my eyes. "You don't believe a word of that."

"Hey, it's partially true. Do you ever read about me in the tabloids? Ever? It's because I'm boring now. Much to my publicist's chagrin."

"So, do you miss it? Being interesting, I mean."

"God, no," he scoffs. "I was such an asshole back then."

"Ah, so you *are* suited to play Rigsley."

Colin glares down at me.

"Rude."

"I'm sorry. Please, continue."

"There's nothing more to be said, really. I just wanted to call you out," he admits. "So what about you?"

"What about me?"

"You've heard of the admittedly questionable choices I've made in my time. What kind of trouble have you gotten yourself into?"

"Oh wow, you are not going to like the answer to this one," I warn him.

"Uh oh," he grins.

"You think you're boring? I'm like stale bread compared to you."

"Ouch. That's a bit harsh, don't you think?"

"Not if it's true. You know those senior superlatives that everyone votes on in high school? Most likely to succeed... most likely to have a dozen kids... biggest flirt...? I was unironically voted biggest teacher's pet."

"You're joking," Colin laughs.

"I wish I was. But I was like, the epitome of good girls. I never had detention. I never stayed out past curfew. I've never even had a cavity."

"So, in other words, you're literally the last person that anyone would expect to write a book like *The Queen's Surrogate*."

"Pretty much."

"It's always the good girls," he comments, casting me a devilish smirk.

"We don't have scandals of our own so we have to make them up as we go," I explain.

"I don't know. Last night was pretty scandalous. Especially considering you don't have a crush on me."

"You're never going to let me live that down, are you?"

"Never," he confirms. "So, if I'm not your type, then who is?"

"You ask a lot of questions."

"I'm a curious person."

"No, I think the correct term here is nosy. You are a *nosy* person."

"I've been called worse. So, tell me."

"No."

"Why not?"

"Because then you'll *really* never let me hear the end of it."

"Oh, jeez. It's Benjamin, isn't it?"

"No, it's not Benjamin," I promise.

"Matthew, then?"

Is there any point in denying it? The rest of the world knows I have a crush on Matthew Kent. Might as well let Colin into the loop as well. Even though, to be fair, I really haven't thought about Matthew since Colin kissed me last night. Which is saying something considering he's been my number one celebrity crush for like, seven years now.

"I may have... at one point... found him aesthetically pleasing," I confess.

"Interesting," he adopts a pensive expression and strokes his stubbled chin.

"Okay, so who's *your* celebrity crush?" Two can play at this game.

"I don't have one," he says.

"Oh, come on."

"It's true. I've dated all of mine. And as you may have surmised, I've got a lousy track record when it comes to relationships."

"We have that in common." The words are out of my mouth before I can stop them. He raises an eyebrow.

"Sounds like there's another story there."

What is with him anyway? I'm not used to guys actually paying attention to what I say, let alone wanting to know more. But Colin is so... inquisitive. Maybe it's because he's older. Or maybe years of starring in Hollywood blockbusters have taught him exactly what to say to make a woman think he's interested. Either way, I'm not telling him.

"Nope," I answer, shifting away from him and climbing up onto one of the rocks that sit on the shoreline.

"Are you sure?"

"Positive."

"You're going to break your ankle up there."

"No, I'm not. I'm an adventurer."

"Tell me your story."

"No."

"Why not?"

"Because there's nothing to tell," I insist.

"Bullshit. There's always a story."

"All right. Let's say for argument's sake that there is a story, but it's one that I have no interest in sharing because it is a beautiful day and I'm standing here on castle grounds, looking out over a shimmering lake that is home to one of the most legendary unsolved mysteries of our time and frankly, I don't want to ruin it."

If Colin is taken aback by my lengthy and aggressive reasoning, he doesn't let it show. He simply says, "All right." Then, after taking a moment to let our old conversation die, he asks, "So, do you think Nessie's really out there?"

"Um, of course I do. Do you?"

"Let's say I'm a healthy skeptic. But I like the idea of a monstrous sea dragon swimming around out there beneath the blue."

"Well sure, who doesn't?" I ask. "I can't imagine there are many folks out there who can honestly say they'd rather live in a world where the Loch Ness Monster doesn't exist."

"You'd be surprised," Colin remarks.

Before I can ask him to elaborate, I catch the sound of Gemma's voice, calling out our names. I turn to see her and Benjamin, traipsing their way down the long stairway to where we are. I look back to Colin.

"Think we should go meet them?"

"Might as well," he sighs. "They'll just keep following us if we don't."

Then, he holds out his hand to help me off of the rocks. I take it and jump, landing perfectly at his feet.

"Thank you."

"Don't mention it."

After exploring Urquhart's ruins, we drive a little further down the shoreline, park, and spend the next hour or so kicking our shoes off, walking the beaches, and skipping stones across the surface of the loch. Well, Benjamin is the only one who's truly mastered the art of skipping stones. Gemma and I are okay, but Colin is absolutely dreadful. It's equal parts sad and hilarious.

For lunch, we drive back to Inverness, where we spend the rest of the day playing tourists, seeing the sights, and visiting one or two of the local shops.

Okay, that's a bold-faced lie. Gemma and I drag Benjamin and Colin into every store that even remotely looks like it might sell souvenirs and by the time we climb into Benjamin's car to drive back to our hostel, we're toting three bags each, full of scarves, t-shirts, magnets, key chains, bumper stickers, coffee mugs, and stuffed Nessies which we claim are for our friend's daughters but are totally for us.

The drive back to Dunadhar Highland Lodge seems to go by much more quickly than the drive out to Inverness and before I know it, we're pulling into the parking lot. Even though I know I'll see Benjamin and Colin tomorrow, I'm not ready to say goodbye to them yet.

"Thank you for the adventure, ladies," Benjamin bids us as Gemma and I grab our numerous purchases and climb out of the car. "Let's do it again."

"Oh, we will," Gemma promises.

Once their tail lights have disappeared into the cool evening air, Gemma shrieks and throws her arms around me.

"Oh my *God*! Did that really just happen?" she asks.

"I think it really did. By the way, you have to tell me everything."

"Oh, I will. You know I will."

And she does. And I listen. And I laugh. Her stories of her night with Benjamin carry us all the way to our room, all the way to the community showers, all the way to the sink to brush our teeth, and all the way back to our room. She's still talking about him as we climb into our respective bunk beds for the night.

"... and the best part is he's so gentle. I wasn't expecting that from him. He's so playful, you know? Kind of cheeky. But he's actually very considerate. A real gentleman."

"I'm happy you had a good time," I tell her.

"God, I had the best time. And it's all thanks to you."

"I think it's all thanks to Benjamin, but I'm open to taking credit."

She tosses her Nessie doll down at me.

"You know what I mean," she laughs. "If you hadn't brought me here, I never would have met him. I never would have had an opportunity like this, period. So, thank you."

"I'm just glad to have you here with me," I tell her. "I can't imagine going through all of this alone."

"Well, you wouldn't have been alone. You'd have Andrew and Louise. Benjamin.

Matthew. And hey, you and Colin seem to be getting pretty chummy. What's going on there?"

I shrug even though I know she can't see me.

"He's fun. He's funny. I like him."

"Yeah? You like him? Or you *like* like him?"

"I thought we stopped *like* liking boys when we were twelve."

"Oh my God! You *do like* like him! So, does this mean you're over Matthew?"

"I barely know Matthew. I'm not sure there's anything to get over."

"Okay, so tell me what you know about Colin."

What do I know about Colin? Sure, we spent a little bit of time together, but that doesn't necessarily mean I know him all that well. Though he did tell me that really moving story about his mom and how reading my books helped her through her cancer treatments. And he showed me that really cute video of his nephew learning to walk. And he admitted that he doesn't miss being as famous as he used to be.

Where do I even begin?

"Well," I finally say, a coy smile playing on my lips. "I know he's a damn good kisser."

Excerpt from *The Queen's Surrogate*

"Mistress Fletcher." The way Rigsley says my name sends a loathsome chill all the way through to my very core. "His Majesty is ready for you."

I am numb. I am dizzy. I am trembling. But I must not show any signs of fear or hesitation. I have been chosen for this. It is my duty. And it is too late to turn back.

Breathing deeply to try to calm my erratically beating heart, I step into the King's bedchamber. The room is alight with fire glow which casts long shadows across the stone walls, the King's fur and trappings, and the golden emblems adorning the table tops. Everything about this room makes me feel small and out of place. Including the man sitting on the canopied bed.

At first glance, I do not recognize him. He's very handsome, easily the most handsome man I've ever seen in my life. Firelight dances in his light blue eyes and thick golden locks. His cheekbones are sharp and his bearded jawline is strong. Although he's dressed only in a white, flowing nightshirt and brown breeches, he is dignified; strikingly so. But he's so much more than that. This man is noble. This man is powerful.

This man is the King.

I finally recognize him now. I've seen him once before, at the tournament. But I've never been so close to him. He's captivating.

"Your - Your Majesty," I breathe as I sink into a feeble curtsy.

The King watches me, the expression on his face somber. I wonder if he resents what he's about to do. I wonder if he resents me.

Finally, he holds his hand out and motions for me to approach him.

"Come," he says.

I obey.

When I reach the bed, he stops me. Then he looks me up and down with those blue, blue eyes.

"You're young," he observes. "You're beautiful."

"Thank you, Your Majesty."

"What is your name?"

"Corrine. Corrine Fletcher."

"Mistress Corrine." He finally rises. "You do your sovereign and your country a great favor. We are indebted to you."

It is then that my words abandon me, so I simply bow my head. But the King takes my hand and softly brushes my hair away from my face.

"I promise I will be gentle with you," he says.

"Thank you." My voice is barely a whisper.

I'm profoundly aware of every sensation, every sound, every thread woven into the King's bed as I lie down atop his burgundy cushions. I close my eyes and try to trick my mind into concentrating on the warmth and comforting softness of the sheets and blankets. But I can still hear the King breathing beside me, his clothes rustling as he removes his breeches. I'm not ready for this.

And yet, I don't have a choice.

Afraid of being perceived as disrespectful or ungracious, I open my eyes as he climbs into bed and then on top of me. He must know that I've never lain with a man before, for he presses a hot hand to my face.

"Shh..." he whispers. "Take a deep breath. Be still. You're doing fine."

Chapter Ten

"I can't believe it."

"It's been fourteen hours."

"I still can't believe it."

"It only happened once," I remind Gemma as we prepare to head downstairs to meet Andrew and Louise. Since today is Sunday and a read-through day, call isn't until two o'clock in the afternoon, which gave us a few blessed hours of extra sleep.

"I don't care. My best friend made out with *Colin Ward*. Colin. Alexander. Ward."

"Is that his middle name?"

"Delaney, you have no idea how proud I am of you!"

"For kissing someone?"

"For kissing Colin Ward! Do you know how many women in the world can boast that they've kissed Colin Ward?"

"Actually, based on what he's told me, there are a fair few," I comment. "Not to mention all the women he kisses in movies."

"Oh, they don't count. You're missing the point. The point is you made out with one of the hottest movie stars on the *planet*."

"So did you," I remind her.

"Yeah, but I make out with everybody. You're different. You're stingy."

"I'm *what*?"

"Stingy. You're a stingy kisser. You know, stingy means you don't do it a lot."

"I know what stingy means, Gem. I've just never been called that in reference to kissing."

"Well, keep making out with Colin Ward and you never will be again."

"I told you, it was probably just a one-time thing. He didn't try to kiss me at all yesterday."

"Yeah, but we were out in public all day. Benjamin didn't try to kiss me either," Gemma reminds me.

"Plus, I told him about Matthew."

"You *what*?!" Gemma snaps.

"Relax, I didn't tell him that Malcolm is based on Matthew, although he's probably figured that out by now. I just said that I had a crush on him."

"Delaney, that is the exact opposite of what you tell a guy when you want to make out with him again. Wait... do you want to make out with him again?"

"Are you kidding? That was the best kiss I've ever had in my life."

"So you have got to let him know that. Trust me, guys can't take a hint. And if he thinks you're interested in someone else? You've got no chance."

Good to know. Am I actually going to take her advice? That's still up in the air. I don't want to force things with Colin. After all, chances are slim to none that I'll actually see him again once we wrap and we all jet off back to our real lives. And in spite of what my initial pining for Matthew may imply, I really didn't come here looking for any kind of relationship.

But kissing Colin was a *lot* of fun...

I try to act as natural as I can in front of Andrew and Louise, but they both want to know how we enjoyed our short excursion to Inverness. Thankfully, Gemma is playing it uncharacteristically coy.

"It was fun! We saw Loch Ness, explored a castle, did a little shopping..."

"And by that, she means we're each going to have to buy a new suitcase if we want to get all of our new souvenirs back to the United States," I comment.

"It's probably going to have to be more than one," Gemma says. "We still have seven weeks of shopping to go..."

"Well, there goes every paycheck I'm making off this show."

"Same. Hey, can I have a raise?" Gemma asks.

"Sure." I reach into my purse and pull out a stick of gum. "There you go."

"Gee, thanks, boss."

When we arrive back at Lot B, Gemma practically flies out of the car and into the building. My first thought is that she's eager to see Benjamin. My second is that she might be rushing off to find Colin.

No, no, no.

I hurry in after her, down the hall, and into the same conference room from our first day here in Scotland. The room is so much smaller than the open studio and especially the halls of Dunadhar Castle. I've barely set foot inside and yet I'm already profoundly aware of Rose and Genevieve standing in the corner, laughing and scrolling through their phones. Matthew is discussing something with Carl and Elizabeth, but he offers me a smile and quick wave of his hand when he sees me. I'm not going to lie; he's still super attractive to me. Celebrity crushes don't just evaporate overnight. But I'll admit, I'm not seeing stars the way I did the first time he looked at me. Finally, I spot Gemma on the far end of the room, swooning over Benjamin by the coffee pot. Colin, on the other hand, is noticeably absent.

"Good morning, lovely Lorelei," Benjamin smiles as I weave my way through the room over to him and Gemma. I swear, he greets everybody as if it's the first time he's seen them in years. And I kind of love it.

"Why hello there, beautiful Benjamin."

"Aw. That's disappointing," he sighs.

"What is?"

"I was just hoping you'd go for bodacious."

"Next time," I promise him.

"Oh! There's Colin!" Gemma squeals. *Very* loudly, I may add.

Upon hearing his name, Colin turns, but he doesn't seem very startled. In fact, he looks almost bored. I guess hearing girls cry out his name isn't exactly a new experience for him. He does smile, however, when he catches me watching him.

"Why Miss Lorelei, are you blushing?" Benjamin grins.

"No!" I exclaim a little too quickly. But having been accused of blushing only makes me blush harder. Why would Benjamin ask me that, anyway? Unless...

Unless Colin said something to him. The very same way I said something to Gemma. Do guys do that? Do they talk about women the way that we talk about them? I honestly don't know the answer to that one.

"Why is it you're always the last one to show up?" Benjamin asks Colin as the latter strolls over with that refined and oh so sexy air of confidence. "Even when we were filming

Frankenstein, you'd always saunter in at the last minute. So what's the deal, Ward? Are you trying to avoid everyone? Spend as little time with all of us as possible?"

"No, just you, really," Colin quips.

"Ouch." Benjamin clutches his heart.

"Hey, Colin," Gemma smiles up at him. And when I say she smiles, I mean like the way little kids smile when they're hoping for a treat. Or when they're gloating because they know a secret and you don't. "My goodness, you are *very* handsome, aren't you? Not that I'm interested or anything. But you know, I bet you really know how to show a girl a good time, don't you?"

Oh my *God*. Can she not even *pretend* to be subtle?

Sure enough, Colin raises both eyebrows and glances my way. A look with which I am quickly becoming familiar.

"It's actually been a while since I last *entertained*," he admits.

Wait. Does that mean what I think it does?

"Oh, *really*?" Gemma sounds intrigued.

Okay, I can't take this anymore.

"You know, I just remembered I have a phone call I need to make. Excuse me." And with that, I duck into the crowd and sprint out the door, down the hall, and into the cool morning mist.

Standing alone in the parking lot, I take a few deep breaths and force myself to concentrate on the way the sparse sunlight hits the rolling green hills surrounding me and not whatever just compelled me to flee the scene like Cinderella at the stroke of midnight. You know, if Cinderella was really awkward and the Prince was a Hollywood sex symbol.

I'd love to say that the way I felt with Colin the other night was not completely out of character for me. I'd love to say that I have the pride and sense of self-worth that gives me courage and makes me feel invincible. I would love to be the girl Colin thinks he kissed. But those fourteen hours have sobered me up.

I hear the door to the building opening and closing behind me. I'm sure it's Gemma, running after me to see if I'm all right.

But it's not.

Again, it's Colin.

"You told Gemma?" he smirks.

"No, what gave you that idea?" I remark.

Thankfully, he laughs.

"You don't have to be embarrassed," he assures me.

I'm not embarrassed. At least, I don't think I am. I don't know what I'm feeling. Anxious? Afraid? Overwhelmed? All of the above?

"I know. And I'm sorry. I don't know why I'm acting like this. I might actually be crazy."

"Trust me, this isn't crazy," he says. He doesn't say the words, but I know he's thinking back to a few of the other women he's romanced in years gone by. Probably the one who threw an ashtray at his head. Or the one who asked him to buy her a pregnancy test when she thought she was pregnant with someone else's baby. Or the one who genuinely thought that the *Titanic* was a fictional ocean liner, conceived entirely for the movie.

How does he even meet these people?

Looking up into his dark eyes, remembering what if felt like to be held by him, touched by him, I realize just how easy it would be to lose myself entirely with him. To him. It wouldn't be good for me. And it's not why I'm here.

"You know Colin, we should probably just be friends," I say to him.

"We can be friends."

"I just think it would be easier."

"I agree."

"Then it's settled." I hold out my hand for him to shake it. "Friends."

"Friends." He takes my hand. But he doesn't shake it. Instead, he deftly takes my fingers and brings them to his lips, where he lets them linger. His gentle touch sends shivers down my spine and I know he knows exactly what he's doing to me. All the while, his dark gaze never leaves my face.

And like a mindless moth drawn to a flame, I wrap my arms around his neck. And I feel his hands pressing against the small of my back. And I'm well aware that anyone could step out at any moment and see us. And I am so beyond caring as Colin pulls me into a long kiss that leaves me breathless and barely able to form a coherent thought.

"I'm glad that we... That we worked this out." I tell him, running my hand through his hair, the way that he's always doing. In turn, he strokes my cheek with his fingertips.

"I am, too."

And then he kisses me again.

"You promise you're not mad at me?" Gemma asks for what feels like the thousandth time.

"I promise."

"Because I love you."

"I love you, too."

"And I want you to be happy."

"I know you do."

"But I know you struggle with this kind of thing. And when you ran out, I - "

"Gemma, I promise you. I'm fine. There's nothing to forgive. All is well."

"Okay, if you're sure..."

"I am. And if we stay in here any longer, we're going to be late for the read-through."

As soon as Colin and I reappeared after our parking lot rendezvous, Gemma dragged me off to the bathroom to apologize for her *enthusiasm*, if you will. That, of course, led me to apologize for making her feel like she needed to apologize and yes, we are those kind of people. One apology is never enough. We have to make sure the other one is all right. And you know what? I'm pretty okay with having a friend like that.

Today, just like last week, I find myself sitting next to Matthew. But, unlike last week, Colin and Benjamin take the seats directly across from Gemma and me. Gemma's pretty face lights up and suddenly, it's like we're back in high school. I half expect her to start passing notes with Benjamin under the table. Meanwhile, I purposely avoid eye contact with Colin simply because I know that one look, one smile, will have me fidgeting in my seat. Especially considering the scenes that they're about to read.

"*The Queen's Surrogate*, episode two: *Kingdom Come*."

Well, that's a fun little play on words. Now I *really* can't look at Colin. Or anyone, for that matter.

Just for the record, I didn't make that up. I didn't even know the episodes were going to have titles. But I have to admit, it is clever. You know, in an embarrassingly indelicate kind of way.

The episode opens with Corrine reeling from the announcement that she is expected to sleep with the King and have his baby. As the day progresses, she is formally introduced to her tutor, Tristan, who doesn't seem to like her very much, and Queen Annette, who greets her politely but is otherwise cold and standoffish. And understandably so.

It's in this episode that Rigsley starts to show his true colors. I'll admit, it's a little unnerving to hear Colin's voice so sadistic, so manipulative. I know every girl loves a bad boy and whatnot, but Rigsley isn't supposed to be this handsome rebel with a heart of gold. He's supposed to be a sociopath. And Colin does a very good job portraying that.

I'm almost tempted to run out of the room again when it's time for the bedroom scene. I can practically feel Benjamin's smirk from across the table. But when I hear Rose start to speak, to read the script that Cody and Sarah so masterfully helped me to create, I realize I'm not embarrassed at all. She's proud of the role she's playing and the work she's doing. And so am I.

Now watching them act it out? That may be another story.

But I don't have to worry about that until later this week.

After read-through ends, Genevieve approaches Benjamin and Colin.

"Matthew, Rose, and I are driving into Fort Augustus for dinner and drinks. Would you like to join us?" she asks.

"Absolutely," Benjamin answers after only half a moment of consideration.

Colin glances over at me.

"Mind if we bring the author along?" he asks Genevieve.

"Oh! No, not at all! You're both more than welcome!" she assures Gemma and me.

"That's sweet of you. Thank you," I say.

"Am I driving again, then?" Benjamin asks.

"Looks like it," Gemma grins. "And this time, I'm calling shotgun."

Chapter Eleven

Fort Augustus is a small albeit very charming village on the Caledonian Canal, at the southernmost tip of Loch Ness. Although its population consists of less than seven hundred people, it's a lovely and spirited little town and quite the tourist's destination. Even as we park and head into the restaurant that the others have chosen, I find myself wishing that I had more than just an evening here to explore, to watch the boats on the Canal, and to visit the local shops.

Inside, we're escorted to a table with a splendid view of the water. I go out of my way to take a seat closest to the window. Colin, with his ever cool and carefree demeanor, takes a seat opposite of me while Gemma flounces into the chair next to me. Then, she grabs Benjamin and with a girlish giggle exclaims, "Sit next to me!" Yet even as Benjamin willingly obliges, I can't help but notice Rose glaring at them from across the table.

Once we've all taken our seats, Matthew orders a round of drinks for our entire table, as well as three separate appetizers.

"I'm glad we finally have the opportunity to spend some time together as a group," he announces, flashing that killer smile. That's when I feel Colin's gaze on me, and I know, without even looking, that he's smirking. So I'm purposefully ignoring him. And I hope he's aware of it.

"And I'm glad that I'm not in any sort of corset," Genevieve quips.

"I'll drink to that," Rose agrees, taking a long sip of beer.

"God, I remember having to wear a corset for theater in high school. It was awful," Gemma says. "I definitely don't envy you."

"No, why should you?" Rose asks in one of those sickeningly sweet voices that the mean girls in movies use right before they lunge for the heroine's throat. Or diamond choker. Or whatever they can get their hands on.

Thankfully, since this is *not* a movie and we are, in fact, in a very nice restaurant in a very nice town, that does not happen. But even though there are no physical punches thrown, Gemma knows when she's being challenged. I hate to say it, but I think she's used to it by now. For as long as I've known Gemma, women have felt threatened by her. Her beauty, her confidence, and her large and often very loud personality can be intimidating and as a result, she's never had very many girl friends.

Thank God she has me here to make an awkward situation even more awkward.

"You know, I've never worn a corset, but I went to college with a girl who kept a squirrel in her bra."

Oh my God.

Why, brain? *Why?!*

For the record, if you've never had five beautiful famous people staring at you like you're some sort of three-eyed space alien, I don't recommend it. It's terribly uncomfortable. Much like I'd imagine wearing a corset might be.

Of course, Benjamin is the first one to break the horrific silence.

"And *how* do you know this?" he asks, gazing at me like he's hoping to hear some sort of weird lesbian squirrel confession. Sadly, the story is not that interesting. And honestly, I don't want to tell it. But I really don't think I can get myself out of this one.

I guess as long as it relieves the tension between Rose and Gemma.

"I was eating lunch in the student union and she sat down at the table across from mine and... there was the squirrel."

"And is this... common where you come from?" Matthew asks, not looking particularly certain that he wants to know the answer.

"Oh, God no! No. I mean, it's Texas so I guess you never *really* know, but... No!" Someone else needs to change the subject. Like now. I don't know why I thought it was okay for me to talk, but it clearly isn't.

"Well, I'm glad you didn't write that into *our* stories," Genevieve smiles at me.

"So am I. I'm not overly fond of rodents," Benjamin remarks.

Throughout this entire fiasco, Colin hasn't said a word. He's still just watching me like he can't decide whether he should laugh or try to rescue me from myself. I'm afraid the latter is rather a lost cause.

"So, how did you go from eating lunch with squirrel ladies to writing romance novels?" Rose asks me.

Again, this is why you should never write a book. Because people always want to know things like why you wrote the things you wrote. Or where you got your ideas from. Or if your main character looks like Matthew Kent on purpose.

"I honestly started writing for fun. I never thought anyone would actually read *The Queen's Surrogate*. But you know, if I had known, I probably wouldn't have had the courage to keep writing."

"So, what you're saying is those books really *are* your dirty fantasies," Benjamin teases.

But before I can bury my face in my hands and pray to the good Lord above to smite me where I sit, Rose groans, glowering at Benjamin with blatant disgust.

"For once in your life, Benjamin, could you *try* to have a little class?"

"What's that supposed to mean?" Gemma asks, jumping to his defense.

"Maybe we shouldn't get into this here," Matthew cautions, resting a hand on Rose's shoulder.

"Oh, come on. Any publicity is good publicity. Isn't that right, *Benjamin*?" Rose sneers.

"Rose, please," Genevieve implores her co-star. "Now isn't the time or the place."

"No, you know what? Now is exactly the time. I could tolerate him back when I thought he was just avoiding me. But parading around with another girl? Right in *front* of me?"

"Wait, what are you talking about?" I ask, ignoring the warning glance that Colin shoots me from across the table. Benjamin, I notice, is very pink around the ears and suddenly very interested in his silverware. And then, the answer to my question is clear as day. Benjamin and Rose had a thing. Just like Benjamin and Gemma. Just like Colin and half the women in Hollywood. Only to Rose, it actually meant something.

Is that why Benjamin has been so keen on hanging out with Gemma and me? Because he was hoping to spend as little time as possible with an already-jilted girlfriend? That would be disappointing. I thought he genuinely liked us. Of course, I can't say I blame him for not wanting to be around his ex. I'd rather eat garbage and

138

wash it down with sewer slime than come face to face with Tommy Riggs again.

But you know, having been the jilted lover myself, I can't say I blame Rose either.

Gemma is different. She prefers casual flings to committed relationships. She'll be able to walk away whenever her whirlwind romance with Benjamin ends and look back on it with a smile on her face and perhaps even a strange sense of accomplishment.

Me? I'm not like that. I'd love to be. But I'm not. And it would seem that Rose Cervantes isn't like that either.

"Do you have any idea what it's like to feel invisible to someone you used to care about?" she demands. "To someone who you thought cared about you? To have felt that connection and then to have it just evaporate into thin air? It's just... it's awful."

"Rose," Benjamin murmurs. "I'm so, so sorry. I thought... I thought we were just having fun. I never meant to hurt you."

"Perhaps. But you never meant to see me again either. Which kind of backfired on you, I guess."

Benjamin looks so ashamed that I can't help but feel sorry for him. I don't like seeing this side of him. Not that I'm stunned by Rose's accusations. He is known as Great Britain's Greater Playboy, after all. It's just that the Benjamin I've come to know over the past week is so sweet, so friendly, who genuinely *does* seem to care about people. But then, maybe that's why so many women fall for him. Maybe it's all just an act. He definitely wouldn't be the first.

What promised to be a fun outing with friends has quickly devolved into a sobering reminder of just how fragile emotions and relationships can be. How no one is immune to rejection or to heartbreak.

And how I want nothing to do with any of the above.

After a very tense and uncomfortable dinner, Matthew, Rose, and Genevieve bid Colin, Benjamin, Gemma, and me a very tense and uncomfortable goodbye.

"We just want to get back to the hotel before dark," Genevieve claims, but we all know that she's just trying to be polite.

Oh yeah, the actors get to stay in a hotel. *Not* a hostel. A very nice, very classy, four-star *hotel*.

What. The. Hell.

I mean, I knew they had to be staying somewhere. They don't actually live in their trailers. But come on. That is so not fair.

Although to be completely honest, retreating to our little hostel in the Highlands doesn't sound so bad after all the drama we just endured. Maybe Gemma and I actually dodged a bullet. Even though the others have gone, I'm somehow still feeling suffocated inside this restaurant.

Colin must be feeling the same way because he breaks the silence asking, "Does anyone want to go for a walk? It's such a great evening. It'd be a shame to waste it."

"I'm down for a walk. Benjamin?" Gemma asks, almost as though to reassure him she doesn't think any less of him.

"Sounds wonderful," he says.

The sun has yet to set, but the gentle chill in the air and the quiet calm of the emptying streets are unmistakable characteristics of the day's end. We start out walking as a group, but soon, Gemma and Benjamin are falling behind, lacing their fingers together and whispering.

And I'm once again alone with Colin.

"That was a fun dinner, wasn't it?" he remarks.

"Oh yeah, lots of fun. Like a root canal but with movie stars," I remark. "Did you know? About Benjamin and Rose?"

"I did," he confesses. "Of course, I only knew what Benjamin told me. And that wasn't very much."

"What *did* he tell you?"

"Just that they went out a couple of times. He liked her. He thought she was cute. But she was a bit young for him and he didn't think she was looking for anything serious. But then, that's always been Benjamin's tragic flaw. He assumes that everyone thinks the same way that he does. Not in a bad way, but in a way that has gotten him into trouble from time to time."

"Especially with women," I mutter.

Colin shrugs.

"I can't judge him too harshly. I *was* him. Hell, I was worse than him."

"And you're not anymore?"

"You make it sound like that's hard to believe." Yet even as he speaks the words, he flashes that smile. The one guaranteed to sweep a woman off her feet.

"Well, I am talking to the man who is rumored to have stolen a girl away from her *royal* fiancé." Seriously. I think I was a sophomore in high school when Colin made international headlines after having been caught sneaking around with the girlfriend of some Prince in Greece. Although both parties denied any wrongdoings, the engagement was called off shortly thereafter.

"Rumored. Never confirmed," Colin reminds me.

"Did you?"

"Why would I tell you? You're a writer!" he laughs. "For all I know, this conversation could end up in your next book. *The Princess and the Player*."

"Not the best title. I'd probably go with something more like *Her Royal Heartbreak*. Or *Crown Casanova*."

"That's fantastic. My embarrassing past rehashed in excruciating detail at the top of the *New York Times'* Bestsellers list."

"Aw."

"What? Are you taking pity on me?"

"No. It's just sweet of you to think I would make the *New York Times*."

"Cute. You're very cute." But he grins nevertheless.

That's something I really like about Colin. He's got a great sense of humor and he's absolutely able and willing to laugh at himself. I wasn't expecting that when I first met him. But then, I wasn't expecting a lot of things.

By the time we reconnect with Benjamin and Gemma, our moods have all lightened considerably. Benjamin is smiling again as Gemma wraps her arms around his waist and kisses his cheek. And I keep stealing glances at Colin who doesn't even try to pretend that he hasn't noticed.

I wish we could stay in Fort Augustus just like I wished we could have stayed in Inverness. I have a feeling that when it comes to my time spent here in Scotland, it will never be enough. I'll always be wanting one more day, one more hour, one more minute. There will always be something I wish I'd seen. And I don't know how I'm ever going to leave.

Chapter Twelve

Filming for episode two begins, wouldn't you know it, with Rose and Benjamin's first big scene together, when Corrine and Tristan are introduced for the first time. And it just so happens that their on-screen relationship somewhat mirrors their off-screen friction.

In the series, Benjamin's character, Tristan, is actually Queen Annette's cousin, although he is more like a brother in the sense that he is very protective of her. He knows quite well how evil Rigsley is and how he's tormented Annette over the years. So while Corrine is still very overwhelmed by her new surroundings, Tristan is feeling very resentful towards the girl whom, he believes, was brought in just to break his cousin's heart.

Of course, being the trashy romance novel that it is, Tristan ends up falling in love with Corrine, and as the story plays out and the characters evolve, she falls in love with him as well. Which, when you think about it, it a little surprising considering I wrote these books as a wish-fulfillment fantasy about Matthew. Then again, perhaps it isn't so surprising. Malcolm and Corrine could never have ended up together. He wouldn't have been able to divorce Annette and I wasn't about to kill her off. I grew too attached to all of my characters to let any of them die.

I'm not sure why I didn't write a story where my characters could have lived happily ever after. It would have been easy enough to make Annette my protagonist and give her a passionate and loving marriage. She and Malcolm could have had seven children and Rigsley ought never to have been in the picture. But I'm afraid that story would have been terribly dull. Besides, it's not the way that infatuation works. Hell, that's not the way that life works. There are always obstacles.

That's how I know that Colin and I are not going to be the Hollywood fairy tale that Gemma for some reason believes we will be. And that's why, despite the fact that my thoughts keep drifting back to the kiss that we shared in the parking lot a few days ago, I've been trying my best to keep a cool and level head around him. All of my efforts will probably go by the wayside very shortly, however, because today is *the day*. The day that Matthew and Rose film *the scene*. You know, the naughty one. With all the sex.

And it's only the *first* sex scene. The tamest too, for that matter. From here on out, this series is going to get very raunchy very quickly. I kind of wish I could have called in sick today, but somehow, I don't think that's an option.

As has become something of a ritual for us, Gemma and I meet Benjamin and Colin in the main trailer at the breakfast table. I'm sincerely hoping that no one (okay, mostly Benjamin) makes any dirty jokes or asks me to compare what's happening on set to what I envisioned while I was writing. Basically, it would just be great if no one talked at all this morning.

Of course, silence is rarely an option with Gemma.

"How do you film a sex scene anyway?"

Well, it didn't take very long to broach *that* subject, did it?

"Very carefully," Colin answers.

"It depends on how intimate the scene is," Benjamin adds. "I actually haven't filmed very many."

As if on cue, we all turn our eyes on Colin, who pulls his hair back off his face and groans. We all know that he cannot boast the same as Benjamin. Most of his early roles involved some kind of sex scene. And not the romantic *Shakespeare in Love* kind of sex scenes either. The hot and sweaty after dodging assassin's bullets and blowing up the local chemical lab kind. The adrenaline-fueled, heat of the moment kind.

To be honest, those sex scenes have never really done anything for me. I prefer tender, intimate moments of love and passion. Kate

146

Winslet and Leonardo DiCaprio in the backseat of an early twentieth-century automobile. Ryan Gosling and Rachel McAdams in a beautifully restored southern plantation. King Malcolm and Corrine Fletcher wrapped in a tender embrace in the dark and quiet of his royal bedchamber.

Okay, the first scene isn't going to be all that romantic. It's actually very formal, almost business-like. But as they grow to know one another, their intimacy evolves into real lovemaking. And the first time she kisses him? She's so hesitant, and yet, he falls desperately in love with her for allowing herself to be so vulnerable, so beautifully sweet and innocent.

With all this in my head, is it really any wonder I'm still single?

"You know, when you're a young unknown in Hollywood, you'll take any role you can get," Colin remarks, summoning me back to our conversation.

"Oh, so you're telling me that you didn't enjoy getting *paid* to pretend to have sex with all those beautiful women?" Gemma asks.

"No, it was nerve-wracking," Colin insists. "Besides, pretending to have sex is not nearly as fun as you'd think it would be."

"Not as good as the real thing, huh?" Gemma smirks. Then she winks at me.

It's going to be one of those days, isn't it?

After the actors are called back to hair and makeup, Gemma and I follow Elizabeth and Carl over to the castle and wait to go over notes for the day.

It turns out that Colin and Benjamin only have one scene each today, and Genevieve doesn't have to be here at all. Matthew and Rose will be the ones doing most of the work.

Of everything I've learned in the short week and a half that I've been here, what's been most surprising to me is how long shooting a single scene can take. I guess somewhere in the back of my mind I knew it took a while. But I'd never given it much thought before now.

By the time we break for lunch, Benjamin and Colin have wrapped filming for the day and are dismissed back to their trailers to change. I probably won't see either of them for the rest of the day, and as much as I would love to say that Colin's presence doesn't affect me one way or the other, I'm not looking forward to the rest of the day without him.

It's because he's your friend, I tell myself. *He makes you laugh. And he's fun to talk to. It's not like you have a crush on him or anything.*

Right. Because why would I have a crush on this guy who's handsome and charming and confident and a downright amazing kisser?

And who I'll likely never see again after these two months are up.

Remember that, I implore myself. *He's not yours. He never will be yours. Now forget that you*

148

ever kissed him and enjoy watching Matthew Kent take his shirt off.

What's funny is that even though I still think Matthew is drop dead gorgeous, he doesn't have the same effect on me that he did when we first met. Probably because I have spent every waking moment since last Friday night either making out with Colin or trying not to think about making out with Colin. I guess, though, after stealing a girl away from a real-life Prince, it's not that surprising that he managed to steal my attention away from Matthew.

My melodramatic and overcomplicated thoughts carry me through lunch and back into Dunadhar Castle where, to my delight and surprise, Colin is lounging in the entry hall, dressed in jeans and a black t-shirt, and scrolling through his smart phone.

"There really is just no reception out here, is there?" he grumbles.

"Did you forget something?" I ask him.

"No." He stands up and slides his phone into his pocket.

"I thought you had the rest of the day off."

"I do."

"So, why aren't you out enjoying it?"

He opens his mouth as if to answer, but before he can get the words out, Gemma appears on the scene.

"If there's one thing that I am looking forward to this weekend it is - hey, wait a minute," she interrupts herself as soon as she lays eyes on Colin. "You're not supposed to be here."

"Or am I?" Colin asks.

"Let me guess. They asked you to stick around in case Matthew needs a crash course in on-screen love-making."

Colin shrugs.

"Someone's gotta teach him."

I can't help it. I laugh. Colin grins at me.

"Maybe while you're at it, you can give Lorelei a more private lesson," Gemma quips, waggling her eyebrows.

That shuts me right up.

You know, a *real* personal assistant would be fired for that kind of comment.

She must know that's she's crossed some kind of line because the next thing I know, she's scampering back towards the door asking, "Do you want some coffee? I'll go get you some coffee. Or a cookie. Do you want a cookie? I'll get you a cookie."

And then she's gone.

Colin waits a beat before breaking the silence.

"I like Gemma."

"Yeah, she's fantastic," I mutter with a generous dose of sarcasm.

"She's not very subtle, is she?"

"What was your first clue?"

"So, was she saying that because you're interested in private lessons or...?" he asks with a mischievous grin.

"No!" I exclaim far too hastily. If I were talking to anyone other than Colin Ward, I'd be afraid that I'd offended him. As it is Colin, however, I'm not very concerned about his ego. It's probably about as fragile as stainless steel. "I - I mean... You know, we're friends. You and I are friends. And Gemma..." I take a deep breath, reminding myself that no matter how big a fool I've made of myself in front of Colin on several occasions now, we are still in a professional setting. "She just wants me to be happy. Sometimes I think she wants it more than I want it for myself."

"She's a good friend," Colin observes. Then he glances around. "You know, there's still a lot of this castle I haven't seen."

Okay, he's hinting at something. I may not know a lot about men, but I do know something about dialogue. It's the only thing my editors say I'm really good at. Because it's fairly obvious I don't excel at grammar. Or plausible storylines.

"Yeah, same here."

"Do you want to go exploring?"

"Right now?"

"No, I know you're still working. But after we wrap, once the crew has all gone? Maybe we sneak back in. See what all this place has to offer..."

Tempting. *So* tempting. I should say no. But I really do want to see the rest of the castle.

And as much as I'd love to deny it, I really, *really* want to be alone with Colin again.

"Okay."

It turns out that filming a sex scene is a lot less sexy than watching it on television or in the movie theater or on Netflix. There are a lot of retakes, a lot of fumbled lines, and a lot of sporadic laughter. But I think the final product is going to be something worth watching. Hopefully over and over again.

After we wrap for the day, I lie to Gemma and tell her that Carl and Elizabeth have asked me to stay late to go over a few changes to the script. I know she wouldn't mind if I told her that I was planning on a secret date with Colin. Quite the contrary. I think she'd probably get a little *too* excited. I don't want her, or anyone else, making more of this than it is. I don't even know what it is.

After Colin has changed out of his costume and back into his normal clothes, most of the cast and crew have gone home, but there are a few who are still lingering. Colin doesn't seem very worried that we'll get caught, however. In fact, he waltzes right back to the castle and picks the lock like he owns the place. He's so relaxed and confident, that any onlooker would probably think he's right where he's supposed to be.

I, on the other hand, am a little more anxious about breaking in. It's not exactly a habit of mine.

"Are we even allowed to be here right now?" I whisper through the vast, empty halls of Dunadhar.

"Probably not," he grins.

"What if someone's here? What if we get caught?"

"You really are a good girl, aren't you?"

"Well, apparently I like bad boys so..."

"*Former* bad boy. I'm a lot more well-behaved these days."

"He said after breaking into a centuries-old castle."

"You know, technically, we do work here. And when you think about it, none of us would be here if it weren't for you. So, this entire show kind of belongs to you," Colin reasons.

"You do know how to sweet talk, don't you?"

"I've read a lot of scripts," he explains.

"You realize that real-life women aren't the same as all those hot female characters in movies."

"*You* realize that most real-life men aren't some sort of Prince Charming or King Malcolm."

"Believe me, I'm well aware," I mutter.

"So are you going to tell me your story yet or - "

"No."

"Even just one little - "

"No."

"How about if I - "

"No." Colin truly looks at a loss for words. He's probably not used to being told no. Especially by a woman. "Why are you so interested anyway?"

"Because I like you," he answers simply. For some reason, that catches me off guard.

"You do?"

"You find that hard to believe?" he laughs.

"It's not that. I just haven't met very many men who are so direct. The ones I'm used to dating.... they like to keep women guessing."

"It makes them feel like they're one step ahead of you. They don't want to give you any sort of advantage in the dating game." Once again, I get the feeling he's speaking from experience.

"Well, I don't know about you, but I'm sick of all the games," I confess.

"And that's why I like you."

"I like you, too," I tell him.

He smiles at me. Our conversation has carried us down a long corridor to an archway, the entrance to a dark and very steep spiraling staircase.

"What are you thinking?" Colin whispers.

"That we shouldn't go up there." And with those famous last words, I step under the archway and up onto the first couple of stairs.

Colin follows so close behind that I can feel his hot breath on the back of my neck. His proximity in this dark and enclosed space ignites every nerve in my body and for a brief moment, I don't trust myself to take another step.

Slowly but surely, however, we carefully ascend the stairs and my mind begins to wander. How many souls have walked these same steps over the centuries? How many of their lives and secrets are etched in these stones? And how lucky am I to be here now, on this fantastic adventure?

The staircase leads us to an open landing, an empty room with two windows, a high ceiling, and a single door. Without a hint of hesitation, Colin crosses the room and opens the door. Golden evening light pours in, transforming the dull, gray tower into someplace warm and magical.

Whatever inhibitions I may have had evaporate into thin air as I follow Colin out onto the tower balcony. The view leaves me utterly breathless. Mountains painted shades of green, blue, and even a hint of violet in the glow of the evening sun. Clouds that dance and line the sky like a spectacular work of art. And Colin smiling beside me, looking like a fairy tale hero come to life.

"So, is this what it's like being in one of your books?" he asks.

"I don't think I could imagine anything this beautiful," I admit. Sure, I sought inspiration from pictures posted online, but images on a screen pale in comparison to experiencing it first-hand.

"I think I could," Colin says, glancing at me out of the corner of his eye.

I should know better than to take him seriously, and I think the rational part of me does. But rationality has never been my strongest suit. And Colin is so very difficult to resist. So when he steps forward to kiss me, I don't resist.

There in his arms, his delicious mouth pressed to mine, I realize that if ever I wanted to engage in a shameless tryst with a man who is the walking definition of a guilty pleasure, this is my chance. It won't be a romance for the storybooks. But it could be everything I never dared to hope for.

Chapter Thirteen

"What are you doing?" Gemma asks, peering over my shoulder.

It's Friday morning in our tiny hostel bedroom and I'm trying to be discreet. Apparently, I'm not doing a very good job.

"Nothing."

"It doesn't look like nothing."

"I'm looking for my lipstick."

"Left it on the counter."

"Oh, good. Mystery solved then."

Gemma grins at me.

"You're packing a just-in-case bag, aren't you?"

"No!" Gemma raises an eyebrow. "Maybe..."

"Oh, my little Delaney Bird. You're growing up so fast," she declares, hugging my shoulders.

"Stop," I blush.

"Imagine how teenage you would have reacted if someone had told her that one day, she'd be engaged in a rapturous affair with Colin Ward."

"She probably would have said, 'He's not my type. Give me Legolas from *Lord of the Rings*.'"

"Yeah, you always have had a thing for the blond pretty boys, haven't you?" Gemma asks. She's probably thinking of the time I dragged her to a Hanson concert in ninth grade. Colin doesn't need to know about that. "Regardless, this is a big night for you. Are you excited? Nervous? Do you have any questions?"

"Gem, you know this isn't my first time. *If* it even happens tonight."

"Oh, I'm pretty sure it's gonna happen," Gemma smirks. "And I'm pretty sure it's going to be the best thing that's ever happened to you. Besides having me as your best friend, of course."

"Of course," I echo.

For the first time in two weeks, Colin is already there and chatting with Benjamin when Gemma and I meander into the main trailer for breakfast. The moment I see him, memories of yesterday evening come flooding back to me. I don't know what it is about him. Maybe it's his carefree air of casual confidence, or perhaps his near-devastating good looks, but something about him makes me forget all of my insecurities and all of my reasons *why not*. Why not to take chances. Why not to share. Why not to trust. Why not to embrace every whim and every desire and every moment. Something about him makes me feel *alive*.

"Happy Friday, ladies," Benjamin greets us. "I hope you've packed your just-in-case bags." Then he winks at *me*. I guess Gemma must have told him about my lack of modern-day preparation skills. Right before he loaned me his underwear.

"Why? You don't want me sleeping in your boxers again?" I ask him.

"Nonsense. I'm always happy to come to the aid of a damsel in naked distress."

Oh, good Lord.

"And they say chivalry is dead," I remark.

"Not to mention when I got them back, they smelled like flowers and vanilla," Benjamin adds.

"You do smell nice," Colin tells me.

"Why thank you," I smile. "So where are we going?"

"*That* is up to the two of you," Benjamin says. "Be advised that we get next Friday off so we were thinking of hitting up Edinburgh next weekend."

"Oh my God, I'd love that," I gasp.

"Here we go," Gemma sighs.

"I finally get to visit the Elephant House!"

"You mean the one and only birthplace of Harry James Potter?" Benjamin asks, his eyes lighting up.

"Nooo," Gemma groans.

"What? Are you not a Potterhead?" Benjamin asks her.

"Don't get me wrong, I love *Harry Potter*. I just don't worship at the altar of Rowling like she does."

"Good. Because I was about to change my mind about you being my date for this weekend," Benjamin says.

Gemma rolls her eyes.

"Colin, are *you* this into *Harry Potter*?" she asks.

"I've never read the books," he admits with an exaggerated grimace, like he's afraid of the berating and chastisement that will surely befall him. "I enjoyed the movies though."

"Ugh..." Now it's my turn to groan.

"You didn't like the movies?" Benjamin gapes at me.

"No, no, the movies were fine. But they're *nothing* compared to books."

"You're a *Potter* purist, are you?" Benjamin asks.

"You're not?"

Benjamin shrugs.

"I'm an actor. I like movies. Though to be honest, I'm still rather bitter that I wasn't asked to be in them."

"Life is so unfair," I comment.

"I know," he sighs.

"So, Edinburgh next week," Gemma says loudly, clearly eager to change the subject. "What are we doing this weekend?"

"Like Benjamin said, it's your call," Colin says.

"What's close? Within driving distance?" I ask.

"Eilean Donan isn't too far," Benjamin says. "In fact, it's only about a thirty-minute drive. In Dornie."

"Really?" I ask. I had no idea we were so close to such a famous Scottish landmark. Then again, as previously stated, I'm *really* bad at geography and directions.

"Maybe we could drive out there tonight. Explore the area a bit. Find us a nice hotel and go from there," Benjamin suggests.

"Sounds like Heaven," Gemma grins. "As long as the two of you keep the *Potter* talk to a minimum."

Benjamin grasps a hand to his heart. I turn to Colin to see if he feels the same way.

"I once sat and listened to my niece talk about *My Little Pony* for eighty-four minutes straight. Do your worst."

I smile. Not because Colin has granted me permission to talk his ear off about *Harry Potter*, but because imagining him with his nieces and nephews is just about the cutest thing ever.

On his way back to hair and makeup, Colin slips past me, brushing my fingers with his.

I know I'm blushing, and judging by the smile on his face, I'm fairly certain that was his intention.

Today, he's shooting a scene with Genevieve, and in my opinion, it's one that makes the character of Rigsley so despicable. He goes out of his way to remind her of all of her shortcomings, that if a child is, in fact, conceived, it will never truly be hers. Although I've never admitted it aloud, Rigsley is something of a representation of the men I've known and dated who have, in one way or another, made me feel inadequate. I wasn't pretty enough. I wasn't smart enough. I didn't give them what they wanted. To them, I wasn't a person with thoughts or feelings. I was an object. And a disappointing one at that. It's sad, but you wouldn't believe how many women I've met who've been made to feel the same way.

And here I am, preparing to go on a date with the guy who's about to embody all of that. Thank God it's all an act.

But it's an unnervingly good one.

"It must be dreadful for you," he gloats over Genevieve, a dark and sinister smirk plastered on his handsome face. "Knowing that right now, your husband is in the arms of such a lovely *young* woman. Soft skin, dark golden hair... pure as a spring flower."

"Leave me be," Genevieve hisses back.

"Now, now, you know this is not my doing. If you had given the King a son, the young lady would have no purpose here. You are the one who has failed. Failed your husband. Failed your kingdom. *Failed yourself.*"

The scene ends with Annette bursting into tears and Rigsley sauntering out of the room, certain that he will be rewarded for his brilliance once Corrine gives birth to a son.

Here's one of those behind-the-scenes set secrets that very few people actually know. When I was collaborating with my fellow screenwriters, Sarah and Cody, we debated throwing in a lust arc between Rigsley and Annette. Of course, no such lust exists in the book, but after Colin was cast as Rigsley, Cody suggested it might be hot to have him hook up with Annette. Not out of love, but out of disdain and anger. And passion. A lot of passion. The idea behind it was that perhaps the reason Rigsley was so horrible to Annette was that he was in love with her and he was jealous that she had married Malcolm instead of him. At the end of the day, that idea was scratched because neither Sarah nor I wanted to perpetuate the emotional-and-mental-abuse-is-romantic-if-the-guy-is-hot-and-in-love-with-you trope.

Shooting wraps early today, so as soon as Colin and Benjamin are out of makeup and back into their street clothes, we climb into Benjamin's car and make the quick journey to Dornie and Eilean Donan Castle.

By the time we arrive, the castle is closed to tourists for the day (not that that should discourage Colin in any way), but even from the car park, it's still a vision to behold: majestic and proud, sitting atop a small island in the middle of blue-green waters, the late afternoon sun casting long shadows across its towers and turrets. The scenic setting reminds me of how few pictures I've taken, how absent I've been from social media. As Delaney Brooks, I can't post anything about this trip. But as Lorelei Dubois, bestselling author and much cooler person in general, I can share a few pictures and updates.

I pull out my phone and snap a few photos of Eilean Donan. Colin glances over my shoulder.

"Pretty," he says.

"Thank you."

I know from internet stalking him that Colin isn't very active on social media. He has a Facebook page and a Twitter account, but I'm pretty sure his team runs them. None of his posts are ever very personal. They're always promotions for his latest projects or recaps of awards shows.

I open Instagram and select my favorite picture of Eilean Donan, captioning it, "*Head over heels in love with Scotland; its castles, its landscape, its history, its people.*"

"You forgot to mention Colin and me," Benjamin remarks, staring at his own phone.

"Are you creeping on my Instagram?" I ask.

"More or less," he replies. "Don't you want all your friends back home to know that you get to hang out with us all the time?"

"I think they already know that." At least, the ones who know about my secret identity do. And those friends are few and far between.

What I don't tell Benjamin is that while I'm sure I'll share that I got to meet and work with him, I won't go into details. I might mention that we became friends, but I'm not going to tell them about our weekend getaways or morning meetings by the coffee machine. And I'm certainly not going to tell anyone about Colin. Other than that he was handsome and charming and an all-around wonderful guy. No one needs to know that we've been sneaking around and making out in castles.

After dinner in a small restaurant called Seafarer's, we check into a local bed and breakfast for the night.

"What shall it be?" Benjamin asks. "Three rooms again?"

"I think we can get by with two," I reply. "That is, if you boys don't mind bunking together," I add with a mischievous grin.

"Not a bit. Colin is fun to cuddle," Benjamin quips. Colin narrows his eyes, but I can tell he's trying not to laugh.

I guess the sweet middle-aged woman who runs the bed and breakfast thinks we must be serious, because she hands one set of room keys to Gemma and me and another set to the guys. Afterward, she looks up at Colin and says, "You're in the movies, aren't you?"

"Oh. Yes. I am."

"I always enjoy watching you. You're very handsome."

"Thank you," he grins.

Benjamin clears his throat, waiting for her to recognize him. She doesn't. Gemma pats his slumped shoulder.

"You know, if you need anything at all, don't hesitate to ask. It's isn't often we get a famous face around here."

"Thank you. You're very sweet, Ms...?"

"Sophie. Sophie Dunbar," the woman beams. "You know, now that I think about it, I remember my daughter mentioning they were going to be filming a new television series here. The one that's based on that book. Oh, what is it called?"

"*The Queen's Surrogate*," Colin supplies. "And as a matter of fact, this gorgeous woman is the one who wrote it," he says, motioning to me.

"No," Sophie eyes me up and down. "My goodness, you are not at all what I expected."

"Really?" I laugh nervously. I never know whether that sort of statement is a compliment or not.

"You look so... innocent."

Okay, I *have* heard that before. I'm not sure what it is about me. It could be the blue eyes that

166

so often appear wide and overwhelmed. Or maybe it's my age. I've had several people tell me that they expected someone older. I guess that makes sense. Most young people these days don't even have time to read a book, let alone write one. Or a whole series.

"Well," Sophie continues. "I do hope you'll all enjoy your stay here. And that you'll... behave yourselves," she adds with a quick glance in my direction. Maybe she doesn't think I'm so innocent after all.

The bedrooms themselves are cute, cozy, and very welcoming. Not at all the setting I'd have imagined for a secret sexy rendezvous with Colin Ward. But then, when does life ever turn out the way we imagined? As far as I'm concerned, none of this was supposed to happen to me. I was supposed to earn my doctorate, become a literature professor, settle down with a nice, normal husband and raise a nice, normal family. But someone somewhere absolutely obliterated the beetle that was supposed to keep the space-time continuum in check. Now I'm living in this strange butterfly-effect alternate universe where I write dirty books and hook up with movie stars. I couldn't have planned for this. I couldn't have dreamt any of this was even possible.

But it is. It's here and it's now. And Colin is here. And he's watching me as I try to make sense of every moment that led us to this one.

And suddenly I know I've spent far too much time trying to make sense of things. Trying to understand the whys and the hows of life when I'm simply meant to be living it.

And as I close the gap between us, as I take his shirt in my hands and breathe him in, as he leans down to kiss me in the golden glow of the evening sun, I know I'm finally ready to live.

Chapter Fourteen

It happens in a series of fleeting moments.

In the first moment, he's sitting down on the bed, fully clothed, waiting for me to make the next move. I'm standing over him, running my fingers through his hair as he leans forward and kisses my collarbone. His hands work their way around my waist, toying with my shirt until they find my bare skin. I lean in closer.

In the next moment, he's taking my hands and pulling me onto the bed with him with a gentle tug and a mischievous grin. I fall on top of him, laughing, as he smiles and kisses me again. My mouth. My neck. My shoulder. Then he looks to me, as if for permission.

He doesn't need to ask for it.

Once we've shed our clothes, we tumble back into bed, entangled in crisp white sheets and wrapped in one another's arms. His strong, sturdy body is hot against my stomach, my breasts, and his proximity leaves me craving him, desperate to draw him even closer. Closer. *Closer.*

The next moment is one of surrender, one of pleasure, and ultimately, one of trust. It's human connection at its most intimate and most passionate. It's in this moment that I lose myself to primal instincts; to shallow breaths and blissful desperation, to rising pressure and hastening rhythm, and finally to a dizzying burst of ecstasy and starlight.

Afterward, he buries his face in my neck and sighs. I rest my arms around him, trailing my fingers down his neck and across his shoulders. When he lifts his head up again, he gives me one gentle, contented kiss and says, "You know... It's been a long time since I've been that nervous."

"You were nervous?" I ask. "Why?"

"I'm making love to a romance author," he explains with a grin. "Your standards are high."

"My standards are fictional," I remind him. "*I'm* the one competing with hundreds of real-life models and movie stars."

"Okay, not *hundreds*," he says. "Maybe a few dozen. But if I may say so, you blew them all out of the water."

"Yeah, I don't buy that for a second."

"Why not?"

"Because just as I make things up for a living, you recite lines for a living. You've probably said that to every single woman you've ever slept with."

"Not true!" he insists. Then he backpedals. "Maybe I've said it once or twice. When I was younger. And foolish."

"But now you're older and wiser?"

"I think the older part is a bit obvious," he remarks, running a hand through his dark, disheveled hair.

"I actually think you look better older," I tell him.

"What are you talking about? Younger Colin was beautiful."

"Yeah, but older Colin is distinguished, which is even better."

"Thank God you're a writer," Colin laughs and kisses me. "Speaking of..."

"No, I'm not going to turn this into my next novel."

"That's not what I was going to ask, but since you mentioned it, I'm a little offended," he jokes. "No, I was going to ask what it is you've made up."

"What?"

"You called me out for parroting lines. Now I'm calling you out for making things up."

I'm glad my cheeks are still flushed, otherwise, I'd be blushing at his accusation. To be fair, I really haven't made up *that* much. True, he doesn't know my real name and thinks that I live full-time as some glamorous romance author when, in reality, I still wear my yoga pants to the grocery store, eat ice cream straight out of the tub, and only shave my legs if I know I'm going to be wearing a skirt. But other than all that, I've been completely honest with him.

"I haven't made anything up."

"See, I'm not buying *that*," he tells me.

"Maybe I haven't *told* you everything, but that's not the same as making things up."

"Okay. So what haven't you told me?" he asks, propping himself up on his elbows and staring down at me.

"We've known each other two weeks. There's a lot I haven't told you."

"Then I'm going to ask you what you asked me last week. Tell me something that I can't find online. Because I've looked."

"You've what?"

"You think I don't take advantage of what little Wi-Fi we have out here?"

"You looked me up online?" Colin shrugs. "What were you hoping to find?"

"Anything. I liked reading through your Twitter," he grins.

Oh, God. My Twitter is ridiculous. It's just a bunch of personalized memes and pictures of cats with the occasional book quote thrown in. And a lot of embarrassing tweets to Matthew Kent.

Fantastic.

If he's a gentleman, he won't bring those up.

"Well, if you've read my Twitter, you know everything about me," I remark.

"No. I know what you *want* people to know about you."

"I've already told you, I'm boring. I like books and cats like every other introvert. My favorite holiday is Christmas. I don't like carrots. I have trouble spelling the word 'mischievous.' And sometimes, when Gemma and I are feeling sad, we get together, drink wine, and binge-watch the *Twilight* movies."

"You're kidding."

"Oh, no. We can quote them."

"Thank you for waiting until *after* we'd had sex to tell me this."

"Shut up," I laugh. "Like you don't have any guilty pleasures." He presses his lips together and tries not to smile. "You do! What are they?" He sighs but he still doesn't say anything. "Come on, you know you want to tell me."

"Can I plead the fifth?"

"No."

He groans and falls back down onto the pillows, burying his face in his hands.

"You're going to laugh."

"You laughed at me."

"I didn't laugh. I grimaced."

"If you don't tell me, I'm going to assume that you also binge-watch *Twilight* when you're sad."

"Fine," he finally breaks. "Two years ago, my sister and her husband wanted to take my niece to see *Wicked* for her birthday. Well, my sister got sick so her husband called me up and asked me if I wanted to use her ticket."

"And you liked it?"

"No. I *loved* it. I went home and downloaded the whole soundtrack. I took time out of my New York trips to see it on Broadway. It's just so good."

"I haven't seen it," I confess.

"I'm going to take you," he tells me.

"Oh yeah?"

"I'm going to fly you out to New York. We'll eat ice cream in Central Park. We'll watch Times Square light up at sunset. And then we'll go see *Wicked*. And it will change your life."

It sounds so wonderful that for a moment, I'm tempted to believe that it could happen. But I have to remind myself that this is not the beginning of anything. This is a temporary albeit glorious break from reality. I can have fun with him. I can even pretend to make plans with him.

But no matter what, I absolutely, positively *cannot* fall in love with him.

Morning breaks much sooner than I thought it would.

I don't know why I thought I would sleep last night. I guess I figured like most of my former hook-ups, once would be enough for Colin.

It wasn't.

And if I'm being completely honest with myself, once wasn't enough for me either.

Now, as daylight streams into our room, I'm resting with my head on his chest while I listen to his deep, steady breathing.

Benjamin was right. He is a lot of fun to cuddle.

I'm just starting to doze off when I hear my phone begin to buzz. Colin shifts in his sleep but doesn't wake. I decide to let my phone ring. It's probably Gemma.

But then it buzzes again.

And again.

Oh, well. Mornings like this are why we have coffee.

Careful not to wake Colin, I slide back over to my side of the bed and grab my phone off of the nightstand.

3 Missed Calls From: Gemma

She calls again. I answer on the first buzz. "Hello?"

"So, how was it?" she asks. Then, before I can answer, she starts to ramble. "Oh, wait, he's probably in the room, isn't he? Never mind. Just give me a number. Scale of one to ten."

"He's asleep," I assure her. "And eleven."

Gemma squeals. I guess that means Benjamin is awake. Gemma's excited voice is so shrill, it could wake the dead.

"Okay, well, I just wanted to call and let you know that we're about to head down to breakfast if you two would like to join us."

"Okay," I yawn. "Sounds good."

"See you soon! But you know, take your time. But not too much time because Benjamin and I were talking about going to the Isle of Skye today to see the Fairy Pools. It's only about two hours away. Of course, if you and Colin don't feel up to it, we completely understand, but I know you wanted to see them."

So many words. So early in the morning.

"No, I definitely want to go," I tell her.

"Great! See you in just a few!" she exclaims. Then she hangs up.

I wonder how much sleep I can get in just a few. Probably not a lot.

"An eleven, huh?" Colin murmurs, smiling at me from his back.

I blush.

"She was asking me for the time."

"It's eight-thirty."

"Huh... I guess my phone is wrong."

Colin laughs. Then he leans over and reaches for my arm.

"Come here." His voice is low and rough as he pulls me down into the best good morning kiss of my life. Then he strokes my hair and asks, "So, what are we doing today?"

For a split second, I forget my conversation with Gemma. I forget coffee and brunch, Fairy Pools and the Isle of Skye. I forget everything that isn't Colin and his arms and his chest and his eyes and his mouth. Why do we have to do anything today? Why can't we just stay here all morning? All week? For the rest of our lives?

But then I catch a glimpse of the world outside my window, the vibrant green hills quite alive and beckoning me out to see and explore.

I turn back to Colin and say, "Catching fairies."

He looks politely confused.

"Is that code for something?"

"We're going to the Fairy Pools," I translate.

"Oh, right. You'd mentioned them last week."

I'm surprised he remembers that.

Even though I know we're both eager and excited to see what Skye has to offer, neither of us seems willing to move. We simply lie in silence, enjoying the warmth of each other's embrace. It isn't until Gemma calls again asking where we are that we finally climb out of bed. But before we dress, Colin pulls me into one more long kiss and says, "You know, what I said the other day was true. It has been a while since I've been with someone."

"Why is that?" I wonder aloud before remembering that that is absolutely none of my business. "I'm sorry. That's so personal."

"I don't mind," he assures me. "I think I just became disenchanted with it all. After watching my sisters settle down and especially after my nieces and nephews were born, I began to realize how shallow all my relationships were. And to be honest, it got to the point where it just really wasn't fun anymore. So, I took some time off from dating, if you could even really call it that. I wanted to wait until I knew that it would mean something. And you, Lorelei... you were worth the wait."

I'm glad he kisses me then, because his words have left me absolutely speechless. None of the other guys I've been with have made me feel like I'm worth anything. But Colin... God, he makes me feel like I'm the only person in the world.

Even if we're not meant to last, even if I never see him again after our two months are up, I know I'm never going to regret him.

Stepping out into Skye is like stepping into another world. Like so much of Scotland, its hills and slopes are a lush emerald green and I can't help but think that if I were to climb far enough, I could actually touch the clouds. The Fairy Pools themselves are every bit as magical as their name suggests. Their waters, so crystal clear and rich

178

in shades of blue and turquoise, even in the shade of the misty, gray skies, must be enchanted.

How can anyone visit this place and not leave believing in fairies?

"So, does this setting remind you of your river?" Benjamin asks.

"Who?" I ask.

"You. Do these pools remind you of your Rhine River?"

I blink.

"I have no idea what you're talking about."

"What?" he declares. "You've never heard the legend of Lorelei?"

"I don't think I have," I answer. I guess I should have done more research when I was trying to pick a pen name. I have no real reason for choosing Lorelei. I honestly just liked the name. I didn't know it came with a legend. Or jokes about a river.

"According to German folklore, a beautiful maiden named Lorelei was betrayed by her lover and threw herself into the Rhine River. But when she died, she became a Siren, sitting atop a rock overlooking the river, enchanting men and luring them to their deaths with her voice. There's even a poem about it."

"There's a song about it, too," Colin adds. "I sang it when I auditioned for a movie based on the tale. I didn't get the part, but I remember every word."

"Well, don't just tell us about it," Gemma says.

"What, you want me to sing?" Colin asks.

"Yes." We all answer as one.

"You might regret asking."

"We won't," Gemma promises. And then she holds up her phone, fully prepared to capture every moment.

"Oh, great," Colin groans. "Just do me a favor. Please don't post this to YouTube."

"Wouldn't dream of it."

Sure she wouldn't.

Colin closes his eyes just as a brisk wind begins to blow in, gently toying with the dark locks of hair falling into his face. He brushes them back with his fingers and begins to sing.

> *"Brother, mine*
> *Are you going*
> *To the River Rhine?*
> *To hear the murmuring mountain*
> *And echoes from the East?*
> *Can you stay?*
> *Can you stay?*
>
> *Have you heard*
> *The story told?*
> *A maiden fair,*
> *A curse of old.*
> *Love, it turned away*
> *And left her shattered on the shore.*

Can you stay?
Can you stay?

They say her name
Is Lorelei.
And she sings
Her broken lullaby
To the souls upon the waters,
The farers of the waves.
Can you stay?
Can you stay?

Brother, mine
Sail ye safely
To the River Rhine.
Hearken not
The Siren's song
Or to the grave
You'll soon belong.
Can you stay?
Can you stay?"

Once the song ends, we all applaud. Colin grins and takes a bow. He actually has a wonderful singing voice.

"So, now you know," Benjamin tells me. "Your parents named you after a heartbroken woman who lures sailors to their deaths."

Actually, my parents named me after a character from their favorite sitcom. But that's not important, especially considering it's an entirely different name than the one that Benjamin and Colin have in their heads.

"I'll have a word with them about that," I tell them.

We hike a little further, Colin and Benjamin leading the way, when Gemma grabs my elbow and pulls me back. I expect her to press me for more details about my night with Colin. But that isn't what she asks at all.

"Do you think... Maybe you should tell them?"

"Tell them what?"

"You know, who you really are."

"They know who I really am." Sort of.

"Colin doesn't know your real name."

"Why would he need to?"

"What if he wants to see you again? Or get in touch with you after filming ends?"

"That's not going to happen."

"How do you know?"

"Because I'm a realist."

"Please, you're a romance author who runs around boasting about her honorary Hogwarts degree. You're the worst realist ever."

"Be that as it may, they still don't need to know. Besides, it's not like I'm withholding that much. I don't have a secret lover or a paid ghostwriter back home. I'm still me. I just... go by a different name."

"Well, I don't think you're giving them or yourself enough credit. Delaney Brooks is my best friend and my favorite person in the whole world. And I think Colin would be just as taken with her as he is with Lorelei DuBois."

Deep down, I know she's right. I know that what I call myself, the name my parents gave me, won't matter to Colin. Or to Benjamin. But having that name all to myself, knowing that name is mine and mine alone, is a bit like having a security blanket. It's reassuring to know that if I get hurt or embarrass myself, if something bad happens, it isn't happening to Delaney. It's happening to Lorelei. And Lorelei can handle it. Lorelei can brush it off like it's no big deal. Lorelei is strong.

Delaney, not so much.

But Gemma doesn't need to know all of that.

"I'll think about it," I say solely to appease her.

"Promise?"

"I promise."

Excerpt from *The Queen's Surrogate*

My nightly visits with King Malcolm have become almost routine. Every night, Rigsley comes to escort me to His Majesty's bedchamber. Every night, I undress and present myself. Every night, I lie in silence as he enters me, not for love or for personal pleasure, but for the sole purpose of putting his child in me. A child which I do not yet carry. A child who may never come at all.

And what will become of me if he doesn't?

This is your duty, *I tell myself.* Lie with the King. Bear his child.

Tonight, when I arrive at His Majesty's quarters, I can see that something is troubling him. We rarely exchange words or sentiments. I do not speak unless I am addressed. But the look in his beautiful blue eyes saddens me, and I find myself wishing there was something I could do to ease his mind and bring him comfort.

I let my dressing gown fall to the ground and take my place on the bed. I try not to observe as the King sheds his own clothing and prepares to take me once again. But I cannot stop my eyes from wandering, from drifting across his broad, muscular chest, up to his strong, bearded jaw, to his devastatingly handsome face. And those eyes, those haunted blue eyes, so full of concern, of responsibility, of the weight of his crown. And I begin to wonder if perhaps he needs more than a servant tonight.

"Your Majesty," I whisper. "What is it?"

"What is what?" he growls.

"You just... You seem distraught. Are you all right?"

"I am fine." His answer is harsh. His eyes are cold.

I should not have spoken. Fearful that I have gone too far, I bite my lip and try to hide my tears from the King.

"I am sorry, Sire," I whimper. "Please forgive me."

It is only then that he looks at me for what truly feels like the first time. His eyes soften. The grimace fades from his face. And then, he sighs and sits down on the bed.

"No. I am the one who should be asking your forgiveness. You showed concern for me and I... I fear I've lost whatever sense of decency I may have once possessed."

"You cannot think that," I insist, sitting up so that I may look at him more directly as I speak.

"You are a great King and a wise and virtuous ruler."

"You are too kind, Mistress Corrine. I am none of those things. Just a man who has failed to do right by his crown, his country, his own wife. Our people are starving. Our Kingdom owes a great debt that we cannot pay, a debt that my dear father saw fit to bury us under..." Then he gives a mirthless laugh. "I cannot imagine why I'm telling you all of this. You're just a country girl, after all. You can't possibly begin to comprehend."

"Perhaps, Your Majesty, but that doesn't mean I can't listen."

"That is not why you're here."

"I'm here to serve my King and my sovereign, howsoever he desires."

He observes me then, his eyes taking in my every feature. And it is only then that I truly begin to feel vulnerable, exposed. What does he see when he looks at me? A poor, plain, simple country girl? Or the woman who has proven herself strong enough, smart enough, beautiful enough to bear the next King of Edin?

And I wonder then... how is it that I see him?

As a King, of course. Powerful, handsome, intelligent. A man to whom I have no right to look upon or speak... or touch. But here in the sanctity and silence of his bedchamber, we may as well be the only souls in the Kingdom.

"You wish to serve me?" he asks. His voice is low and so deep, I can feel its timbre throughout my entire body.

"Yes, Sire. With all my heart."

The King then reaches out to me and brushes my hair back away from my face. I feel my body begin to tremble.

"Then treat me as you would an ordinary man. Talk to me. Touch me. Embrace me."

I couldn't disobey him if I wanted to.

Chapter Fifteen

It probably goes without saying that sex with no strings attached is addictive.

After our journey to the Fairy Pools, Colin and I spent a second night in Dornie, and it was even better than the first. Then Sunday morning dawned and forced us back to Lot B, back to scripts and the lingering smell of day-old coffee, back to the real world where no one is supposed to know that I spent the weekend in Colin's arms. I went home to our hostel Sunday night wondering how I was supposed to wait until Thursday night to be with him again. Possibly Friday. I don't know when we're leaving for Edinburgh, which makes the wait even worse. Monday night was equally excruciating, especially considering the *two* incredibly steamy scenes I watched Matthew film, first with Rose and then with Genevieve.

Now it's Tuesday afternoon and Elizabeth has just called for our thirty-minute lunch break. I plan to take mine as I usually do; with Gemma and, if they don't have lines to run or additional work to discuss, Colin and Benjamin. Since there's no sign of either one of them, I'm guessing it will be another girls' lunch.

"Did you hear about Lisa?" Gemma asks me.

"Oh God, do I want to know?"

Lisa Bateman is a girl we went to high school with and she is actually insane. She's manipulative, she's controlling, and last spring, the guy she was dating ended up in the hospital after a very serious fall down the stairs. Gemma is convinced that he was pushed and that one day, she and I are going to end up on *Dateline* talking about how we always knew there was something off about our former classmate.

"Don't worry. She didn't kill anyone."

"Well, that's a relief." It probably is only a matter of time, though. "What's going on?"

"She's reading your book. And apparently, she's obsessed with it," Gemma gloats.

"Fantastic," I remark. Thankfully, I doubt she'll recognize my picture in the back of the book. The last she saw of me, I was a scrappy eighteen-year-old who didn't know how to style her hair or apply mascara.

"According to her new boyfriend, she's just ordered a new bow and arrow and a gold crown... so they can role play."

Gross.

"Why are you friends with her new boyfriend?" I ask her.

"I'm not. He just posted about it and tagged her. Wouldn't it be awesome if she knew that you - " She stops mid-sentence and glances at someone over my shoulder.

"Knew that you what?" Colin asks, taking a seat next to me.

"Hey," I smile. "I thought you weren't going to join us."

"Actually, I'm not. I came here hoping to steal you. I have a few questions about the script."

"Oh. Okay." This is the first time he's ever asked me for help with anything work-related.

"We won't be long," he tells Gemma.

"Take your time," she grins.

I follow Colin outside and around the castle, back to the lot where their trailers are parked.

"I'm sorry. I hope I wasn't interrupting anything too serious," Colin says to me.

"You weren't," I assure him. "Just hometown gossip. Nothing important."

"I see," he says, unlocking the door to his trailer.

I'd never imagined anyone could live comfortably in a trailer, but Colin's has a couch, a closet, a small kitchen area, and a bathroom. It's not very personal or homey, but it's enough.

Once we're inside and he's closed the door, I ask, "So, what questions did you - "

But before I can finish, Colin presses his lips to mine, silencing me with a deep, craving kiss that leaves me trembling. Sad to say it isn't until he wraps his arms around my waist and lifts me right up off the ground that I realize he never had any questions about the script.

Our first night together, we took the time to explore each other, to kiss, to touch, to admire. Our second night was very much the same but preceded by the rapturous anticipation of knowing just how good we are together.

Here in the trailer, there is no anticipation or tender exploration, just a wild desire to be as close to Colin as I can possibly be, to feel his body and his heat as he takes from me everything that I'm willing to give and more. We don't speak. I barely even breathe. It's fast and it's exhilarating and it's almost more than I am able to withstand.

And then it's over.

Once I finally catch my breath, I look Colin in the eye.

"Something tells me... that wasn't your first time in the trailer."

"It's my first time with one of my bosses in the trailer," he answers, sounding just as winded as I feel. "Does that count?"

"I'm one of your bosses?"

"Well, I think so. It's your story. I'm the one who's supposed to make you happy, not the other way around."

"Yeah, but I make way less money than you. And I'm staying in a hostel," I remind him. Though to be fair, I'm making a pretty decent amount of money from this project. I really can't complain.

"True, but if you wanted me gone, all you'd have to do is say the word. They could replace me easily. You...? Without you, this show doesn't happen at all."

"Actually, it does. I signed the contract."

"You know what I mean." And to prove his point, he kisses me again. "By the way, I'll probably have a few more questions for you before the week is up."

"And I will be more than happy to answer them for you," I assure him.

Then, after running my fingers through my hair and helping him reposition his tunic, we step out of his trailer and make our way back to the castle.

Thursday finally arrives and with it, a renewed sense of excitement. As much as I love our castle in the Highlands, I'm eager to see what the rest of the country has to offer. Especially Edinburgh.

Beautiful, historic, magical Edinburgh.

"We have two options," Benjamin told us this morning. "We can either head out tonight as soon as we wrap, maybe stop for dinner along the way, or we can all get a good night's sleep and drive down first thing in the morning."

The vote is unanimous and once we've been dismissed for the day, we embark on the three-hour drive to Edinburgh. Again, I sit in the back with Colin, only this time, I let myself slide over to the center so I can be closer to him. He doesn't seem to have any objections as he wraps an arm around my shoulder and plays gently with my long brown hair.

I must be sleepier than I thought because I doze on and off the whole way there and before I know it, we're pulling into the car park of a Riordan Suites hotel. It's a beautiful building, gothic in design and detail, but the florescent sign hanging near the base of the tower looks very out of place. Very commercial.

"I know it's a bit touristy," Benjamin claims, "but it's in a great location. And as charming and quaint as that bed and breakfast was last week, I will admit to being accustomed to a slightly finer way of life."

"Slightly?" Colin comments.

"I missed having room service. There. Are you happy?"

It's really no wonder he and Gemma get along so well.

I will admit, touristy though it may be, the Riordan is *really* nice. Crystal chandeliers in the lobby, cozy white bathrobes in the closets, not to mention a fantastic view of the Royal Mile from our fifth-story balcony. The sun has finally set, though the distant horizon still glows a brilliant golden orange and the sky remains a dark mix of blues and violets. Still, it's dark enough for the city lights to flicker to life, bright white beacons adorning an ageless skyline.

I haven't even been here an hour and already, Edinburgh is the city of my dreams.

"I need this."

"No, you don't."

"Yes, I do. You know I do."

"People are watching."

"I don't care. Take the picture," I insist, pressing my phone into Gemma's hands.

We're standing in front of the Elephant House, next to the large sign in the window proudly identifying the coffee shop as the building where J.K. Rowling penned the *Harry Potter* series. And I'm getting a picture of me smiling and pointing to the sign to share with the entire world. Or at least, the people who follow Lorelei DuBois on Instagram.

"You are so embarrassing," Gemma sighs.

"Just be grateful I didn't bring my wand."

Gemma rolls her eyes while Colin and Benjamin laugh from the sidelines.

After walking the Royal Mile, we visit Edinburgh Castle. Overlooking the city from the grassy hilltop of the Castle Rock, the fortress itself looks as though it has been carved from the very stone upon which it sits. It is powerful yet elegant, lavish yet wholly inviting to anyone fortunate enough to find themselves standing at the castle gate. These are doors and walls and windows that have seen kings and queens, saints and sinners, voyagers from all corners of the world. And now us.

"Yeah, I think I could live here," Gemma declares, taking in the splendor of the great hall. "In fact, when the rest of you go back to the Highlands, you can just leave me here."

"But then who will bring me my coffee and make inappropriate jokes about my love life?" I ask her.

"Colin, what's your phone number? I'll text them to you," Gemma jokes.

At least I hope she's joking.

"It's her! Look she's wearing the same outfit! Lorelei!"

I turn to see two young women, both of whom look to be about my age, gaping at me from across the great hall. They approach me with an air of timid confidence that I've come to find characteristic of readers who recognize me in public.

"I'm sorry, we don't mean to bother you, but you're Lorelei Dubois, right?" One of the girls asks. She's wearing glasses and an adorably geeky shirt with a picture of a cat dressed as Shakespeare. She and her friend are also American tourists.

"Yes," I answer with a smile.

"I knew it!" the second girl squeals. She has long red hair and is wearing black pants and a white button-down shirt. She looks like she belongs here. "We saw your post on Instagram! We're huge fans."

"I'm actually a writer, too," the first girl tells me. "Your books inspired me so much."

"Oh my God, thank you. What do you like to write?" I ask.

"I actually write fantasy. Mostly dragons, but with a little magic and witchcraft thrown in."

"Sounds like Scotland is the perfect place for you," I tell her.

"It really is. Are you here for - COLIN WARD!" The writer with the cat t-shirt almost faints right on the spot when she realizes who I'm with. "I love you. I love you. Oh my God. I've seen all your movies. Your performance in *Boundless* was just brilliant. And - " Then she spots Benjamin and I truly begin to worry that she might *actually* keel over.

"Hello," Benjamin grins.

"So wait, are you filming here? I mean, we know that you're working on the miniseries," the redhead says.

"Today is actually our day off," I explain. "We're here as tourists. And *Harry Potter* enthusiasts."

"Oh, I love it!" the writer exclaims. "Can we please take a picture with all of you?"

Benjamin doesn't think twice.

"Of course!"

We spend the rest of the afternoon on the castle grounds. We visit Saint Margaret's Chapel, the National War Museum, even the whiskey shop. Watching Colin peruse the bottles, I can't help but wonder if being here is difficult for him. Maybe we should leave.

Benjamin, on the other hand, doesn't seem to share my concerns.

"Imagine if those girls had asked to take your picture in here," he says to Colin.

"Geoff would have loved that," Colin remarks.

"Geoff?" I ask.

"My publicist. And when I say he would have loved it, I truly mean he would have loved it. I could have made all kinds of headlines: *Colin Ward, Off the Wagon!*"

"*Falling Back to the Bottle!*" Benjamin chimes in.

"But that's terrible," I declare. I hate to interrupt their fun, but to me, that just doesn't seem like the kind of thing you joke about.

"That's the business," Benjamin sighs.

"Geoff isn't a bad guy," Colin assures me. "We just... don't always see things eye to eye."

"Is he flying in next week for the interviews?" Benjamin asks.

"I think so."

Oh, right. Next week, we're going to have a few bloggers and reporters on set interviewing the cast, the producers, the director, and yes, the writers. Sarah and Cody will be flying out too, and I'm excited to officially meet them. But knowing that Colin's publicist will be there stirs up a new sense of fear and anxiety that stems from age-old insecurities and moments I wish I could forget. It's irrational, I know. But after what Colin has said about Geoff, I'm not altogether certain that I can trust him. And I definitely don't want him to even *suspect* that I may be anything more to his client than a casual acquaintance.

I like Colin. I really, *really* like him.

I just don't need the world to know how much.

Chapter Sixteen

The girls we met at Edinburgh Castle shared the pictures that they took with us and lo and behold, the media got a hold of them. Just to be clear, a picture with one of us, maybe even two, would not have been enough to get the gossip bloggers talking. But all three of us out and about is apparently worth a few headlines.

All the Queen's Men: Lorelei DuBois Hangs Out in Edinburgh With TWO of Hollywood's Brightest (and Hottest!) Stars!

Colin Ward, Benjamin Wyndham, and Lorelei DuBois Greet Fans in Edinburgh!

Benjamin Wyndham and Colin Ward Take a Break from Filming... And Take Lorelei DuBois to a Real Castle!

Everyone living in the Internet age knows that the world wide web is immortal. That can be a very empowering thing. It can also be very destructive. I'm no stranger to interviews, articles, or even the occasional headline. And as long as I get a say in what's written about me, I have no qualms about those interviews and articles being published. It's the stories that get written without my consent, the anonymous observations and speculations that go over my head and behind my back, that I wish I could do without.

Thankfully, these articles all seem to be written with amiable intent. There's no hint of scandal, no mention of romance. Just reports of three colleagues enjoying their time in a beautiful and historic city.

"Maybe I should be a gossip blogger," Gemma muses as we stroll the hills and meadows of Holyrood Park. It's Saturday, our second and last day in Edinburgh, and I haven't seen nearly enough of it. "After all," she continues, "I've got an in with the stars of the steamiest miniseries since that one that was actually about a guy who worked on a steam engine."

"We could start with a tell-all piece about yours truly," Benjamin grins. "I was born in Wembley, which a lot of people don't realize. For some reason, everyone seems to think I'm from London, which personally, I find to be a bit presumptuous..."

"More presumptuous than assuming that someone out there wants to read the story of your entire life?" Colin asks, taking a playful jab at his friend.

"Colin, my life is fascinating," Benjamin argues. "Though not nearly as fascinating as yours. I'd wager *your* tell-all could fill an encyclopedia. Have you ever considered that? Writing a book, I mean?"

"Yes, because even though everyone already knows how much of an idiot I used to be, I thought they might like to read about it from my perspective."

"All right, then hire someone to write it for you. Like the girl you're currently shagging," Benjamin comments, knowing full well that I'm going to start blushing. Colin just grimaces.

"No. That would be even worse."

"How come?"

"Because after all is said and done, I still want her to like me," Colin explains.

And like it does so often when Colin is involved, my heart skips a beat.

"Mate, she was a teenager with internet access. She already knows everything."

"Actually, in high school, I only had dial-up," I tell them. As if that's relevant.

"Okay, so she had very, very slow internet. But it was still a connection. And I bet she read everything they wrote about you. Didn't you?"

"Not really," I answer. "I mostly used the internet to Instant Message my friends and read fanfiction."

"Fan-what-now?" Colin asks.

"You know, stories based on books and movies."

"Written by fans?"

"Exactly."

"And did you ever dabble in fanfiction?" Benjamin asks.

"No." That is a bold-faced lie.

Thankfully, before Gemma can call me out on it, Colin's phone rings. As he steps aside to answer it, Benjamin leans over to me and murmurs, "I knew you'd be good for him."

"I'm sorry?" I ask.

"Colin. I haven't seen him this happy in... To be honest, I don't think I've ever seen him this happy."

"What do you mean though, you knew I'd be good for him?"

"Colin is a good friend, one of the nicest people you'll ever meet. But his past still troubles him. Truthfully, I think he's so ashamed of the life he used to live that he doesn't always allow himself to really live the life he has now. Not to its fullest extent, anyway. He has his family, of course, and his work. I still worry about him, though. Which is why I'm so glad that we met you."

"Are you saying that you... You tried to set us up?"

"I'm not a double dater, Love."

"Does Colin know?"

But Colin returns before Benjamin can answer.

"Sorry about that," he tells us. Then he looks at me. "What's wrong?"

"What?" I ask.

"You look concerned. Is everything okay?"

See, this is why I'd never make it as an actress. Or a gambler. I have no poker face. If something's bothering me, the world is going to know that something is bothering me.

"I just told her that I set the two of you up and I think she's a bit scandalized," Benjamin admits.

Gemma, meanwhile, casts me a sympathetic glance. She knows exactly what's going on in my mind right now and I can almost hear her voice in my head telling me, "*Calm down. This isn't like the last time. You're overreacting. Everything is going to be okay.*"

Colin just rolls his eyes.

"I think you're giving yourself a little too much credit," he says.

"Am I? Who was it that suggested that weekend trip to Inverness?"

"I thought that you and I had been planning that all along."

"Okay, but who suggested we invite the girls along? It was all part of my brilliant plan," Benjamin gloats.

Colin turns to me and murmurs, "Sometimes you've just got to let him think what he wants."

"I heard that," Benjamin says. "So, who was on the phone?"

"It was just Geoff, calling about next week," Colin answers. "He's looking forward to meeting you," he says to me.

"Wait, you... You told him about me?" Even as I speak the words, I can feel the blood draining from my face and my heart threatening to beat itself out of my chest.

"No, no, nothing like that. He asked if that was really you in all the pictures. I guess he had a different image of you in his head. He wasn't expecting someone so gorgeous," Colin winks.

It takes everything within me not to heave a sigh of relief.

As we wander further into the park, Gemma and Benjamin break away, leaving Colin and me with a little more privacy.

"Do you ever get used to it?" I ask him.

"What?"

"The articles, the tabloids, the gossip..."

"I might not be the person to ask," he confesses. "After twenty years, I'm afraid I'm numb to it. But I do know from friends' experiences and from my family's experience that sometimes, what's written can be devastating. And that's what I regret more than anything. I know how much it hurt them, my parents, my sisters, to see me in such a selfish, destructive state. What's even worse is that at the time, I didn't care." Then he offers me a nervous grin and brushes his hair back away from his face.

"That just got a lot heavier than I'd hoped it would."

"No, it's fine. You were only answering my question."

"It won't be like that for you. I promise," he says. "You're smart. You're kind. You're beautiful. You've got nothing to worry about."

There's so much that I know I should tell him. I should tell him that I'm not afraid of words. Most of them, anyway. I'm not afraid of rumors or even criticism. When you write trashy romance, criticism is all but guaranteed.

It's betrayal that I fear. The kind that can utterly break your heart, your spirit, your ability to trust, your ability to love... And perhaps worst of all, your ability to love yourself. Because when that betrayal happens, you feel small and stupid and worthless. You're not a person, you're a plaything; one of little value.

I know that if I told Colin, he would understand. But the thing is I don't want him to have to understand. I don't want to be the weird writer girl with all the baggage and insecurities. I want to be the person I feel like when I'm around him, and that person is confident and sexy and everything I, more than often, feel that I'm not.

Finally, I look up at him and smile.

"Thank you, Colin."

"You don't have to thank me," he says. "And I just want you to know that I would never tell Geoff anything about my personal life or yours until I discussed it with you."

"I know. And I'm so sorry I overreacted. I just... I still really like to stay out of the limelight. As much as I can, anyway."

"And I don't blame you," he assures me. "To tell you the truth, that's something that I... well, that I really admire about you."

"Really?"

"Not to sound conceited or anything, but I've had more than my fair share of girlfriends who were only sleeping with me because I'm Colin Ward. They wanted that celebrity notch on their bedpost. And I was so full of my own bullshit back then that I didn't even care. I did anything and everything for some of those women. I let them be photographed with me. I put in good words with agents, directors. I let them use me however they wanted, as long as I got what I wanted in return. I was a jackass." Colin shakes his head. "But you... you're just so different. And I think that's why I can't get enough of you."

Again, I feel my breath catch in my throat. Doesn't he know by now what he does to me? Especially when he says wonderful things like that.

"I don't think I'm ever going to get used to you," I admit.

"Is that a good thing?" he grins.

"Oh, yeah," I assure him.

It's a *very* good thing.

We decide to call it an early night for several reasons, the first of which being two days of non-stop touring, exploration, and yes, shopping, have left all of us exhausted. We also have to wake up bright and early if we want to make it back to the Highlands in time for call tomorrow afternoon.

And of course, I want to make the most of my time with Colin.

Before we say goodnight to Benjamin and Gemma, however, Gemma takes me aside and says, "I know you're going to say you're fine, but I'd be a lousy assistant and a terrible friend if I didn't at least ask. So tell me right now. Are you okay?"

"Yes, I'm fine," I promise.

"Because I saw the look on your face earlier."

"I was being a little melodramatic. I was afraid... Well..." I don't have to explain it. Gemma knows exactly what I was afraid of.

"Did you tell Colin?"

"No."

"You know, it would probably be a huge weight off your shoulders. And mine."

"Gemma, I love you and I love that you're so protective of me. But this is a conversation that I *really* do not want to have tonight."

"You never want to have it and that's why it keeps eating you up."

"It's not eating me up!"

"You almost had a panic attack in the middle of a very public park because Colin mentioned you to his publicist."

"He caught me off guard, that's all."

"You know if you're going to date a movie star, you're going to have to get used to people talking about you. And your love life."

"I'm not dating him. I'm not going to date him. This is strictly sex."

"I know you want to believe that and I am so proud of you, but Delaney... This just isn't you. And I don't think it's Colin, either."

"Are you kidding? That's all his relationships have ever been."

"Be that as it may, I see the way you act around each other. I think he really cares about you. And I think *you* really care about him but you don't want to admit it because that would mean feeling something and feelings scare the crap out of you."

"Do you blame me?" I ask her.

"No. I blame Tommy Riggs and his merry band of assholes. But that was over ten years ago. You can't let what they did dictate your entire life. Or there's a very real chance that you'll miss out on the best thing that's ever happened to you."

"I thought this already *was* the best thing that's ever happened to me." Isn't that what she said to me last weekend?

"That was before."

"Before what?"

"Before I saw the way that Colin looks at you."

As I follow Colin back to our room for the night, I try to forget the conversation I just had with Gemma, and not because I'm hoping she's wrong. I know that if I let what she said to me go to my head, I may very well lose my heart. And if I lose my heart to Colin, there is a very real chance that I won't get it back.

Like I said, I'm trying not to think about it. Thankfully, Colin knows exactly how to distract me.

After pulling me into a long kiss, he takes my hips in his hands and toys with the waistband of my jeans.

"I think I'm going to take a shower," he says.

"Okay."

"Care to join me?"

Deep breath.

"Okay."

We walk in silence to the bathroom, where Colin watches with eager and, dare I say it, adoring eyes as I undress. Like so many women, I don't care for the sight of my naked body. If you were to ask me, my flaws far outnumber my positive attributes. And yet, somehow, standing here in front of Colin, I find myself feeling beautiful.

Now it's his turn to strip for me.

Colin isn't built like your typical Hollywood heartthrob. Don't get me wrong, his body is sexy as hell. In fact, if you ask me, he's even sexier than those guys with the perfectly chiseled features and the airbrushed abs that you often see in movies. And no, I'm not just saying that because I'm sleeping with him. Colin has a very natural, very masculine quality to him. His body is strong. Rugged.

Like I said, sexy as hell.

After he turns the water on, Colin holds my hand while I step into the shower. As soon as the water hits my skin, I begin to shiver.

"Too cold?" Colin asks me.

"A little."

He turns the hot water up and immediately, I feel myself begin to relax.

"Better?" he asks.

"Better."

"Good."

Then he slips his hands around my waist, leans down, and presses his forehead to mine. I lift up my arms and wrap them around his neck. For a moment, we just stand there, savoring one another. Then, acting purely on instinct, my hands begin to roam, exploring his back, his chest, his stomach. When I come across a particularly sensitive spot, I feel Colin tense. His fingers tighten around my curves. His pleasure is intoxicating.

"Do you want me to stop?" I ask him.

"No, Lorelei," he breathes. "I never want you to stop."

Chapter Seventeen

Today is the first of three days of filming the behind-the-scenes featurette and interviews with the cast and crew and, in spite of what Gemma has been telling me all morning, I don't think I look as nervous as I feel.

"You're pale. Your smile is forced. You've got dark circles under your eyes. You need to style your hair. And change into something that shows off a little more cleavage."

"Are you kidding me? No!" Okay, first of all, of course I'm pale. I've been in Scotland for three and a half weeks. But I guess I could apply a little bit of blush. And I could stand to fix my hair. And dab some concealer under my eyes. As far as my smile goes, I'll think happy thoughts.

But I'm not going to change into something that shows off a little more cleavage.

"Aw, come on! Why not? I bet Colin would appreciate it," Gemma grins.

"He isn't the one interviewing me."

"He's still going to be watching."

"Look, all I want is to get through the day without embarrassing myself."

"And you will. You just have to exude confidence."

Right. Confidence. I have confidence.

I am confident that I am going to embarrass myself.

I don't know how. I just know that it is bound to happen.

As we make our final preparations to head downstairs to meet Andrew and Louise, my phone rings. My first thought is that it's my publicist, or I guess technically, my publisher's publicist. But it isn't. It's my mom.

"Hello?" I answer.

"Hi there, sweetheart!"

"Mom, you're still awake?" I'm happy to hear from my mom. In fact, her voice is so comforting that I could cry. But it's past midnight back home and my mother is not exactly what you'd call a night owl.

"Yes, believe it or not. I've been watching a documentary on American con artists."

"Well, that's interesting." And a little bizarre.

"How are you doing? Are you okay?"

"Yeah, I'm fine. Everything is great. Getting ready to go film a couple of interviews."

"I know."

"Wait, you know?" I ask. "How do you know? I didn't tell you."

"Gemma texted me. She said you might be a little nervous."

Here's the thing about my mother. She is the sweetest person living on God's green earth. She is also the least subtle. I have no idea how she's managed to keep my life as Lorelei a secret all these years.

"I'm going to be okay. Thank you, Mom."

"I saw your picture with Benjamin Wyndham and Colin Ward the other day. Where was Matthew? Wasn't he there with you?"

Like I said. Not subtle. At all. Which is exactly why I haven't told her that my new celebrity crush is actually Colin. Or that just yesterday, I was climbing him like a tree in his trailer.

"No, Matthew wasn't there," I tell her.

"Oh, are you all right? I know how much you were looking forward to working with him."

"Yes, Mom, I'm fine."

I seem to be saying that a lot lately. Is that a thing? Having to constantly reassure your loved ones that you're okay? Maybe I need to ask my therapist. Of course, I'm pretty sure I already know what she'd say. It's the same thing she's been saying to me since I first started seeing her.

"It's okay to open up. It's okay to not be fine. It's not easy, I know, but bottling up your emotions, closing yourself off, is not good for you. Nor is it fair to the people around you."

I get that. And maybe I should tell my mom everything. Maybe I should tell Colin everything. But telling would mean explaining and explaining would mean reliving. And reliving is the very last thing I ever want to do.

"Well, you know that you can always call me, no matter how late it gets," she reminds me.

"Thank you. I love you, Mom."

"I love you, Delaney."

My name. Hearing my name in my mother's voice brings unexpected tears to my eyes. It's the name that she gave me. The name I've known my entire life.

The name that no one here knows me by.

Including Colin.

When we arrive on set, a new camera person is already there, filming the goings on, the set-up, and of course, the actors. Benjamin is hamming it up for his adoring audience while Matthew and Genevieve look on and laugh. Rose is nowhere to be seen. She may already be back in hair and makeup. Or hoping to stay as far away from Benjamin as possible. Meanwhile, Colin is standing off to the side and looks to be in no mood to perform for anyone or anything until he's had his morning coffee. His face lights up, however, as soon as I catch his eye.

But before I make it over to say good morning, a man approaches him. The moment I see him, my blood runs cold and a knot begins to form in the pit of my stomach.

It's Rigsley.

Or I guess I should say Rigsley as I imagined him. A slight, sickly-looking man with greasy brown hair and beady, weasel-like eyes. I have no idea who this man is, so I can't say for certain that he's a scheming, manipulative, self-serving bastard like Rigsley, but there's certainly something about him that I don't trust.

"Lorelei!" Colin calls out to me.

And suddenly, those beady, weasel eyes are staring straight into mine.

Run! the anxious little voice in the back of my mind hisses. *Run away, change your name again, and find a blanket fort where you can take refuge until Colin and the rest of the world forget you ever existed.*

Miraculously, I'm able to disobey. I flash what I hope is a bright smile and not a nauseated grimace as I walk over to them.

"Good morning, Mr. Ward," I greet Colin as professionally as possible. He looks politely confused.

Okay, maybe calling him *Mr. Ward* was taking it a bit too far. Thankfully, he's over it in about two seconds.

"Geoff, allow me to introduce Lorelei DuBois. Lorelei, this is Geoff Martin, my publicist."

So, this is the publicist. The one who seems to be so disappointed that Colin is actually a decent, mature human being. I knew I wasn't going to like this guy.

"It's a pleasure to meet you, Miss DuBois. I've heard good things about you."

Ew. His voice is just as oily as I'd imagined Rigsley's might be. The only thing missing is the British accent.

"It's nice to meet you, too," I reply.

Then, much to my chagrin, he reaches out and grabs my hand. His palm is cold and clammy, almost sticky with sweat, and it's all I can do to not immediately jump back, out of his reach.

"You know, I never would have pegged you for a girl who likes to write dirty books, but I guess looks can be deceiving. I bet you're a wild one, aren't you?" Geoff grins, eyeing me in a way that makes me feel disgusting, as though his gaze has somehow left a layer of dirt and grime on my skin.

"Leave her be, Geoff," Colin warns.

"Come on, son, you know I'm just teasing her. She's so beautiful, she ought to be used to it by now."

Right. Because that makes everything he just said to me A-okay. Creep.

Unsure of how to respond to that, I excuse myself to the restroom. Maybe if I stay in there long enough, I can convince people that I've got food poisoning and that I need to go home. Like *all* the way back home. To Dallas.

I'll blame it on the haggis.

Of course, I haven't been in the bathroom for more than thirty seconds when Elizabeth walks in and informs me that Milo Harris, the man behind the featurette, will be interviewing me first while the actors are in hair and makeup.

I think I squeak out an "Okay."

The interview itself is to be conducted in the great hall of Dunadhar Castle. By the time I arrive, Milo's crew has already set up the cameras, the lighting equipment, and a red cushioned chair that actually reminds me of a throne.

Milo Harris is a tall, wiry man, probably in his early thirties, with wavy light brown hair and wide blue eyes, framed by thick hipster glasses. I can't help but wonder if he actually needs them to see or if he's wearing them as a fashion accessory. Judging by his multi-colored hand-knit scarf and faded orange shoes, I'm going to go with accessory.

"Miss Lorelei DuBois?" he asks as I walk up to him.

"That's me."

"Right on time. I like that in a writer."

I laugh and suddenly, I'm not feeling nervous at all. I like Milo. He seems sweet and very easy to talk to.

"Are we typically tardy?"

"Not all of you. But my boyfriend is a writer and he thinks that showing up thirty minutes late is the same thing as being fashionably early. It drives me crazy."

"That would annoy me too. I appreciate it when people are punctual."

"Then you would not appreciate him," Milo grumbles, sounding for all the world like half of an old married couple. It makes me smile. "But enough about that. Would you like to have a seat?"

"Sure."

Once I'm seated in the incredibly comfortable red chair, I turn my attention to Milo, who goes over the standard interview basics and protocol.

"Remember, this is supposed to be a fun project. I want you to enjoy yourself, laugh, don't over-think things. If there's anything you don't want to tell me, just let me know and we'll skip right over that question. Sound good?"

"Sounds good."

"Okay then, let's get started." He nods to his cameramen, waits for the go-ahead, and begins. "First of all, I want to ask what do you think of this project? The miniseries? Is it living up to your expectations?"

"Honestly, it's exceeding them," I answer.

"How so? And I should mention to you that I'm not going to be featured in this at all, so tell the story as though you're speaking directly to your audience. Pretend that I am not even here."

"Oh. Um, okay." I take a deep breath and try again. "This is a dream come true for me. I've loved every moment. And um... it probably goes against everything I believe in as a reader and as a writer to say this, but what the cast and the crew and the directors have created here... it outshines every word of every page of every book that I've ever written."

"So, what you're saying is you think this miniseries will be better than the books?"

"I do. I really do. Elizabeth and David, Sarah and Cody, all the actors, our amazing crew... they've brought *The Queen's Surrogate* to life in a way that I'd never imagined possible. They've turned it into something beautiful. And I'm completely in awe of them."

"Let's talk about the story itself and what it means to you."

"Oh God, it's supposed to mean something?" I laugh. Then I remember what Colin said to me that night in Inverness. "To be honest with you, for a while, it really didn't mean anything to me. It was just something I wrote. And you know, it really isn't that good." That garners a few chuckles. "But then I started to meet people who told me what the story meant to *them*. And you know, that's been the best part of this whole experience. It's not really about the story or the characters, it's about the way that those stories and characters shape and impact real lives."

"Good answer, good answer," Milo says. "Now tell me what hopes you have for the show."

"I can only hope what every writer hopes: that my readers will enjoy it as much as they enjoyed the books."

"What's been the best thing about working here on set?"

"See, all my answers have nothing to do with work..." I answer with a laugh. "I think the very best thing is being here in Scotland. I'm still having trouble believing that a place so beautiful actually exists. But as far as work goes, I'm going to have to say the people. The cast is extraordinary, the crew is phenomenal, everyone is so kind and creative and they've really made this a wonderful and worthwhile experience."

"Okay, final question. I've been reading up on you, doing a bit of research. There isn't a whole lot out there about you personally, and I was wondering if that was intentional?"

"That's a little tricky," I answer. "I don't intentionally withhold information about myself... But I don't go out of my way to share a whole lot either. I do try to keep my professional life separate from my personal life."

"That said, there have been rumors, never confirmed or denied, that Lorelei DuBois is actually a pseudonym. Care to divulge?"

Oh, God.

That's it. I've said too much.

"Not today. Sorry, Milo," I answer with as bright a smile as I can muster.

"I understand," he assures me. "Well, *Miss Dubois*, thank you for joining me today. It has been a pleasure."

"The pleasure has been mine." Even though he tried to call me out on my pen name. Oh well. No harm done.

Then I stand to gather my purse. And I see them. The three figures standing in the entrance of the great hall: Gemma, Benjamin, and Colin. They must have stepped in to listen after Colin and Benjamin got out of hair and makeup.

And they've heard every word that Milo and I have just said.

Chapter Eighteen

"You mean to tell us that we've known you for three and a half weeks now and we don't even know your real name?" Benjamin asks, sounding incredulous.

I look to Gemma for help and guidance. For once, she looks as lost as I feel. Of course, she's been nagging me to tell Colin the truth since the Fairy Pools so she's probably not going to be very much help at all.

"I didn't say that Lorelei wasn't my real name," I remind him.

"But it's not, is it? That's why you're talking in riddles and refusing to answer the question!" Benjamin declares. Then he turns to Gemma. "Do *you* know her real name?"

"Of course I do."

"Gem!" I exclaim.

"What? They're going to find out eventually."

"What is it?" Benjamin demands. He's surprisingly far more scandalized by all this name nonsense than Colin is. Colin is just standing there, listening and looking rather amused, actually.

"Does it really matter?" I ask.

"Yes, it absolutely matters!"

"Why? What's in a name, really?"

"Your very identity, for starters. And you've been keeping yours a secret from us! And don't you dare try to tell me that a rose by any other name would smell just as sweet because I guarantee you, no one would sniff it if you called it a festering pustule."

"So, are you saying that my pen name is a festering pustule?"

"To an extent, yes, I am," Benjamin huffs. Then he looks at Colin. "I can't believe you've got nothing to say about this. You're shagging a girl and you don't even know her name!"

Colin shrugs.

"It wouldn't be the first time."

And with that, I burst out laughing. Not that I like the idea of Colin sleeping with anybody else. I'm just so relieved that he's not holding this against me.

To my relief, before Benjamin can scold me further, two new people enter the great hall. I've never met them in person, but I recognize them immediately: Sarah MacTavish and Cody Wagner, my co-writers.

"It's so nice to finally meet you," I greet them with genuine enthusiasm, all the while silently praying that Benjamin doesn't make some stupid, off-handed remark about how I still haven't *officially* introduced myself to him or something. Convoluted? Perhaps. But I definitely wouldn't put it past him.

"Ask her what her name is," Benjamin hisses.

See?

"I'm sorry?" Sarah asks, looking politely confused and slightly flustered by Benjamin's command.

"Ignore him," I tell her.

Sadly, I don't get to spend much time chatting with Sarah or Cody before they're whisked away for their interviews with Milo and the rest of us are called for the first scene of the day. Hoping to avoid any further discussion concerning my name or my reasons for keeping it a secret, I hang back and wait for everyone to go on without me. But of course, Colin stays behind too.

I expect him to interrogate me, to demand some kind of explanation. But he doesn't. Instead, he keeps his dark eyes locked on my face and, taking a few seductive steps toward me, says, "You know, it's supposed to be a clear night tonight. How about we go somewhere? Just the two of us? We could set out a blanket, sip on an Irn Bru, watch the stars come out..."

"But it's the middle of the week," I remind him.

He shrugs.

"We don't have to go far."

Today, they're filming Corrine's first childbirth scene and Rose is not looking forward to it. I really don't blame her. She's the one who's going to be doing most of the work today. Genevieve just has to stand by and look concerned, then elated when Rose "gives birth" to a healthy baby girl. Similarly, Matthew is supposed to pace back and forth outside the bedchamber while Colin reminds him that this was all his idea and that he's the one that deserves glory and praise when the young Prince is born. Of course, when the baby turns out to be a Princess, Colin finds himself in a bit of trouble with Matthew, which in turn gets Rose in trouble with Colin. Then Benjamin valiantly comes to her defense.

I'll admit, all the drama was fun to write. And I have a feeling it will be even more fun to watch. Especially the scenes with Matthew and Colin. My two celebrity crushes in one glorious frame. They actually work really well together. Matthew exudes the charismatic arrogance of a King and the heartfelt concern of a new father for the well-being of his child and lover. And Colin? He's just so damn sexy as a villain, even one as vile as Rigsley. He's transformed him from a sniveling scumbag to a confident and intelligent and yes, a very dark man of ambition and

226

corruption. And yeah, I know that is not supposed to be sexy at all. But it's Colin. What do you expect?

"So, are you going to tell him?" Gemma asks me between takes.

"I don't know," I answer honestly.

"It's just a name."

That's the thing, though. It's not just a name. Like Benjamin said earlier, my name is my identity, my entire history. Delaney Brooks isn't a bestselling author. She doesn't travel. She isn't adventurous. She doesn't hook up with movie stars in hotel rooms. That's Lorelei DuBois. Delaney Brooks is the girl who lost herself trying to be something that she wasn't. The girl who still likes to pretend to be more than she is.

Why would I want to be her when I can be Lorelei? Why would Colin want her when he could have Lorelei?

"You know Benjamin is going to pester you about this all night," I tell her. Since I'm going out with Colin, Gemma arranged for Benjamin to give her a ride back to the hostel, which will more than likely end up being a ride to the middle of nowhere to snog in the back of his car.

"Let him try. I know exactly how to distract him."

"Thanks, Gem. Way to take one for the team."

"I do what I can."

Once filming wraps for the day, I try my best to lie low until Colin is changed and ready to go. I don't want to take the chance of having Benjamin confront me in front of the rest of the cast and crew. Or worse, Colin's eel of a publicist. Geoff.

Thankfully, by the time Colin finds me, we're two of the only ones left on set. He looks so good in black jeans and a charcoal gray t-shirt that I almost miss the leather jacket and black helmet that he's holding underneath his arm.

Wait a minute...

"So," he says, handing me the helmet. "Are you ready to get out of here?"

I've never been on a motorcycle before. I'm not even sure I *know* anyone who's been on a motorcycle before. Well, except for Colin, obviously, who's been riding around on one since before I got my learner's permit.

Of all the crazy, reckless, totally out-of-character chances I've taken since the moment I set foot on Scottish soil, climbing on the back of a shiny black motorcycle has got to be the craziest.

As Colin takes his seat in front of me, he glances back and grins.

"Hold on tight!"

He doesn't have to tell me twice. I'm bracing myself before we've even started moving.

Then the motorcycle roars to life and we tear out into the summer evening. Every fear, every reservation, every care in my world evaporate as the Scottish Highlands fly by. I don't remember the last time I felt so free, so weightless. Like nothing can touch me. I've forgotten why I ever worried about anything at all.

I don't know how long we ride before Colin pulls off and parks on the side of the road. Wherever we are, we're overlooking a small body of water, surrounded by gold, green, and even purple hills. Climbing off the bike, Colin holds out both of his hands to help me down before grabbing his ever-trusty backpack, which he'd secured to the seat behind me.

"That. Was. Exhilarating," I tell him.

"Fun, huh?" he smiles. "I've been wanting to ride out here since the first time I visited the Highlands at least ten, maybe twelve years ago."

We cross the road and hop the guardrail. Colin pulls a navy plaid blanket from his backpack and lays it down on the level ground before the land slopes into a hill. Then we sit and he immediately pulls me into his arms. I lean back into his embrace and savor the feel of his warm breath on the side of my face.

"It's so quiet out here," I whisper.

"I like it."

"I do too."

"So, who are you?"

The question is simple, sincere, like a lover's caress. I want to be honest with him. I want him to know me. But I'm also afraid. And I don't want to admit that to him. Or to myself.

"I'm not even sure I know," I finally answer.

"Were you ever going to tell me?"

"I don't know."

"Why not?"

"It just seemed so much easier to be who everyone thought I was."

"But you *are* Lorelei DuBois. That just isn't your name."

"That's true... to an extent."

"What do you mean?" he asks, tucking a stray lock of hair behind my ear.

I pause to think for a moment. I know what I want to say. I'm just not entirely sure how to say it. Writing is so much easier than speaking.

"Have you ever done anything completely outrageous for a part?" I ask him.

"Have you seen some of my earlier movies?" he deadpans. "I once ran naked through the frozen foods section at Wal-Mart."

"I did not see that one."

"Please don't."

"No promises."

"Okay, I believe you were making a point." Oh my God. Is he blushing? I think he's blushing.

"My point is that that's something that you could do because it wasn't you. It was a character.

You can do anything when you're not the one doing it. Does that make sense?"

"Yeah, it does," he says. "So, you feel braver when you're Lorelei?"

"It's more like she makes me feel protected," I explain. "If she screws up or makes a fool of herself, it doesn't matter because she doesn't actually exist. But it's even more than that. When I'm Lorelei, I can pretend that whatever happened to me in the past didn't happen. It's like having a completely clean slate."

"I understand that," Colin says.

"Really?"

"Of course. There are days I'd love to not be Colin Ward. As you know, that name comes with some *really* dirty laundry. But I'm also very proud of the person I am today. I'm proud of the choices and the changes I've made. And I definitely have better taste in women..." He trails off and gently presses his lips to mine. Then he looks at me and says, "It is a bit strange though."

"What is?"

"Judging from past experiences, most women do not appreciate it when you can't remember their names. And you... You've gone out of your way to keep yours a secret." It isn't an accusation. It's a fact. I don't know what to say. Colin, sensing my hesitation, holds my gaze and says, "You know you can trust me, right?"

"I know," I whisper.

It's true. I didn't realize it until now, but I *do* trust him. And although the walls that I've spent the last eleven years building around myself won't be easily demolished, here in the heart of the Highlands, I finally feel them start to crumble.

So I take a deep breath and I tell him my story. The one that he's been asking to hear since the very beginning.

"My senior year of high school, I went to Prom with a guy named Tommy Riggs. He was everything. Tall, handsome, varsity quarterback. He was smart, too. Not National Merit material, but he was always in the top ten percent of our class. All the girls wanted him, all the guys wanted to be him. When he asked me to Prom, I was elated. He could have had anyone he wanted. And he picked me.

"I was so excited about that night, and my parents were excited for me. We didn't have a lot of money back then, but my mom saved every penny she could to buy me the most beautiful dress. It was just like a fairy tale. Or at least, it was supposed to be.

"After the dance, Tommy told me that he'd reserved a hotel room for the evening and asked if I wanted to go up with him. I wasn't naïve. I knew what he wanted, and although I hadn't admitted it to anyone, I wanted it, too. Gemma encouraged me. She'd lost her virginity a year earlier at Junior Prom. It seemed like the thing to do. And Tommy was just the perfect guy. I wanted him to be my first. Hell, back then, I wanted him to be my only.

"Following him up to his room, letting him kiss me... That's the last time I genuinely remember feeling beautiful. Because after..." My voice cracks and my lips begin to tremble. I don't want to cry. I've wasted far too many tears over people who don't deserve them. But I can't stop them.

"We didn't stay the night. Once it was over, he was ready, almost eager to leave. I tried to tell myself that he was tired, that his parents were expecting him at home, that there was nothing off about his behavior. But I didn't hear from him the rest of the weekend.

"As soon as I got to school Monday, I knew something wasn't right. For the first time in my life, people watched me as I passed by to go to my locker. Girls whispered. Guys grabbed at my skirt. But it wasn't until Tommy's best friend, Gabe Abrams, cut me off on the way to first period that I found out."

I can still hear his words in my head, clear as a bell. I can still see the ugly, amused smirk on his face as he looks me up and down like a predator eyeing its next meal.

"Well, if it isn't little Miss Freak Show. Heard you've actually got a nice ass under all those layers."

"Wh - what are you talking about?"

"Cut the crap, Baby, the whole school knows. And I have to say, kudos to you. When I bet Tommy that he couldn't get you to give it up for him, I really thought he was up for a challenge. Guess you're easier than I thought."

By now, I can barely look Colin in the eye.

"They'd made a bet. And everyone knew. And for the rest of the school year, I was propositioned and heckled. I had *Skank* and *Easy* and *Slut* graffitied on my textbooks and crude illustrations taped to my locker. A few guys even tried to feel me up. Thankfully, through it all, I had Gemma. She stood up for me, protected me. She felt guilty about what had happened, for being so adamant, even though it wasn't her fault at all."

"My God..." Colin whispers.

"Anyway, that's why I created Lorelei. Because even though I haven't spoken to those people in years, I just couldn't bear the thought of them finding out what I wrote. And I know it's silly of me to let what happened then dictate my life now, I just..."

"No, it's not silly," Colin assures me. "What happened to you was traumatic. It shattered you. And I... I can't imagine dealing with something like that at such a young age."

"You dealt with a *lot* of stuff like that at a young age."

"Yeah, but I was never the victim. You were innocent. And that sort of cruelty... That's

234

something I never experienced. And I wish there was something that I could do or say to take it all away from you."

"Just promise not to look at me any different. I don't want you feeling sorry for me." Finally, I turn to look at him. "I want you to see me the same way you did that night in Inverness."

"I'm sorry, but I can't promise you that," he says, reaching up to trail his fingers across my cheek. "Because you are so much more beautiful to me now than you were that night."

Then, wiping the tears away from my face, he leans down and kisses me. It's a kiss that comforts. A kiss that draws every doubt and every fear and every hesitation from my being.

A kiss that says, "*I finally know you*."

Excerpt from *The Surrogate's Princess*

My Princess is growing. Every day, she learns something new. Every day, she smiles a little brighter.

They named her Violet, after Malcolm's mother. It's a beautiful name, one that suits her. For she is surely the most beautiful creature to ever grace this or any land.

Yet while my heart is fit to burst with love for my daughter, my mind is plagued with uncertainty. She is not the son that Malcolm desires or the Prince that the Kingdom so desperately needs. She is lovely. She is perfect. But she is not enough.

I was not enough.

So what will happen to me?

Violet will be loved and adored and treated like the royalty that she is. She is already cherished by every soul within these castle walls, especially by Malcolm and the Queen. But Edin still needs an heir. Am I to remain here? To once again bed the King in the hopes of producing a son? Or will *he rid himself of me, the woman who has already failed him once, in favor of someone new?*

I will know the answer soon enough. Tonight, for the first time since Violet's birth, he has summoned me back to his bedchamber.

Rigsley arrives to escort me. I dare not look him in the eye.

"So superior," he sneers. "So certain that His Majesty will not cast you out. Even after you've failed him. Do you truly believe that he cares for you? That he loves you? The King does not love you. He never will. You are nothing to him."

His words linger in my mind and in my heart as I step into Malcolm's chambers.

He is there, tending the fire. The King. My King. He glances up as the door closes behind me. And then he smiles.

"Corrine." The way he softly speaks my name, the same way one might utter a prayer of reverence in church, lays to rest all of my fears and doubts.

"Malcolm," I whisper.

He stands and beckons me with a single wave of his hand. I walk to him and he welcomes me into his arms with a gentle kiss. I cling to him, breathe him in. He smells of cinder and smoke, of ashes and fire... With his passion and heat, he seems the very embodiment of fire.

"How I've missed you," he murmurs.

"And I, you."

Then he pulls away ever so slightly to look at my face.

"I hope you know that you have given me the most precious gift any man could hope to receive. My Violet... Our Violet... She is everything."

"But she is not a son."

Malcolm turns his eyes down to the ground.

"No, she is not."

I wait with baited breath to hear what he will say next. When he remains silent, I raise my voice to speak.

"We could try again."

Malcolm meets my eye once again.

"You would be willing?"

"I am your most humble servant," I remind him. "Command me, and I will do as you say."

"Oh, Corrine." He takes my hands in his. "You are no one's servant. You are grace. You are radiance. You are my sanctuary, my truth, and my joy. And you will be mother to the future King of Edin."

Then he presses his mouth to mine and his fire begins to blaze in me as well.

Chapter Nineteen

"Kimberly."

"No."

"Zoe."

"No."

"Alicia."

"No."

"Are you sure it isn't Kimberly?"

"I promise you, Benjamin, my name is not Kimberly."

This has become our new gimmick. Benjamin rambles off a list of generic names in an attempt to guess mine. A week and a half later, he has not had any success.

"I think you're lying to me. I think I *have* guessed your name and you're just denying it. Colin, help me out."

"I've already told you I don't know," Colin tells him.

"And that doesn't keep you lying awake at night?"

"Actually, I've been sleeping pretty well these last couple of weeks."

"What about you, then?" Benjamin asks me. "You wouldn't rather be with a man who actually knows your name?"

I shrug.

"It'd be nice, but honestly, watching you get all worked up over this is just so much more fun."

Exasperated, Benjamin turns to Gemma.

"You're on my team, aren't you, Love?"

"Baby, I've been on her team a lot longer," Gemma answers. That is true friendship right there.

Today, we're in Fort William and we're debating how to spend the afternoon. Gemma, of course, wants to do the tourist thing, explore the town, and shop. Benjamin wants a day of relaxation and a night at the local pubs. But Colin has his sights set on Glen Nevis.

Glen Nevis is known far and wide for its beauty and its mountains, particularly Ben Nevis, the highest mountain in Britain.

"I've heard there are some amazing hiking trails there," Colin says.

"Colin, if you think I'm scaling a mountain after five straight weeks of non-stop work, you're as crazy as all of your ex-girlfriends said you were twelve years ago," Gemma remarks.

"That's not nearly as crazy as some of those ex-girlfriends actually were," Colin argues.

I don't doubt it. Then again, he was the one sleeping with the crazy so is anyone really sane in this scenario?

"Especially the one who showed up in the middle of the night with a baby elephant," Benjamin comments.

Okay, seriously, where the hell did Colin find these women?

"If it's all the same to you, let's not revisit them one by one. I want to enjoy today," Colin says.

"I thought you said you wanted to hike up a mountain," Benjamin quips. Colin casts him a sidelong glance.

"You don't want to go hiking either?" I ask Benjamin.

"Do I look like I'm built for conquering the rough terrain?" A long, lanky British guy with alabaster skin and famously delicate ankles. I guess I see his point. Then he asks, "What about you, Kimberly? Are you one for hiking?"

"I am, actually," I answer.

"Really?" he asks.

"You find that hard to believe?"

He shrugs.

"Writers aren't known for being a particularly athletic lot."

"Perhaps, but a few of us are known for our propensity to retreat into nature for shelter, solace, and rejuvenation."

"There's also whiskey for that," Benjamin comments.

"Oh, but mountains are so much prettier."

I'm sure we could banter back and forth like this for hours upon end, but then we'd waste the entire day trying to figure out how to spend it. So we agree. Benjamin and Gemma will stay and enjoy Fort William while Colin and I explore the glen.

Maybe we'll even climb a mountain.

All writers have their strengths and weaknesses. Some excel at weaving a series of twists and turns into their stories, keeping their readers on the edge of their seats. Others may find they have a flair for witty dialogue.

Me? I'm not sure what my strengths are, besides totally and completely objectifying Matthew Kent, but I'm well aware of my weaknesses. Any professional writer or instruction guide will tell aspiring authors, "Show, don't tell." In other words, make your written world as real as the one we live in.

I don't think I'm very good at that.

When I was writing for myself, I didn't really think about it. I didn't really have to think about it. I could see the country of Edin inside my mind. I knew exactly what Malcolm's castle was supposed to look like. Writing it all out, describing it for myself on paper, wasn't necessary. But when I began editing and rewriting for actual readers, that's when things got tricky.

It didn't matter what I wrote. Nothing was ever good enough. My descriptions paled in comparison to the world I'd so long only been imagining. I tried my best to show my readers fields of gold and purple flowers, trickling streams so clear that even the rocks beneath their waters glistened in the sunlight, mountains that guarded their surrounding forests like watchful deities, powerful and loving. But those words still fell short.

I should have just told them to visit Glen Nevis.

Here in Scotland, I've often found myself wondering if what I'm seeing is, in fact, real. The beauty of this country far surpasses anything I could ever imagine, especially the wild and regal splendor of Glen Nevis. There's something in the air that feels secret, sacred. I wish there was a way to bottle it up and keep it with me.

"I think we made the right decision," Colin says.

"I think I agree with you."

"After this is done, after I've finished with my upcoming projects, who knows? Maybe I'll buy a cottage out here," he says.

"Can I come and visit?" I ask.

"I'm hoping you will," he answers.

I smile, thankful that my cheeks are already flushed from our hike.

"I can't believe we've already been here five weeks," I say.

"I can't believe we've only got three weeks left."

"That too."

"So, what are your plans?" he asks. "What does the future hold for you?"

"I... really don't know," I answer honestly. It's sort of exciting, imagining a future of endless possibilities. But it's also intimidating and more than a little frightening. Where do I go from here?

"More books?"

"Perhaps." I'd like to write more. I'd like to be known for more than just *The Queen's Surrogate*. Who knows? Maybe the next book I write will actually be good.

Oh, who am I kidding? It will probably end up being about a Princess who falls in love with the wrong man. Like the spare to the throne of a neighboring Kingdom. Of course, she's betrothed to the oldest brother, the heir. But it's the second brother, the one with the dark hair and the darker past who ultimately wins her heart.

Actually, that would be a lot of fun to write. I wish I'd brought my notebook.

"What are you thinking?" Colin asks with a laugh.

"Huh?"

"You have a bit of a far-off look in your eyes."

I shrug.

"Just plotting."

"A new idea for a book?"

"Maybe."

"Care to share it?"

"Not really, no."

"Just a hint?"

"Sorry."

"Tell me this, then. Does this one at least have a happy ending?"

So, I'm no stranger to criticism. *The Surrogate* series has, in the past few years, received its fair share of negative reviews.

"It's stupid."

"It's shallow."

"It's poorly written."

"It's too raunchy."

"It isn't raunchy enough."

But the most common complaint has always been about the ending.

"I hated the ending. It felt like a cop-out."

"Where was the happily-ever-after? No one gets their happily-ever-after!"

"That can't possibly be the end of the story. What was Lorelei DuBois thinking?"

Here's what I was thinking. I never intended for that story to have an ending. Remember, I was writing purely for my own enjoyment. And stories you write for your own enjoyment can be as sloppy as you want them to be. You don't have to write those pesky yet necessary filler scenes. You can write what you want to write and let it all go unresolved.

But once a publisher picks up your manuscript, you need a proper ending. So I wrote one. It wasn't the one that readers wanted, but it was the only one I felt truly fit the story.

In the final chapters of the final book, Corrine becomes pregnant again. But her relationship with the King has shifted. Malcolm wants Corrine all to himself but at the same time, he refuses to divorce Annette. Rigsley has poisoned his mind into believing that he deserves both of them. Meanwhile, Corrine has grown ever closer to Tristan, whom she admires for his intelligence, his kindness, and his gentleness. She realizes that she is, in fact, in love with him, not Malcolm. When Malcolm finds this out, he becomes enraged. He banishes Tristan and locks Corrine in the tower.

It all ends with Annette breaking Corrine out of the tower and seeing her off in the middle of the night with Tristan. Tristan, after all, is Annette's cousin and she wants to protect him and to make sure that he's happy. Along the way, Corrine goes into labor and gives birth.

To a son.

And okay, yeah, I get why that ending wasn't particularly well-received. There are several loose ends that I never tied up. For example, how did Malcolm react when he discovered that Corrine and his unborn child had escaped? What became of Princess Violet? Will Corrine and Tristan find their own happily-ever-after or will they forever be fugitives? I don't know, really. I guess that's up to each individual reader. I'm sure there's a whole other book there waiting to be written, and maybe one day I will put it all to paper. But when I think about it, life offers no guarantee of a happy ending, an explanation, or a resolution. Why should my stories be any different?

Right now, however, Colin is still waiting for an answer. Will my next book have a happy ending? I can't know that for sure. I probably won't know until I'm down to the last chapters. And so I answer honestly.

"I don't know yet."

"What about your story, then?" he wants to know. "Do you foresee a happily-ever-after?"

My heart begins to pound. I don't know what he's asking me. When he says happily-ever-after, does he mean for the two of us?

No. It's not possible.

Is it?

"I'd like to believe that..." I begin but I can't seem to find the words. Not the right words, anyway.

"What?" Colin presses.

I take a deep breath, terrified that if I say the wrong thing, whatever magic that has brought Colin to me will evaporate. But I suppose that's a risk we all take when admitting to someone else and to ourselves how we really feel, what we really want.

"I guess I'd like to believe that anything is possible."

"Like us?" The question is casual, simple, yet it all but takes my breath away. I freeze in my tracks and turn to look up at him. His dark eyes are warm and sincere as he takes both of my hands in his. "This has been a whirlwind, I know. Trust me, I've had my fair share. And I've never really been sad to see them end. But I don't want to say goodbye to you in three weeks. I want you in my life. And I want to be part of yours."

"Colin, I..." What do I say? What do I *want* to say? Never in a million years could I ever have imagined this.

"I know. You didn't come here looking for a high-profile relationship. Considering everything you've told me, it's probably the last thing that you want."

"I don't even know what I want," I admit to him. Then my eyes begin to sting with unbidden tears and a hard lump rises up in my throat. I don't want to cry in front of him again. I don't want him to think he's upset me. I'm not upset at all. I'm just everything else. I'm excited. I'm elated. I'm overwhelmed and hopeful and terrified. But not upset. Finally, I find my voice again. "All I do know is that I don't want to say goodbye to you in three weeks, either."

And with that, he crushes me to his chest and buries my mouth in a kiss that could very well move the mountains that surround us.

Chapter Twenty

Here's the thing about hiking up a mountain: it's a lot harder than you think it's going to be.

I guess there are logical people in the world who think to themselves, "Yeah... climbing a mountain... you should probably prepare for that. Do some leg stretches or breathing exercises."

But then there are the people like me who think, "I hike all the time. I can totally handle this." I didn't stop to consider, however, that my hiking experience is limited to the great albeit very flat state of Texas where the air is heavy and everything is around sea level.

Suffice it to say, neither my legs nor my lungs were prepared for Scottish elevation.

"Are you going to make it?" Colin asks.

"I.. don't... know..." I wheeze. This is horrible. I thought I was in amazing shape. Okay, maybe not *amazing* shape. It's not like I couldn't stand to lose a few pounds. But I can usually hike for miles without getting winded.

"I promise you, it'll all be worth it."

"Worth... dying...?"

I was fine for the first two-thirds of this adventure. It was just like hiking back home. I felt wild and free and strong, like I could conquer just about anything. Then the fire began burning in the backs of my lower calves and it became harder and harder for me to fill my lungs with air.

Now, with the summit in view, I'm in complete agony.

"Sit, take a deep breath," Colin tells me. "We're in no hurry."

I do as he says and immediately, pure and glorious relief floods my entire being. Colin kneels down beside me, reaches into his backpack, and offers me his bottle of water. I've already finished mine off and if I'm not careful, I'll drink his dry as well. I take a small sip and hand it back to him.

"Thank... you..."

"Drink as much as you need."

I nod and take another sip. Then I ask, "How... are you... okay...?" Seriously, he's barely broken a sweat.

"I spend a lot of time in the mountains back home," he answers. "The hike down is much easier."

Oh, right. I forgot we're going to have to make it all the way back down.

"Can you... carry me?"

"If you need me to. But I don't think you will," he grins.

"I'm glad... Gemma decided... to stay in town," I remark. I'm finally catching my breath. "If she saw me like this... I'd never hear the end of it."

"You mean she'd make fun of you?"

"No, she'd make me sit through some bizarre, self-satisfied lecture about how I should have listened to her and how I'm definitely going to regret this in the morning and, by the way, I smell like nature which, coming from her, is not a compliment."

Colin cracks up.

"I guess you need to prove her wrong, then."

Damn.

With Colin's help, I lift myself back up onto my aching feet and follow him onward and upward, limping every step of the way. Again, I find myself struggling to breathe, but with the summit drawing ever closer, I implore myself to keep going.

Just a few more steps.

I can make it. I can make it. I can make it.

And then, after an excruciating final ascent, we're there. And it's *spectacular*. I can see for miles, over the tops of the tallest trees, across rivers and meadows, right along the mountain range. The sun, positioned between the peaks, illuminates the vibrant magenta and yellow flowers that decorate our mountain.

"Oh, wow..." I sigh. Not very eloquent, I know. But sometimes words simply aren't enough.

"Pretty fantastic, huh?" Colin asks.

"It's everything," I answer.

While I scamper around snapping pictures with my phone at every imaginable angle, Colin unzips his backpack and lays out the same navy plaid blanket from our excursion last week.

"You know what the most amazing thing is?" I ask him as he sits himself down on the blanket.

"What's that?" he asks, smiling up at me.

"I'm looking down at the shadow of a mountain. Usually, I'm standing in the shadow, completely consumed by it. But right here? Right now? I'm part of that shadow."

"How do you do that?"

"Do what?"

"Make everything seem so whimsical."

"I guess it's the writer in me." It's a silly answer. But I'm in a bit of a silly mood. The magnitude of what we've just done and the magnificence of the world around me have left me in a tizzy. It's an incredible high, one from which I'm not eager to come back down.

I stand for a few more moments, taking in as much as I can, before joining Colin on the blanket.

"Look at this," he says, holding up his phone.

It's difficult to see in the bright light of the afternoon sun, but displayed on the screen is a candid picture of a young woman with windblown hair and a look of pure wonder in her smiling eyes. It takes me half a second to realize that the woman is me.

"I don't remember the last time I looked so happy," I admit to him. "Thank you."

"For what?"

"For showing me the picture. For bringing me here. For everything."

"You know you don't have to thank me. But you're welcome."

Then he pulls me into a soft, gentle kiss as a cool mountain breeze sweeps in from the east. After our long hike, the wind is welcome and refreshing, but I'll more than likely be shivering by the time we head back to Fort William. Honestly, I'd never thought I'd be wearing a jacket in July. Good thing I brought along my souvenir tartan scarf.

One of them, anyway.

"You know, I first started going into the mountains when I was struggling to stay sober," Colin admits to me.

"Really?"

"Yeah. My therapist suggested it. She said it would be beneficial to disconnect from the constant demands and expectations of my life in L.A. My life in general, really. She was right."

"My therapist suggested I keep a journal."

"That should be easy for you," Colin grins.

"Actually, I don't enjoy writing about myself or my feelings nearly as much as I enjoy writing trashy fiction about hot guys who live in castles."

"Does your therapist know who you really are, then?"

"If you're asking if she knows my real name, then yes. If you're asking if she knows that I'm Lorelei DuBois, then no."

"Really?" Now he looks genuinely surprised. "Not even with doctor-patient confidentiality?"

"It's actually not something I've purposefully withheld from her. It's just never really come up. Maybe it's because Lorelei doesn't need therapy. I do."

"Well, if you ask me, there's no better therapy than mountain therapy. We spend so much of our lives consumed by what's going on around us. It's easy to forget that places like this, that moments like this still exist."

He's right. For so long, I've sought to control how people see me, what they know about me, and in doing so, I've forgotten what it's like to simply exist. But it's more than that. I've forgotten that for all my worries and problems and cares that there is something greater out there. What that is exactly, I can't say. But I believe that whatever it is brought me here to this mountain.

And I think that maybe it's been trying to get through to me for a very long time.

I regret everything.

That's my first thought when I wake up next to Colin on our second and final morning in Fort William.

Yesterday, I truly believed I was the queen of the universe. Today, I feel like I got hit by a truck. As much as I hate to admit it to myself, I'm pretty sure the hike alone would have been enough to render me useless today, but after we met back up with Gemma and Benjamin, we let them talk us into a late dinner and then dancing at one of the local pubs.

Granted, when Benjamin said dancing, I was expecting something... I don't know... traditionally Scottish. Like a jig or step dancing. I never anticipated the pub having an actual DJ who spun out all the latest hits from artists like Bruno Mars and Griffin Valentino.

At first, I had no intention of setting foot on the dance floor. I think it probably goes without saying that I really haven't been one for dancing since what happened at Prom. Or I guess, technically, what happened after Prom. But it only took one look from Colin and a particularly steamy song by a singer I know but couldn't name to get me out of my chair and into Colin's arms. I followed his lead, moving my body with his, running my hands through his hair, and losing myself to his touch and to the music. I didn't care for a single moment that anyone could have recognized us. And clearly, Colin didn't either.

After we finally made it back to our hotel room, we fell into bed with every intention of going straight to sleep. But then Colin reached over and began running his fingers up and down my arm. So I snuggled myself up next to him and began trailing my lips down his neck. And then, suddenly, neither of us was tired anymore.

I'm definitely tired now. Tired and achy and even a little queasy. That mince and tatties that I ate last night is not agreeing with me. I feel like I have a stomach full of rocks. I would try to climb out of bed for a glass of water but my legs are killing me. Absolute and utter agony. I'm truly wondering if I'm going to survive the ride back to Dunadhar Highland Lodge and the read-through this afternoon. Maybe I'll just have Gemma fill in for me while I try to sleep off my entire weekend.

I'm ready to go home.

The thought is unbidden and frankly, comes as a surprise. Since the moment I arrived in Scotland, I've been wondering how I'm supposed to leave this place and go back to life as I knew it before. How do I trade in the mountains and castles and small historic towns for the big cities and traffic jams and mindless days binge-watching movies online?

But my family is back home, too. And so are my books and candles on a rainy day. And the smell of magnolia blossoms in the summer and pumpkin spice in the fall. These last few weeks have been an adventure to be sure, but I'm finally missing the little things that make home home.

It could be that I'm feeling sick and am longing for the comfort of my own bed, but I think it's something more. Something to do with the handsome man still sleeping soundly beside me. I haven't only been dreading the thought of leaving Scotland. I've been dreading the thought of leaving him, too. After all, our love affair was never supposed to last. Just yesterday, it was too much to even hope that I would see him again. But now...

"I want you in my life. And I want to be part of yours."

I want him in my life, too. I really, really do. I don't know how we'll make it work. *If* we'll make it work. But simply knowing that he wants to try is enough to make my heart sing.

For the first time in a long time, I'm not afraid of what the future holds or what might happen. For the first time in a long time, I feel like I'm finally free.

Chapter Twenty-One

Benjamin Wyndham Finds Love... Again!
She Could Be the One... But Who Is She?
Benjamin Wyndham Steps Out with Mystery Blonde!

Does British heartthrob Benjamin Wyndham have a new leading lady? The actor was seen embracing a young woman whom, sources claim, he met while filming The Queen's Surrogate *in the Scottish Highlands. Wyndham, 33, will portray Tristan Bray opposite former flame Rose Cervantes in the highly anticipated miniseries, based on the bestselling books by Lorelei DuBois. Ms. DuBois, 29, has also been pictured socializing with the actor in recent weeks.*

Although little is known about Ben's new beauty, those close to the star say that he is absolutely smitten and that he's already planning to introduce her to her parents.

"It's a big step, but Benjamin feels he's finally ready," one anonymous source confirmed. "He knows he's got a bit of a reputation for being a player. He wants to prove to her, to his family, and to himself that he's a changed man."

Reps for Benjamin Wyndham have declined to comment.

"Well, I guess I've made it," Gemma remarks,

"Made what?" I ask.

It's Monday morning and I'm still trying to drag my poor, sorry self out of bed while Gemma, already awake, refreshed, and looking like a million bucks, scrolls through articles on her phone.

"You know, I've *made* it? Like, made it big? It's a joke, Morning Glory."

"Oh."

"I can't believe this. They have pictures of me on *People.com*."

Oh, great. Last night, when the story first broke, I thought it was going to pass under the radar, especially since Benjamin having a new girlfriend is kind of old news. Now it's spreading like wildfire.

"That's not good. What if someone back home recognizes you?"

"Oh, these pictures are so blurry, no one will be able to tell it's me. Even I barely recognize myself. Still, I guess these articles will be something for the scrapbook."

"And will this scrapbook be on display at your wedding to Benjamin?" I tease.

"No. Shut up."

"What? He does seem to really like you."

"He's Benjamin. He likes everyone."

"But especially you."

"Delaney, I am just going to stop you right there. I see those stars in your eyes and I know you're about to go all romance writer on me so please, allow me to spare you the trouble. I am not in love with Benjamin. He is not in love with me. We are shallow, selfish people who have no interest in feelings, commitments, or giving up our personal sense of freedom."

This doesn't really come as any sort of surprise. Gemma has never shown any interest whatsoever in being somebody's girlfriend. She claims the thought of only being allowed to sleep with one person at a time makes her feel smothered. I guess that still applies even when that person is Benjamin Wyndham.

Of course, as it turns out, Benjamin isn't the only celebrity whose love life is making headlines today.

Matthew Kent Steps Out With* Surrogate *Co-Star, Rose Cervantes!

The King and His Rose: Matthew Kent and Rose Cervantes are Dating!

Love Blossoms on the Set of New* Surrogate *Series!

I don't have time to sit and read the articles but from what I can gather, Matthew and Rose went out last night after the read-through and were very public with their display of affection; holding hands, touching, teasing, even kissing.

I'm not jealous. Not really. I have Colin, after all, and I care about him more than I know how to adequately express. I guess what I'm feeling is kind of the same thing as when you see an ex with someone new. Even if that ex is someone you know that you wouldn't get back together with, it still isn't fun to watch them move on. Granted, I never dated Matthew. Not even close. He was just my celebrity crush. But my infatuation with him changed my life and I think he'll always have a place in my heart because of it.

"This can't be real," Gemma remarks.

"Why do you say that?"

"Because we saw Matthew and Rose just *yesterday*. They barely even glanced at each other."

"Maybe they've been seeing each other in secret." You know, like we've been seeing Colin and Benjamin in secret for over a month now.

"It's possible, but if you ask me, this so-called relationship reeks of publicity stunt."

"Does that actually happen?" For someone who likes to fawn over famous people the way I do, I really don't know all that much about the way Hollywood operates.

"Of course it does! Benjamin told me that at least half of his relationships were set-up by publicists for whatever project he was working on at the time. It's a brilliant marketing scheme."

Huh. Interesting. Now I'm wondering how many of Colin's girlfriends were actually girlfriends that he asked out himself and how many were suggested to him by slimy Geoff.

"It's a little unnerving," I remark. "I mean, letting someone dictate your personal life?"

Gemma shrugs.

"They're actors. It's what they do. Besides, you know Rose is just loving this."

"How come?"

"Because now she can parade her new romance around in front of Benjamin, who, by the way, she is still far too hung up on for her to have moved on so quickly."

"But maybe that's why she moved on, so she can get over him," I argue.

That's when Gemma looks at me like I've just shed my own skin to reveal Old Man Jenkins from the *Scooby Doo* cartoons.

"What's going on?" she asks.

"What do you mean?"

"You, Delaney Georgia Brooks, are the queen of trust issues. You always assume that somebody has an ulterior motive. That's why we all love you and that's why you won't let yourself love or be loved by anybody else. And yet, here you are, trying to convince me that what Rose feels for Matthew Kent is genuine. *Matthew Kent*! The man you've been fantasizing about for the better part of your adult life! And yes, I know the dashing Colin Ward managed to sweep you off

263

your feet and away from most of your senses, but is it possible that he changed your mind?"

"About...?"

"About everything! About love and life and really, really good sex. About confidence and trust. Maybe even about yourself."

Now it's my turn to shrug.

"Yeah, maybe," I admit with a coy grin.

Gemma squeals.

"What was it? How did he do it? Did he tell you that he loved you?"

"No, no, I don't think we're there yet," I answer. "But he did say that he wanted to keep seeing me. You know, after we go back home."

"Oh my God! Delaney! That's huge!" I can't help it. I smile. "So what does this mean? Are you exclusive? Are you going to move in together? *Did you tell him your real name yet*?"

"Not *quite* yet."

"Delaney!"

"I know, I know, I will. As for the other stuff, I don't really know if we're exclusive or not. I don't know what's going to happen. I just know that I really don't want to let him go."

Gemma takes both my hands and looks me in the eye.

"Then don't."

I don't believe this.

The paparazzi are here. At Dunadhar Castle!

There aren't very many of them. In fact, they're so inconspicuous that I may have mistaken them for tourists just passing through had it not been for the rapid shutter speed of their fancy cameras. Gemma and I were walking into the main trailer when I first heard it. And of course, I turned to look and found myself staring directly into a shiny black telephoto lens.

Now we're inside and I'm trying to remind myself that this is not a big deal. Certainly nothing to lose my feeble cool over. After all, I know they aren't here hoping for a shot of me. They're here for the headliners. For Matthew and Rose. And Gemma. Who isn't concerned in the slightest that her image may very well soon grace every celebrity gossip site on the world wide web.

"They took a blurry picture of us walking. So what? They're still not going to know who I am."

"But they're going to know who *I* am," I remind her. "And what if they trace me back to you?"

"They're not going to and you know why? Because as far as the rest of the world knows, Gemma Price has never met Lorelei DuBois."

I wish I had time to dissect, identify, and explain every flaw in her flippant argument, but frankly, we'd be here all day. Of course, no one else seems even remotely bothered by the paparazzi. I suppose after you've been in the entertainment industry long enough, you get used to people stalking you with cameras.

Fortunately for Gemma and for anyone else who might find themselves subject to my obsessive fretting (Colin), this week, we have two little girls on set who are so sweet and adorable, it's extremely difficult to dwell on anything negative.

Maya and Cecily Davies are the three-year-old identical twins playing Princess Violet and we simply cannot get enough of them. In the books, Princess Violet is much younger, less than a year old, when her younger brother is conceived. But Sarah and Cody suggested making her a little older for the miniseries in order to give her a real relationship with Corrine. Initially, I was concerned that seeing that bond form between mother and daughter would make the way that Corrine's story plays out even sadder than it already was. Then I realized that that was the whole idea.

Now, whenever the cameras aren't rolling, we're all fawning over the twins. Genevieve and I sneak in all the cuddles that we can. Rose and Matthew take turns showing them all of the medieval toys and trinkets that the producers have collected for the episode. And Colin gets down on his knees and tries to convince the girls that he isn't *really* as mean or scary as he's pretending to be. Maya seems to be warming up to him, but Cecily is still keeping a safe distance.

Then there's Benjamin.

Just as we can't get enough of the twins, the twins can't get enough of Benjamin. They love the way he picks them up and whirls them around and speaks to them in silly voices. Whenever he's around, they latch themselves to him like little magnets and it's as though the rest of us don't even exist.

"They are pretty cute, aren't they?" Gemma muses, watching the little girls squeal with delight when Benjamin presents each one with a rose. For the record, that is probably the nicest thing she's ever said about anyone under the age of twelve.

"Especially in their little princess dresses," I add.

"You know I can read your mind so you know that I know that at this very moment, you're imagining having daughters of your own just so you can dress them up as princesses every single day and take pictures of them in the rose garden that you planted in the backyard in between your daylilies and your pumpkins."

Sometimes it's a little scary how well Gemma knows me. Although I really don't know if I could successfully grow pumpkins, as much as I'd love to.

Aloud, I say, "I don't think I'm ready for kids *just* yet."

"But when you are, they're going to be princesses."

"Oh, absolutely."

"I wonder if Colin wants kids?"

"Gemma!" I hiss.

"What? You know he'd be like, the world's hottest dad."

Okay, yeah, this is absolutely true. But she still doesn't need to be saying that kind of thing out loud. I don't want Colin to overhear and think that I'm planning on trapping him in some kind of baby net. And I especially don't want this conversation getting back to our photographer friends outside.

Thankfully, by the time we wrap for the day, the paparazzi have packed up and moved out, restoring peace and privacy to our little community here at Dunadhar Castle.

"So, I've got an idea for a getaway this weekend," Colin says to me as the rest of our colleagues pass us by.

"Really? What is it?"

"I can't tell you. It's a surprise. But it's going to be just the two of us this time. No Benjamin, no Gemma. Are you all right with that?"

As if on cue, Benjamin darts past us, with Maya and Cecily right on his heels.

"I think I'll survive."

Chapter Twenty-Two

I spoke too soon.

It turns out that in order to survive a weekend without your two best friends, you first must survive the preceding week. Well, I'm still alive, but just barely.

It all began late Tuesday afternoon when little Cecily announced that her tummy hurt. Her mom, who is on set with us, gave her a glass of water and told her to sit down and rest. Maya, who never leaves her sister's side, began wailing and claiming that she was sick too and that she needed to stay with Cecily even though we were just about to shoot their final scene for the day.

In a valiant, if not slightly misguided, attempt to cheer them, Benjamin grabbed three plates and announced that he was going to juggle for them. Well, that would have been really sweet and adorable if he actually knew how to juggle. Perhaps he did at one point, but he certainly doesn't now. Less than ten seconds in, he fumbled, dropped all three plates, and cut the palm of his hand wide open as he went to catch them.

Everyone immediately sprang into action. Elizabeth ran to fetch a wet washcloth. Louise called an ambulance. And I scampered back to the main trailer for the first aid kit. As I scampered, however, I caught sight of our friendly neighborhood paparazzi. Desperate to remain unseen, I tried to duck out of their line of vision. Of course, in doing so, I tripped and toppled over onto the graveled pathway, in full view of the people who make their living taking pictures of their fellow humans in awkward and embarrassing situations.

Five hours later, Benjamin left the hospital with eight stitches and I left with a wrist brace and strict orders to keep my arm iced, elevated, and rested.

The next morning, images of my graceless tumble were circulating online with stupid captions like *Lorelei DuBois is Head Over Heels... Literally!* and I was considering dyeing my hair blue and assuming yet another false identity. However, Gemma managed to convince me that the pictures weren't that bad and that I wouldn't get laughed off the set. She was mostly right. The only person who laughed was Benjamin. So I called him Frankenstein, you know, because of his stitches. But of course, since he actually played Victor Frankenstein in that movie with Colin, it wasn't offensive or even remotely funny. Then he made me sit through the "Frankenstein is the doctor, not the monster" lecture even though I've read *Frankenstein* twice for two different literature classes.

The rest of Wednesday really wasn't too bad. Until Gemma and I got back to the hostel, that is. That was when the poor girl at the front desk informed us that they'd discovered infestations of earwigs in a few of the bedrooms. She assured us that it was nothing to worry about and that they were in the midst of trying to get rid of them. However, Gemma and I might want to sleep with bits of toilet paper stuffed in our ears, just in case.

Yeah, for the record, even though earwigs don't actually crawl into your ears in order to burrow into your brain and build a nest, they sometimes do crawl into your ears just for the hell of it. Granted, so do a lot of other bugs but they didn't choose to take up residence at the Dunadhar Highland Lodge. Earwigs did. And earwigs are particularly disgusting.

Needless to say, there was not a lot of sleep to be had that night. Especially after Gemma found two earwigs *in her bed*.

To top off an already shit-tacular week, Thursday morning I woke up (and I use that phrase very loosely) to an emailed receipt from my bank stating that I had withdrawn a significant amount of money from my checking account. Except that I hadn't. So, on top of the strained wrist, the stupid pictures, and the earwig-induced insomnia, someone hacked my bank account. That meant I got to spend a good two hours on an overseas phone call verifying my identity (in private, of course), canceling my debit and my credit cards, and identifying the false transactions in my recent banking activity.

May I just say that if I didn't believe in Murphy's Law before, I certainly do now.

Honestly, the only thing that's kept me going is the promise of a romantic weekend with Colin. I still have no idea where he's taking me, but as long as it's free of earwigs and all the other things that like to go creepy crawling in the night, I will be a happy camper. I just wish I didn't have to wear this stupid wrist brace.

Okay, so maybe I'm still not in the best mood. But at least it's finally Friday. And that means that for the next forty hours or so, I get Colin all to myself.

Now if only I knew where he was.

He finished filming his last scene of the day about two hours ago. He told me that he was going to change and shower and to text him when I was free.

I've just grabbed my phone out of my backpack when Benjamin passes by.

"Hope you and Colin have fun this weekend without us. Though I can't imagine you will," he teases.

"Like you and Gemma will even notice we're not there," I reply.

"You wound me, Kimberly. Your absence always weighs heavily on my heart. Though it might not weigh so heavily if you told me your real name."

"You already know my real name. Kimberly"

"Bollocks."

I giggle.

"Watch out for the paparazzi, Benji."

"That is a name for a dog. Please do not call me that."

"But it's adorable."

"It makes me feel like your pet. And I don't think Colin would like that at all."

Actually, he'd probably think it was hilarious. In fact, I make a mental note to tell him all about Benjamin's new nickname. But first, I need to find him.

Free! I text him. **Where are you?**

He writes back almost immediately.

Trailer. Come on over!

Keeping a sharp eye out to make sure there are no paparazzi around to catch me sneaking off for a secret rendezvous with Colin Ward, I casually make my way back to the lot where the actors' trailers are all parked. When I reach the one I know very well to be his, I glance around once more to check for cameras before I knock on the door. When he answers, it's all I can do to keep my knees from giving out.

He looks... *wow*. Just wow. His dark hair, still damp from his shower, falls naturally and gracefully into his eyes and he's dressed in a white button-down shirt that's not actually buttoned all the way and a pair of amazing jeans that hug his body in the best and most enticing way.

I don't care where we're going or what he has planned. He could take me down to the creepy, haunted Edinburgh Vaults and I'd still be all over him.

"Okay, you are *really* hot," I tell him.

He laughs.

"So are you."

"Not like you. I feel like I shouldn't be allowed to touch you."

"Oh, well, we can't have that, can we?" He takes my hand and gives a gentle tug, pulling me up the steps and into his arms. Once we're inside, he closes the trailer door and leans down to kiss me. Then he asks, "Feeling better?"

"No, not yet." And I press my mouth to his again. I know how easy it would be to just have him right here, right now, and after the week I've had, I'm absolutely considering it. But I also know that he's had our weekend planned for a while now. I don't want to ruin it by jumping the gun. Or you know, him. "So," I finally say. "Where are we going?"

"You'll see. We can't leave just yet, but I've just about got everything we need."

Huh? None of that makes any sense at all.

"Can you at least give me a hint?"

He stops to think about it.

"It's in Scotland." He is clearly impressed by his own wit. I am not.

"Oh boy, what a great hint."

"I try."

"Okay, if you can't tell me where we're going, can you tell me what we're waiting for?"

"I could... But it might give it away."

"Give what a - "

"Hey, you've had a long day. You should sit down," he interrupts. Then he goes to clear a space on his couch. "Here. Relax while I finish getting things together."

"What things?"

"You're not very good with surprises, are you?" he grins.

"Actually, I love surprises. But I'm a curious person by nature. They're conflicting personality traits."

"Just be patient."

I heave an overly dramatic sigh, but I do as he says.

Finally, after forty minutes or so, he grabs his backpack and what looks to be a small ice chest and says, "Okay, I think we've given it enough time."

"Are we going camping?" I wonder.

"You'll see."

"Are we going on a picnic?"

"Is this what it's like watching movies with you? Because I might have to rethink a few of my ideas for future dates."

Actually, Gemma has told me on multiple occasions that I am one of the worst people to watch movies with specifically because I'm always trying to guess what's going to happen. I can't help it. I like to know things.

"I may have been shushed once or twice..." I admit as I follow him out of his trailer. By now, it's almost eight in the evening and the world around us is calm and still and silent. It almost seems a shame to disturb the peace with the roar of Colin's motorcycle.

Except we're not heading toward the motorcycle. In fact, we're not heading toward the parking lot at all.

I think he's taking me back to the castle.

"Wait a minute, what are we doing?"

"What do you think we're doing?" he grins.

"I think we're about to break into a castle for the second time in the past six weeks."

"That is exactly what we're doing. But we're not just breaking in."

"What does that mean?"

"All in good time."

Again, we step into the vast emptiness and ageless echoes of Dunadhar Castle. In the absence of the liveliness and action of the cast and crew, it seems an entirely different place. One of royalty and reverence, not cameras and cue cards.

"Come with me," Colin whispers, although he has no need to do so. We're the only ones here. He could shout and there'd be no one to hear him.

He leads the way up the grand staircase, past the tapestries and stone carvings, to the King's bedchamber. Or at least, the room that serves as the King's bedchamber in the show. Our set designers have done an incredible job crafting an environment that captures the ambiance of the books; sensual and secret, passionate and powerful. Every detail is exquisite, from the day chairs to the medieval-style candle holders to Malcolm's desk, stacked with antique books, letters, and a small ink bottle. A shield bearing the royal Saxe coat of arms overlooks the fireplace and there's a small table with a silver pitcher and a wash rag in the far corner of the room. Then, of course, there's the enormous four-poster bed, adorned with crimson velvet curtains and a spread to match.

When Colin drops his backpack onto one of the chairs, I finally begin to realize just what he has planned.

"Are we spending the night here?"

"I know it seems like I didn't put very much thought into this, but hear me out," he says. "I wanted you to have a night in a castle. Any other castle, we're going to have to share with dozens of other tourists. We wouldn't be able to wander the halls, explore its secret passageways, make love in the throne room..." And now I'm blushing. Colin takes my hands and continues. "Here, we can do whatever we like. We're alone. We're free. Tonight, Dunadhar Castle is ours."

Chapter Twenty-Three

It's one of those dreams I never expected to come true. In fact, it's one of those dreams that I never even realized I had until it came true. But considering the setting I selected for my trashy romance novel, I guess it comes as no surprise.

Standing at the window, I take in the splendor of the Highlands while Colin makes his way about the room, lighting every candle and then finally, the fireplace. Then he turns to me and asks, "Would you like to set up our banquet here or in the dining hall?"

The dining room is so large, I feel like we'd be worlds apart, even if we were just sitting across the table from each other.

"Let's stay here for now," I tell him.

"Perfect."

He begins his preparations by moving day chairs aside and clearing a large space in front of the fireplace. Then he lays out his blue plaid blanket and begins unpacking the ice chest.

"Do you need any help?" I ask.

"I have dishes and silverware in my backpack if you'd like to retrieve those for me."

Those dishes and silverware turn out to be plastic, which is understandable. I doubt Colin would be running around with fine china or plates of gold or silver in his backpack. Meanwhile, he's prepared a regular buffet of "banquet" foods including black grapes, apples, three different kinds of bread, and a variety of cheeses. He's also brought two bottles of sparkling pressé.

"How did you think of all this?" I wonder once my plate is fit to overflow with fruit, bread, and cheese.

"Actually, it was something that Benjamin said a few weeks back. About these books being based on your fantasies."

"You mean my *dirty* fantasies?"

He chuckles.

"Well, yes, but I'm trying to make this romantic."

"I'm sorry, I'm sorry. Please continue."

"Anyway, I got to thinking that as great as it must be for you to see your fantasies come to life, it would be even better if you could actually live them. Again, I know this doesn't seem like much but - "

I don't give him the chance to finish. Leaning into him, I reach up and stroke his cheek before gently guiding his mouth to mine. The kiss lasts for several sweet and celestial moments and when it ends, I say, "This is the most wonderful thing that anyone has ever done for me. Thank you."

Colin smiles.

"Don't thank me yet. The night has barely begun."

If you had asked me six weeks ago if I believed in magic, my honest-to-goodness answer would have been, "I don't know."

I consider myself a semi-rationalist. I believe in explanations, but I'm also convinced that everything happens for a reason. I put my faith in science, but I also like to think that there really is a mythological monster out there beneath the dark waters of Loch Ness. My way of thinking really doesn't make much sense. But I guess if it did make sense, I wouldn't be standing here, gazing up at a castle ceiling.

That's what I'm doing. Just gazing.

After dinner, Colin and I set out to explore the castle, to really take it all in. There's no rush. There's no one here to tell us what to do or where to be. And so I'm taking it all in and I'm thinking about magic. Not the fairy tale kind of magic or the witchcraft you'd learn at Hogwarts, but the magic that we, as humans, typically tend to overlook. Because it's everywhere. It exists in everything. It exists in books and in castles, in forests and in mountains. It guards secrets and guides spirits and reassures time and time again that there is more to our existence than we could ever hope to know.

And yes, I got all of that from a castle ceiling. But I'm a writer. I think it goes without saying that I'm a little out there.

But then, Colin isn't exactly the poster boy for normalcy.

"You know, I've heard this castle is haunted," he whispers. Of course he'd wait until *after* the sun has finally begun to set to tell me this.

"I've heard that Scotland is haunted," I reply. It's true. From what I've been told, this entire country is crawling with spirits. My favorite ghost hunting show, *Cemetery Tours*, is set to film their Halloween special here. In fact, they might even be here now. I'll have to check. I'm a little behind on my Twitter stalking.

"So are you a believer?"

"Oh, absolutely. Aren't you?"

"I probably believe in ghosts about as much as I believe in Nessie. But you know, maybe if I saw one tonight - "

"No."

"You don't want to see a ghost?"

"No."

"I thought you believed in them."

"I do. And that's exactly why I don't want to go looking for one. Because if we actually found one, there is no way in hell I'd be staying here tonight."

For some reason, Colin finds all of this very amusing.

"I can't believe you're afraid of ghosts."

"Really? I'm afraid of everything: ghosts, germs, vulnerability, the dark, Slender Man, public speaking, earwigs..."

Colin laughs again, although there is definitely nothing funny about earwigs. Thankfully, I don't have to worry about *them* tonight. Given the choice between earwigs and translucent dead people, I'd have to go with the dead people.

"Okay, okay, no ghosts," he concedes. "But how do you feel about extraterrestrials?"

"Oh, I'm afraid of them too. Why?"

"I'm technically not supposed to say anything yet, but my agent called this morning to let me know I've been offered a part in a new sci-fi/horror film supposedly based on actual events. We start filming in Arizona just two days after we wrap here."

"Oh my God, Colin! That's so exciting!"

"If I promise to protect you from aliens, would you come visit me?"

"Wha - Really?"

"Yes, really," he laughs. "If you'd like to."

"I'd love to."

Grinning from ear to ear, Colin takes my hand and pulls me into a kiss. It's a kiss full of promises, possibilities, and pleasure. I lift up my arms and wrap them around his broad shoulders, pressing my body to his.

This is real. This is real. He's real.

Taking a deep breath, I whisper, "Let's go back upstairs."

He nods silently in response.

As we fall into bed, I can't help but think back to the night I began writing *The Queen's Surrogate*. Of course, it didn't have a title back then. It was just a silly story that I decided to write because I was bored and I didn't want to study and I had just watched about half a dozen Matthew Kent interviews on YouTube. I could have written it a hundred different ways, but my mind went directly for the age-old standard: medieval romance.

I can see my fantasies as clear as day, everything I envisioned while writing that very first scene. I wanted Corrine and Malcolm to be more than lovers. I wanted them to fall in love, even though I knew they would never truly end up together.

With Colin, it's a whole different story. Like Corrine and Malcolm, we began as lovers, but I never intended to fall in love with him. In fact, I tried my hardest not to. But after tonight, I know I can't keep denying it. I love him. I'm in love with him. And I'm daring to hope that maybe, just maybe, we'll end up together after all.

Driven by desire and passion and love, I rise up and hoist myself onto Colin's hips. Clutching my thighs, he lowers himself onto his back, his dark eyes dancing with the light of a thousand flickering candles. I reach down for his hands and lace my fingers through his as my body begins to move for him, with him. After a few moments, however, he lets go of my fingers and shifts beneath me.

"This is no good," he breathes.

"No?"

"No. I want to be touching you."

And with that, he sits up to meet me, pulling me into his embrace and pressing his lips to my bare skin. I wrap myself around him, close my eyes, and breathe him in. In my stories, I wrote Malcolm as fire and gold and power, but here in my arms, Colin is cedar, silver, and summer air.

Finally, he lifts his head up to kiss my mouth, and that's when I lose myself completely.

I cling to him as we lay back down together, settling into a state of comfort and bliss. Within moments, he's drifted off to sleep, leaving me alone with the Highland wind, the crackling fire, and the sweet, reassuring sound of his beating heart.

I love him. I love him. I love him.

As a romance author, I'm supposed to know how to make love out of words, and maybe once, I thought I did. After tonight, however, I don't think I would know where to begin. It's easy to fill a page with saccharine dialogue and pretty similes. Yet now it seems that every word of every page I've ever written falls terribly and tragically short.

Glancing up at Colin's sleeping face, I wonder what he's dreaming, if he has any idea how much he means to me.

How can he? The quiet voice in the back of my mind wonders. *You've never told him.*

And suddenly, I know exactly what I need to do.

Silently, I climb out of bed and grab Colin's discarded white shirt off the floor. Slipping it over my shoulders, I tiptoe across the room to where I left my bag. I reach in and pull out my notebook and a pen. Then, in the soft glow of firelight, I tear out a single piece of paper and take a seat on the floor.

It's only then that I hear Colin shifting beneath the sheets.

"What are you doing?" he asks me, his voice heavy with sleep.

"I'm sorry. I didn't mean to wake you," I whisper.

"It's all right." Colin climbs off the bed and, dressed only in a pair of gray sweatpants, joins me on the cold, stone ground. "Are you okay?" he asks, draping his arms around me.

"Mm-hmm." I nod. "I'm wonderful."

"You are," Colin agrees, kissing me behind my ear. "What are you working on?"

I don't answer. I just hand him the sheet of paper, upon which I've written three small words:

Delaney Georgia Brooks

Colin reads the note, then turns his eyes toward me as though he's seeing me for the very first time.

"Delaney," he whispers.

"Don't tell Benjamin," I tease, fighting back tears. I don't want to cry. I don't want to be that girl. But I think I am.

"Wouldn't dream of it," he assures me. "I might hold it over his head a bit..."

"You definitely should."

We both laugh softly. Then, he brushes my hair back away from my face and pulls me in, closer and closer, until our foreheads touch. "I love you, Delaney."

In fiction, a declaration of love is often a grand affair, or at least a soliloquy full of lines that will more than likely end up on Pinterest boards of inspirational quotes. When Malcolm professes his love to Corrine, he says, *From the moment I awoke, I thought only of you. Of the golden softness of your hair, the smell of roses on your skin, the shades of starlight in your eyes. I'm used to spending my days preoccupied with matters so dull and dreary that I begin to envy the lark who perches outside my window and taunts me with his mirthful song. Yet today, I found myself singing along, enraptured by the memory of your warmth and the promise of your kiss. You have brought me to life, Corrine, at a time I thought that life had nothing more to offer me. And I love you. I love you."*

Colin's simple declaration, uttered softly in the quiet of night, isn't one for the storybooks or the silver screen, but I wouldn't rewrite it for the world. Because he's the one who spoke it.

Slowly, deftly, I reach my hand up to stroke his face as I echo his sentiment. "I love you, too. So much."

And with that, our night ends as so many do; with the flicker of embers, the rustling of blankets, and the taste of a lover's kiss lingering on our lips.

Excerpt from *The Surrogate's Tutor*

"... Speak to me instead of that great land beyond the veil, where spirits dance in the mist and flit about the fields as shimmers of sunlight. For that is where she dwells. My love, my hope, my everlasting."

Then Tristan closes the book, a look of reverence and reflection on his gentle face. I love it when he reads to me. I love the sound of his voice, deep and soothing. I love the way that he loses himself to the world inside the story.

"Is it really over so soon?" I ask him.

He smiles at me before returning the book to its rightful place on the shelves of the royal library.

"I asked the same thing the first time I read this book." Then he says, "You seem pensive today. Is something troubling you?"

"No. No, not at all." I assure him. Then I take a deep breath and confess, "I am with child."

"Oh." I am unable to read the look on his face. "Have Their Majesties been informed?"

"Yes. The announcement is to be made in the coming month."

"So what is it that concerns you?" he wonders.

It is not fair that he can read me so easily. Like an open book. But he has become so much more than my tutor. Tristan is my dearest friend and confidante. He is my comfort and my protector. I may be Malcolm's by the cover of night, but I am Tristan's by the light of day. I trust him above all others.

And so I confess to him my fears; my fear of uncertainty, of what the future may hold for me if I bear the King another daughter. Or how my life will change if I bear the King a son. My purpose here will be fulfilled. I will no longer be needed. But if the child I carry is a girl, I may no longer be welcome. Malcolm may claim to love me, but how can I be of use to him if I am incapable of giving him a son?

"Corrine." Tristan kneels down before me and takes my hand. "His Majesty cares deeply for you. No matter what happens, he will see that you are cherished. And if he does not... Then I will."

I look up to meet his eye.

"Tristan..." I whisper.

"I know I have no title, no castle to call my own. I cannot offer you a life of nobility or

290

banquets. But I promise that I will always love you and keep you safe. If you'll have me."

His proposal has left me with an unfamiliar ache in my heart, one that renders me breathless. I love Malcolm, and my body will always yearn for him. But my spirit longs for Tristan, for his compassion and wisdom.

"Of course I'll have you."

And for the first time in the many moons since we first met, Tristan takes me into his arms and there, in the sanctuary of a thousand words and pages and stories, he finally kisses me.

Chapter Twenty-Four

Spending a night in a castle with the man of your dreams is the most romantic thing in the world... Until you wake up shivering at three o'clock in the morning because, oh yeah, age-old castles don't have central heating systems. At least, Dunadhar doesn't. And I don't know if you know this, but Scotland is *freezing*.

Okay, so maybe it isn't actually freezing, but nights here in the Highlands can get pretty cold. Especially to someone born and raised in Texas, where eighty degrees is considered sweater weather.

Colin, of course, slept right through the chill and my chattering teeth and only stirred after I crawled back into bed wearing three layers of clothes, including his sweatpants. He asked if I wanted to go back and spend the rest of the night in his hotel, but in my sleepy stupor, I argued that going outside would be even colder. So he wrapped me up in his arms and blankets and held me until I fell back asleep.

Still, despite the arctic blast, last night was the best night of my entire life, and I wouldn't change a moment.

We are, however, staying in his fancy hotel tonight. And when I say fancy, I mean *really* fancy. This place has crystal chandeliers, gold lions guarding the grand staircase, emerald green carpeting, and a spa. I'm not kidding. A legitimate spa where you can drown your troubles in a heated jacuzzi and have your knots kneaded out by a licensed masseuse. And if you're really stressed, you can settle in for a nice, relaxing pedicure.

Do you know what we have at the Dunadhar Highland Lodge? Showers that never guarantee you hot water, stale dinner rolls with every meal, and earwigs.

Seriously, if you want to live a life of luxury, don't be a writer.

We've actually been here at the hotel since around noon. Shortly after we settled in, thunder began rumbling in the distance and before we knew it, we were caught up in a beautiful Scottish thunderstorm.

"I guess it was bound to happen sooner or later," Colin remarked.

"I like rain. It's soothing," I said, watching the droplets streak across the stained-glass window of his bedroom.

"You're enchanting, you know that?" Colin asked. I blushed. "So, what do you want to do?"

"I know I'm supposed to say something like, 'Let's brave the rain and go have an adventure,' but I'd be just as happy to spend the day here with you, lounging in our pajamas, watching movies, reading..." *Having fancy hotel sex...* I didn't say that last bit out loud, but Colin still got the gist.

So that's what we've done today. And it's been glorious. Now evening has fallen again, the rain is finally subsiding, and I'm famished.

"Do you want me to call room service?" Colin asks.

It's probably pretty customary for celebrities to take full advantage of having meals delivered directly to their doors, but I'm still used to trekking down to the lobby for a midnight carton of chocolate milk or instant macaroni and cheese. Granted, the coffee bar downstairs probably has much better food to offer than that, but the point remains. Besides, I wouldn't mind stretching my legs a bit.

"That's okay. I'll go downstairs and see what they've got. Do you want me to bring you anything?"

"I don't know. Am I supposed to let you wait on me so early on in the relationship?" he grins.

"Okay, I'm bringing you a sandwich. I'm not polishing your silver or giving you a foot rub. You can go down to the spa for that."

Colin heaves a playful sigh but accepts my kiss nevertheless before I step out of the room and into the long hallway.

There are a few guests still out and about, sipping tea and chatting by the fire in the lobby. None of them pay me a first, let alone a second thought. To everyone here, I'm just another girl in plaid flannel pants and a navy-blue t-shirt bearing the Scottish flag, stopping by the hotel coffee shop for a late-night snack.

"Lorelei?"

Or not.

I turn and to my absolute horror, find myself face to face with Rose Cervantes and Matthew Kent, who look to be very much together. Whether it's for publicity or not, I can't say, but there are no photographers or reporters around and they're still wrapped in one another's embrace.

"What are you doing here?" Rose asks me.

"Um..." I truly have no good answer for her. Matthew, meanwhile, is eyeing either my curious wardrobe or the two sandwiches and three pieces of Scottish shortbread that I'm carrying or possibly all of the above.

"Are you here with someone?" he asks me.

"Um... sort of."

Even though I'm the one with all of the secrets, Colin's face will be the one showing up in all the tabloids and celebrity gossip columns if word gets out that Hollywood's favorite playboy-turned-terminal-bachelor is romancing a romance author in the Scottish Highlands. Then again, Colin has proven himself extremely resilient in the face of worldwide scrutiny and notoriety. I wish the same could be said for me.

"Actually, I'm kind of here with - " But before I'm able to make my confession, the lift doors open and a man with greasy hair and a delicate stature steps into the lobby.

Colin's publicist. Geoff.

Rigsley.

And, as if Rose and Matthew weren't already confused enough, I take off mid-sentence, sprinting in the opposite direction, and I don't stop until I'm back at Colin's room. I glance over my shoulder to make sure there's no one trailing me as I pause to catch my breath. Once I've regained my composure, I knock on the door.

"That was fast," Colin comments after he's let me in. "Is everything okay?"

"I should have just let you order room service," I tell him. Then I recount my run-in with Rose and Matthew and my near-miss with Geoff. "You didn't tell me he was staying here too."

"I knew he was flying in sometime this week, but I didn't realize it'd be so soon," Colin admits. "He's probably been trying to get in touch with me."

"How quickly would he sell you out if he found out about us?" The words are out of my mouth before I can stop them.

"Is that why you don't like him?"

"He just... he makes me uncomfortable. And I know that people are going to find out. But I want us to be the ones to tell them. Not the media or press or a gossip blogger seeking a hot new headline. And I especially don't want anything breaking before I tell my parents."

"You haven't told them?"

"They already put up with a lot of weird having a romance author for a daughter. I didn't want to tell them anything until... well..."

"Until you knew I wasn't going anywhere?" Colin grins, taking my hands.

"More or less."

"Well, my mom's known for about a month now."

"*What?*"

"Don't worry, I didn't go into excruciating detail," he assures me, lacing his fingers through mine. "But I may have mentioned that I'd met you. And that I'd kissed you," he pauses to do just that, "once or twice. And I may have mentioned that you were beautiful and amazing, kind and intelligent, and that I can never seem to get you off of my mind."

By now, my hands have slipped out of his and up around his neck, and I'm rising up onto my toes for another kiss.

Then I confess, "I have no idea how I'm going to tell them."

"Why is that?" Colin laughs.

"Because they know who you are! You're Colin Ward! You're the hot guy who takes his shirt off a lot in *Streets of Atlantis*." Which, by the way, is a terrible movie. It came out when I was a freshman in high school and I only saw it because I thought it was going to be about dolphins. It wasn't. It was about a group of guys who discover Atlantis and there's a lot of technology and explosions and it was just so boring, especially to a fourteen-year-old girl.

"My mom knows who you are," Colin reminds me.

"Still, authors and actors are different kinds of famous. Unless you're J.K. Rowling, and sadly, I am not."

"I'm glad you're not. She's married. It'd be a bit awkward."

"Then Geoff would really have a scandal to sell."

"Don't worry about Geoff. He may come off as a bit shady, but he's a reasonable guy. He won't say anything if I tell him not to."

I'm still not fully convinced, but Colin's assurance does bring me a little comfort. Maybe I judged Geoff too hastily. It wouldn't be the first time I've let a preconceived notion cloud my first impression of a person. Or my second.

"If you trust him, then so do I," I say.

Colin smiles and kisses my forehead.

"I love you."

"I love you, too."

The next morning, Colin sneaks me out of the hotel and drives me back to Dunadhar Highland Lodge on his motorcycle. Thankfully, the rain has let up, though the sky is still overcast. Even so, it's a beautiful morning for a ride through the Highlands.

"I'll see you in a few hours," he bids me as I lean forward to kiss him goodbye.

I head upstairs to shower and change and maybe even take a quick nap before Andrew and Louise arrive to take Gemma and me to Lot B for this afternoon's read-through. That is, if Gemma is even here. I know she was running off with Benjamin again, but I haven't heard from either of them all weekend.

As it turns out she is here, looking bright-eyed and beautiful in a short blue dress, leggings, and riding boots.

"You look cute," I tell her.

"You look like you spent the last forty-eight hours riding a motorcycle. And the man who owns it."

"Guilty."

"I guess that means I don't have to ask you if you had a good time this weekend," Gemma winks.

"It was pretty perfect," I admit. "I told him."

"Are you serious?"

"Yeah."

"Delaney, I am so proud of you!" Gemma squeals and wraps her arms around me. "It's really real for you, isn't it?"

"Yeah, I think it is."

"Well, you deserve it."

"Thank you," I smile. "So, what did you and Benjamin do this weekend?"

"We broke up."

"*What*?" That is the absolute *last* thing I expected to hear.

"It's okay, Delaney. We all knew it was coming."

"Yeah, but... I know you really liked him. And you guys seemed so good together."

"I did like him and I still do. But we're only here for two more weeks and with all the paparazzi hanging around, we just figured it was better to quit while we were ahead. Neither of us is bitter or anything. It was very amicable. No tears, no drama."

"Still, I'm sad for you."

"Please don't be. I'm not. Neither of us was ever in this for the long run. Besides, I have a date with Andrew tonight after read-through."

"I'm sorry, what?"

"What? He's cute!"

"Didn't you just break up with Benjamin because we're only here for two more weeks?"

"Yeah, but I'm allowed to have a little fun in those two weeks."

Typical Gemma, leaving a trail of broken hearts behind her everywhere she goes. I know Benjamin was more than capable of handling her, but poor Andrew may be another story. I just hope she doesn't hurt him.

Of course, I can't help but notice that when he and Louise arrive to pick us up, Andrew eyes Gemma with the look of a man eager to have his heart broken by such a beauty.

Perhaps he does know what he's getting himself into.

Gemma and I are among the first to arrive for read-through, along with a few members of the supporting cast and Matthew and Rose. Just the couple I *don't* want to see. I glance over, hoping to catch Gemma's eye, but she's too busy flirting with Andrew to pay me even the slightest bit of attention. She won't notice if I slip away for a moment or two. Or at least until I have a couple of tall allies to hide behind.

I've barely escaped when I run into one of those allies just down the hall.

"Where are you off to, my darling Kimberly?" Benjamin asks.

"Oh, you know, just running away from potentially awkward encounters."

"Does this count as an awkward encounter?" For once, Benjamin looks genuinely concerned, I assume because of what happened with Gemma.

"Of course not. You're my friend. Besides, it's not like you're the first guy to break up with Gemma."

"Well actually, she's the one who broke up with me."

"What?" I seem to be saying that a lot. I guess today's the day for delivering emotional bombshells.

"She didn't mention that?"

"No. She made it seem like the decision was mutual."

"Well, it wasn't."

"Oh my God, Benjamin, I'm so sorry." I truly am. Not just because my best friend is the "bad guy" in this break-up, but because unless I am mistaken, Benjamin Wyndham is, for what may be the first time in his life, suffering from a broken heart. "Do you want to go outside and talk?"

"I don't want to trouble you."

"It's no trouble, I promise," I assure him, reaching out to touch his arm. "Come on."

"I knew it." Benjamin and I both turn to see Rose, glowering at us from outside the conference room. "I knew it!"

"Rose, it's not what you think." I try my best to remain calm but my fight-or-flight instinct is threatening to kick in and carry me all the way back to the hostel.

"You really expect me to believe that? Especially after last night? You forget, Lorelei, that I know what it's like to love Benjamin. I have been there, done that. But at least he gave me the courtesy of not jumping into bed with my best friend before I had time to take the hint!"

"It *isn't* like that," Benjamin insists.

"Oh, just shut up, you pig."

"Rose! Can we take this outside? Please?" I beg. Not only for my sake, but for Benjamin's.

"Maybe I should stay here," Benjamin suggests, looking glum.

"I think that would be for the best," I agree before ushering Rose out of the building.

She doesn't waste a moment before she starts tearing into me again.

"I just can't believe that *you* would sink so low, Lorelei. I thought you were better than this. But you're just as big a slut as your friend. And twice as stupid if you think that - "

"That's enough!" I snap. "Look, you can insult me all you want, but you leave Gemma out of this. Especially when she hasn't done anything to deserve it."

"How the hell are you in any position to defend her when you're sleeping with the man that just broke up with her?"

"Because I'm *not* sleeping with Benjamin! I'm sleeping with Colin! There, you happy?"

Rose's face falls flat in disbelief.

"You... What?" Apparently, I've stunned her into silence. Too bad I didn't figure that trick out earlier. "I don't... I'm sorry, I just... Really?"

"Yes, really."

"But you never act like you're anything more than acquaintances."

"Well yeah, that's because we were trying to keep it under wraps. Until I kind of blew it last night by parading around in my pajamas."

"I guess that does make sense, it's just... Colin Ward? Are you sure that's a good idea? He's like... a legendary playboy. He's even worse than Benjamin."

"He's not, though. And Benjamin isn't bad, either. He just doesn't always handle things the way you might like for him to."

Rose sighs.

"He was the first guy to really break my heart, you know?"

"I know." Boy, do I ever know. "To tell you the truth, if I had to work with the first guy who broke my heart, I'd have quit on the spot."

"I thought about it, but I didn't want to let him stand in the way of what I've been working for my entire life. And if I'm telling you the truth, I really wanted this role. I loved your books."

"Really?" That's a pleasant surprise.

"Really. Being here, bringing Corrine to life, has been a dream come true."

"Well, you've done a fantastic job." And I'm not just saying that because - miracle of all miracles - we're finally bonding. I really mean it. Rose is a fine young actress and I want nothing but good things for her. For every member of the cast.

"Thank you, Lorelei," she smiles. "And listen, I'm sorry about everything I said. About both you and Gemma. I really overreacted."

"That's okay," I assure her. "I'm sorry, too."

"Why?"

"Because I really do know how you feel. And it's the worst."

Chapter Twenty-Five

Walking on eggshells is never easy, but it's particularly difficult when you have a starry-eyed best friend flaunting her new romance in front of her heartbroken former lover, a publicist who may or may not be an eely sleazer lurking about, and the paparazzi relentlessly camped out in your car park. On top of all of that, the cast and crew are sitting through more interviews which means longer hours and less time with Colin.

Gemma and Andrew, however, are making the most of the extended workday and spending as much time together as possible. And it's making poor Benjamin miserable.

"Do you want me to have a talk with her?" I asked him on Tuesday after we spotted Gemma giggling with Andrew over a private lunch. At least, as private as a lunch can be on set.

"No."

"Are you sure? I don't mind."

"I know you don't. But I don't want to be the git pining after a girl who doesn't want him. I can't imagine anything worse than having everyone feeling sorry for me. It's bad enough that you do."

"I'm sorry, I can't help it. I care about you."

"If you really cared about me, you'd tell me your real name."

I'm happy that he was feeling himself enough to tease me, but I still couldn't bring myself to tease him back.

Now it's Thursday and I'm trying to come up with a valid excuse for sneaking into the great hall to listen in on Colin's interview. I managed to catch the second half of Benjamin's yesterday by mistake and I'll admit, it was a lot of fun listening to him talk about his experience and sharing his favorite moments and memories.

I guess I don't have to say anything as long as I don't get caught.

Casually, trying my best to act as though I'm supposed to be there, I slip into the great hall where Colin is just settling in with Aïda Jobe, the woman conducting the interviews for this featurette. When Colin catches me, he flashes me a quick grin and a wink before turning his attention back to Aïda.

"Good to see you again, Ms. DuBois."

First, I'm startled. Then I'm shaken to my core. I didn't even notice Geoff standing off to the side. Now he's leering at me over my shoulder.

"Oh. Uh... It's nice to see you again, too." Even as I remind myself of everything that Colin told me, I take an involuntary step away from him.

"It's a pity, isn't it? Your time here is almost over."

Is he making polite conversation with me? Or is he trying to trick me into saying something I'll regret?

"It is a little sad, but I know I'll be back," I tell him.

"Fallen in love, have you?"

Interesting choice of words.

"How could I not? Scotland is magic."

"You seem to have a touch of magic yourself. That is, if my client is to be believed," Geoff says, indicating Colin. "He speaks very highly of you, you know."

"My, what a compliment." And it is. Even coming from Geoff. "It's been a real pleasure working with him." *Oh, please don't read too much into the word 'pleasure.'*

If he is on to me, however, he never gets the chance to say so. Colin's interview is beginning and we're both here to listen.

"Now Colin, you've been in this business for a while now. You're something of a household name. I have to ask what got you interested in this particular project?" Aïda wonders.

"I'd heard good things about the books. My mother and my sisters are all big fans. The series actually helped keep my mother's spirits up while she was battling some pretty serious health issues. Not to mention I think my sisters were both really eager to see me as the disgusting villain."

"That actually leads me to my next question. You're so handsome and yet, you take on quite a few unconventional roles. Why is that, exactly?"

"It's not really a conscious decision. I take the roles that interest me and at the same time, roles that I hope will challenge me. It was different when I was younger. I was type-cast a lot and although I was always incredibly grateful to be working, I got tired of playing the same characters over and over. Now that I'm older, I have a bit more freedom."

"What's been the best part about playing a character like Rigsley?"

"There aren't very many perks to playing him if I'm being totally honest," Colin laughs. "Well, actually, that's not true. It's been a great honor and privilege to work with our amazing cast and crew. But as for the character himself? He has very few redeeming qualities. He's cruel, he's cunning, he carries with him a lot of contempt for everyone around him. Playing him, getting in his head, is exhausting."

"But it's also got to be sort of fun, right? I mean, everyone loves a bad boy."

"Yeah, I would know," Colin quips. "But Rigsley isn't your charming rogue or tattooed rock star. He's actually quite sinister. He has no empathy. I wouldn't want to make an enemy of him, I can tell you that."

"Yeah, I don't think I would either," Aïda agrees before she goes on to the next question. "The appeal of stories like *The Queen's Surrogate* is largely the romance aspect; the passion, the forbidden love, that kind of thing. Do you wish that you had been cast in perhaps a more romantic role?"

"No, not really," Colin answers. "Don't get me wrong, those roles are great. But for this project, I think I was right where I was supposed to be. And it's been a blast. I wouldn't change a moment."

At that, I can't help but smile.

"I talked to Benjamin Wyndham yesterday and he told me that his favorite part of this experience was getting to work with you again."

"Aw, I wish I could reciprocate," Colin jokes. Aida laughs out loud. "I'm teasing, I'm teasing. Benjamin is a great friend and an extremely talented actor. I love working with him and just having him around."

"He seems like quite the character."

"There's never a dull moment."

"It's a shame that young Wyndham couldn't make it work with his new lady friend" Geoff murmurs.

My heart begins to thud the same way it does whenever I'm about to be caught in a lie.

"What makes you think he couldn't?" I ask.

"I'm more observant than you think." He makes it sound like a warning. "Perhaps you could cheer him up. You seem to have a certain soft spot for each other."

Okay, this conversation is getting far too personal.

"We're friends. Nothing more."

"No need to get defensive, Ms. DuBois. Speaking as someone who only has your best interests at heart, it is not at all becoming."

May I just say that the very last thing I want or need is to be lectured by Geoff Martin. But, be that as it may, I hold my tongue. If I want to be Colin's girlfriend, I'm going to have to get used to dealing with his publicist. And just as Colin said of Rigsley, I'd rather *not* make an enemy of Geoff.

Colin's interview ends shortly thereafter, but instead of waiting around to see him, I exit the great hall quietly. I have a feeling Geoff will want to speak with him and I figure I've pushed my luck with him enough for one day.

It doesn't take long, however, for Colin to find me. And thankfully, Geoff is nowhere to be seen.

"I'm glad I was able to catch you," he says. "I actually don't have very long to talk. Geoff wants to have dinner tonight since I told him that I was unavailable tomorrow."

"Oh."

"You're welcome to join us."

"Oh." I guess *Oh* is the only word I can muster when confronted by the idea of socializing with Geoff.

"No pressure," Colin assures me. "I just wanted to extend the invitation."

"And I appreciate it. Thank you," I smile. "I'll probably stay in and try to have a girl's night with Gemma. Haven't seen a whole lot of her this week."

"Yeah, I kind of gathered." He shifts uncomfortably, running a hand through his hair. I know he feels just as bad for Benjamin as I do. And we both know there's nothing either of us can do to make it easier for him. "I hate to do this, but I really need to get going. Before I do though, I wanted to ask you something."

"Anything."

"Since this is our last weekend here, I wanted you to choose where we go. So just be thinking about that tonight. And pack accordingly," he grins.

"I think I can do that," I tell him. "Do you think we should invite Benjamin? I mean... he is the one who started all of this."

"I was wondering the same thing," Colin admits. "I'll text him tonight and let him know the plan."

"And tell him to be prepared for anything."

"Isn't he always?"

Yes, he usually is. Until Gemma came along and worked her way into his heart.

I don't think he was prepared for that at all.

Our hostel dinner of rigatoni and marinara sauce leaves a lot to be desired. It isn't bad, necessarily. It's just that the pasta could stand to be cooked for a few more minutes. And it would be nice if the sauce wasn't... crunchy. As for the dinner rolls, well, they're the same dinner rolls we've been eating for seven weeks now. But you know, at least the salad is fresh.

"You want to know the first thing I'm going to do when I get home?" Gemma asks. "Drive through McDonald's and order the biggest cheeseburger on the menu."

"You know they have McDonald's here," I remind her.

"Yeah, in the big cities."

"Ask Andrew if he'll take you to one on Saturday."

"I did. He has to work," Gemma sighs. "I suppose you and Colin will be taking another romantic getaway."

"Yeah. We haven't decided where we're going yet. He wants me to choose."

"Is it an exclusive excursion or can your favorite personal assistant tag along?"

"Uh..." Oh boy. This is a tough one.

"If you want to be alone, I get it. It is your last weekend together, after all."

"It's not that," I confess. "We were just thinking of asking if Benjamin wanted to come. That's all."

"Oh. Well, that's not a problem. We can go as friends," Gemma says flippantly before taking another bite of rigatoni.

"Actually, I'm not sure you can." I know I promised Benjamin that I wouldn't say anything, but I can't imagine any of us would have a good time this weekend if Gemma came along.

"And why is that?"

"Please don't tell him I told you, but Benjamin isn't as okay with your break-up as he'd like for you to think he is."

"What? No way. That's impossible."

"Why is it impossible?"

"Because Benjamin Wyndham doesn't do relationships. He told me that like, hundred times when we were together."

"Well, apparently, you changed his mind."

"I didn't change his mind. I may have bruised his ego a bit. But if I hadn't broken up with him when I did, he would have ended it about five minutes after we got back home. I'm not the bad guy here. I was just trying to spare each of us the stress of trying to keep up with the fantasy."

"Is that what you think Colin and I are doing?"

Gemma sighs and sets her fork down.

"I'm sorry. That came out wrong. I think that if you two want to make it work, then you will. I just... don't see that happening for Benjamin and me."

I'm sad to say that it's only then that I begin to truly understand my best friend's motives. For so long, she's been the first to call me out on my near-crippling phobia of trust, commitment, or anything that might involve actual feelings when in fact, she suffers from that very same fear. Fear of letting someone get too close. Fear of uncertainty. Fear of having her heart broken. So she goes out of her way to be the heartbreaker.

All these years, I could have been helping and encouraging her. Instead, I've flat out envied the way she never seemed to let anyone or anything affect her.

"It could, you know," I tell her.

"Yeah, well, even if it did, I don't think I'd ever get used to cameras flashing in my face every time I wanted to leave my own apartment," Gemma remarks. "And please don't think I'm a terrible person or that I don't care about Benjamin. I do. We were great together. I just think I'm finally ready to go back home and get back to my real life." Then she looks at me, her eyes shimmering with love and with pride. "It's different for you. This *is* your real life. This weird world of castles and make believe and movie stars. This is where you belong."

Everyone has a love language, or so I'm told. If that's so, then Gemma's is definitely words of affirmation. She's been with me at my absolute worst, she's seen me at my absolute lowest, and somehow, no matter what, she always knows just what to say. She knows how to make a person feel worthwhile and beautiful.

Granted, she can also be sassy and catty and will definitely tear you a new one if she feels you deserve it. But for the most part, she uses her gift for the powers of good.

After dinner, we retreat to our room and to our respective bunk beds. Usually, we're both so exhausted that it's all we can do to keep our eyes open. But tonight, before I hit the light switch, I say, "I'll talk to Benjamin and Colin. I really would like for you to come with us this weekend."

"Oh, it's all right," she yawns. "You know I can take care of myself."

"I know. But I'm the one who brought you here. I can't just run off on our last weekend and leave you here alone."

"Sure you can. I'm sure I'll find something to do. Maybe I can convince Andrew to sneak me into that fancy hotel while he's working."

"They *do* have a spa."

"Well, glory hallelujah. If that doesn't sound like a dream come true, I don't know what does."

Our conversation ends there, but I'm certain as I lay here in the dark that we're both drifting off to sleep with smiles on our faces.

Chapter Twenty-Six

"So, what exactly are we supposed to do here?" Benjamin wonders, glancing around at the hustle and bustle of the streets and the Firth of Lorn.

It's Saturday morning in the small coastal town of Oban. Benjamin, Colin, and I arrived last night after a two-and-a-half-hour drive from Dunadhar Castle. We haven't seen very much of Oban yet, but I'm eager to experience and explore. I love the atmosphere here. I love the salty sea breeze and the colors of the boats docked in the harbor. I love the brisk, gray clouds hovering overhead and the sound of the wind on the water.

"There's lots to do," I tell him, scrolling through Oban's tourist website on my phone. "There are castles, gardens, sea life adventures... Ooh! We could go diving with basking sharks."

"Absolutely not."

"No." Benjamin and Colin object simultaneously.

"Why not?" I ask them.

"I don't do open water," Colin explains.

"And I don't serve my delicious self up on a silver platter for bloodthirsty sharks," Benjamin says.

"Basking sharks are gentle giants. They only eat plankton."

"Yeah, well, I bet it could still swallow me whole if it really wanted to."

I'm glad Benjamin seems to be in good spirits. I'll admit, I've been worried about him. Hopefully, this getaway will be exactly what he needs.

"There he is!"

"Benjamin! Benjamin Wyndham!"

Or not.

None of us has time to react. In the blink of an eye, we're caught up in a small storm of paparazzi, flashing cameras, and a plethora of invasive questions.

"Benjamin, where's your new girlfriend?"

"Can you tell us how you met?"

"Is it true that you've already asked her to move in with you?"

I'm completely overwhelmed, of course, but Benjamin handles it like a total champ.

"Actually, I'm currently single. The woman in question and I are just friends. Sorry to disappoint you. Carry on," Benjamin tells them.

"What about you?" One of them addresses me. "Lorelei, right? You're very rarely seen out of Benjamin's company these days."

"She's my boss. I have to be nice to her," Benjamin counters. "Now, off you go on your merry way."

"What about you, Colin? Do you have anything to share?" another man with a camera wonders.

Colin just glares at them, which scares them off pretty quickly. Maybe you never fully shake that bad boy reputation.

"Are you okay, Benjamin?" I know that's probably the last question he wants me to be asking, but I'd feel like a lousy friend if I didn't.

"Fit as a fiddle, my dear Kimberly. This isn't my first run-in with those snap-happy camera snipers."

"I know, but - "

"I'm going to stop you right there, Love. This is our last weekend here. I am not going to let anything or anyone ruin it. Now. Let's go see what sort of trouble we can get ourselves into before lunch."

It turns out when you're in a town as charming as Oban, there isn't very much trouble to get into. We spent the morning exploring Dunstaffnage Castle, one of the oldest stone castles in Scotland. It has withstood the trials of time and history, having been constructed in the thirteenth century by a man known as the King of the Isles, conquered and captured by Robert the Bruce, and a prison to Flora MacDonald. Benjamin then went on to tell us all about how Robert the Bruce is actually his great-times-nineteen-grandfather and that he intends to remind Disney of that next time they're casting for a live-action Prince.

Once we'd seen the castle and its companion chapel, we made the thirty-minute journey to North Pier for lunch. That's where we are now, at a charming restaurant with a splendid view of Oban Bay. I think I would be content to sit here and gaze out the window all afternoon.

"Did you know that Oban is known as the seafood capital of Scotland?" Benjamin asks, slurping down an oyster.

"I think the real question here is 'Why do you know that?'" I comment. Colin snickers into his soda.

"I enjoy trivia," Benjamin answers. "Believe it or not, beneath the ravishing beauty lies a ravenous brain."

"In other words, you are living proof that God does give with both hands."

"Are you mocking me, Kimberly?"

"Of course not," I grin.

Once we've finished eating, we board a ferry for a short ride to Easdale Island. Although the guys vetoed diving with basking sharks, they both agreed to a whale watching tour that departs from one of Oban's neighboring isles. In the hopes of keeping a low profile, they're both wearing sunglasses and hats: Benjamin, an LA Dodgers baseball cap and Colin, a charcoal gray flat cap. And you know what? He can actually pull it off.

As soon as we board our boat, I hasten to the railing to take in the view. It's spectacular. The water is the deepest, purest blue I've ever seen. The neighboring islands, shrouded in mist and mystery, all but sing to me of enchantment and ecstasy and ancient magic. This is Scotland as I never imagined, a nautical paradise.

The ride itself is an exhilarating one, although it isn't long before the biting chill of the saltwater wind begins to set in, leaving me wishing I'd packed a heavier coat than the dinky red jacket that I bought at Target.

Colin, as always, tunes in on my discomfort and, without a second thought, slides his blazer off his shoulders and wraps it around mine.

"What about you?" I ask him.

"Don't worry about me. I don't freeze easily."

"I'd kiss you right now if there weren't so many people with cameras around," I smile, snuggling into his large coat, still radiating the warmth of his body heat and the scent of his cologne.

"I'll let you make it up to me later," he winks.

I can't wait.

Once upon a time, if someone had asked me to describe my perfect day, I wouldn't have known how to answer. I'm sure my bullet points would have included books, scented candles, and chocolate ice cream.

Now, if someone asked me to describe my perfect day, I would simply tell them, "This one."

My perfect day is one of castles and forests, islands and harbors, adventure on the open sea and dolphins dancing in the waves. And of course, the company of one of my new best friends and the man that I love. I only wish Gemma had been here.

Of course, if the pictures that she's been sending me all day are any indication, she's had the time of her life at the fancy hotel spa. I'm certain her day has been nothing short of perfect as well.

But now that my perfect day is drawing to a close, a bittersweet melancholy is setting in. I'm happy, content, and in love with Colin and with life, but a small voice in the back of my mind keeps reminding me that this is the end. This is my last weekend in Scotland, my last weekend of adventures, my last weekend with him. True, we'll have a wrap party next Friday to celebrate a successful production, but come Saturday, we'll all be gone.

"God, I'm going to miss this," I whisper to Colin. We're lying together in bed, my back pressed against his bare chest. I can feel his breath on my neck and his warm fingers tracing small circles on my hip.

"It's not forever," he reminds me.

"When do you leave?"

"Friday night."

"What?" I sit up and turn to face him. That can't be right.

He sighs.

"I'll be able to stick around for most of the wrap party, but I have to drive back to Edinburgh that night if I'm going to make my flight the next morning. I'll have about half a day in L.A. before heading out to Arizona Sunday evening."

Try as I might, I can't wrap my head around this. It's really happening. Colin is really moving on. And I won't be with him.

Desperate to keep him as close as I can for as long as I can, I sink back down into his arms. I knew I would be sad, but I didn't expect it to hurt like this. Even if we do have every intention of seeing each other again.

"Just don't forget me, okay?" I mean to tease him, to try to lighten the mood, but I choke on my words and my laughter gives way to tears.

"Never, Delaney. I couldn't forget you if I tried," he promises. "And remember what I said to you that night in the castle. I want you to come visit me in Arizona. In fact, I... " And for what may be the first time since we met, he hesitates.

"You what?" I ask, rising back up on my elbows to look at him.

"Well, I was just thinking that there are coffee shops in Arizona."

"Yes...?"

"Well, if you wanted to, you could bring your computer, get some work done while I'm on set. Or I bet, you know, you could even bring your computer and work there. Or, if it's too loud and there are too many distractions, I know you could work in my trailer. We usually have Wi-Fi." And then he blushes. Colin Ward actually blushes. "Forgive me. I think I'm rambling."

"No, no. It's fine." My heart is beating so quickly I can barely speak. Is he asking me what I think he's asking me?

"I mean, I know you've just spent two months away from home and I know you'll want to catch up with your family and your friends. Take some time to relax and recover. But... what if, when you were feeling up to it, you just... you came to stay with me?" As soon as the words are out, he laughs and says, "I'm sorry, I don't know why I'm so nervous."

"Don't apologize." I'm laughing. I'm crying. I'm dizzy and I'm weightless. "Yes."

"Yes?"

"Yes, I'd love to come stay with you."

Colin's handsome face lights up with a dazzling smile.

"I love you," he says, taking my face in both of his hands. Then he chuckles. "I used to go out of my way to avoid saying that. I'd make excuses, I'd change the subject, I'd do anything to spare myself from having to speak those words. Now they seem to be the only words I'm sure of. The only ones that make any sense to me. And no matter how many times I tell you, I don't think it will ever be enough."

"*You're* enough," I whisper. "And I love you, too. I love you so much."

I have a million questions awaiting a million answers, but I don't care to ask them tonight. There are arrangements to be made and plans to be shared, but they can wait until the morrow. All I want now, in this moment, is Colin.

And so, I take him, drunk on passion and frenzied by the notion that he is mine to keep.

Chapter Twenty-Seven

"Ooh, look at this! You can actually go on a UFO tour in Sedona!" Gemma exclaims. Ever since Sunday, when I told her that Colin asked me to stay with him in Arizona, she's been doing extensive research on the area and on the upcoming film. Now it's the middle of our last week in Scotland and I'm fairly certain I know everything I could ever want to know about Sedona, Arizona and the movie, titled *It Happened to Hannah*.

"Yeah, that's a big no."

"How come? You love weird supernatural things. Like Nessie!"

"Nessie is a docile sea monster who lives a life of peace and serenity beneath the glittering waves of Loch Ness and who inspires the minds and spirits of storytellers and adventurers around the world. Aliens are terrifying."

"Oh Delaney, you're a strange little bird. But I suppose that's why I love you."

Okay, did Gemma even read the synopsis for *It Happened to Hannah*? Yes, it's technically fictional, but it's based on several real-life instances of UFO sightings and supposed abductions in Arizona. In the movie, a teenaged girl named Hannah Gallagher goes missing, only to return three days later, claiming that she's been gone for years, held captive by beings that she can only refer to as "*them*."

In spite of having only been missing for seventy-two hours, Hannah appears ill, emaciated, and exhibiting signs of severe psychological and physiological trauma. Naturally, suspicion falls on her single father, John, and that's who Colin will be playing. Of course, Colin has already received and read the script and he's let me in on a few of the secrets that even Gemma hasn't been able to unearth. For example, while it will never be outright explained why Hannah's mother is not in the picture, it will be hinted that she lost her mind and disappeared shortly before the movie is set. *It Happened to Hannah* is a horror movie to be sure, but it's rather disturbing on a psychological level as well. I honestly can't wait to see it. And to watch Colin battle some aliens.

Fake aliens. Not real ones. I will have no business with real ones.

I have no qualms, however, about visiting the Grand Canyon or camping out under the stars, both of which Colin and I have already scheduled for the days we know he won't be filming. Sadly, those days will be few and far between, but at least we'll still be together, even when he's working late.

As though Gemma has read my mind, she asks, "So what are you going to do all day while Colin's filming? Will you be allowed to bum around on set like you do here?"

"Doubt it." Honestly, I'm surprised Elizabeth and Carl have kept me around as long as they have.

"But if they know that you're Colin's girlfriend... you know, officially..."

"Then they probably won't want me hanging around and distracting him," I quip. "Besides, I'm still not sure how all that is going to work out yet."

"How what's going to work out?"

"The whole making the relationship public thing. I mean, do we tell people that Colin is dating Lorelei? Or Delaney? And if we tell them that he's dating Lorelei, what happens when I want to introduce him to my family and friends? The ones who don't know that Delaney and Lorelei are one in the same? Or what happens if, somewhere along the line, we decide to move in together? How do I explain that?"

Gemma looks like she's giving some serious thought to my predicament. Then she opens her mouth.

"I can't believe you haven't given yourself an ulcer yet."

I am not impressed.

"Really? That's all you've got?"

"What do you want me to say, Delaney? That this is going to be easy? News flash. It isn't. To be completely honest with you, I have no idea how you've managed to keep Lorelei a secret *this* long."

"Very carefully."

"Well, maybe it's time to give yourself a break and just let it go. I didn't want to tell you this, but I counted three gray hairs in your ponytail the other day."

"*What*?!"

"Relax, you can pluck them right out. I looked it up and it's not true what they say about five more growing in their place."

"Great. Thanks."

Gemma smiles and wraps an arm around my shoulder.

"I know you hate uncertainty. But just remember, you've got a lot of good things going for you. A lot of *amazing* things. Don't let your fear get in the way of what should have you dancing on the moon."

See? That's the advice I was actually looking for. But of course, thanks to Gemma's earlier observation, I'm going to be dwelling on those three gray hairs for the rest of the day.

Maybe even the rest of the week.

As it just so happens, the rest of the week flies by, and far more quickly than any of us had hoped it would. Of course, there will be reunions for post-production and what-not, but I doubt I'll be involved in any of that. My work here is done. My purpose is fulfilled.

I expected I'd be sad to hear Elizabeth calling out, "That's a wrap!" for the last time. And I am, a little, when the moment comes. But mostly, I feel a great sense of accomplishment, even euphoria. We've made something great, something that I think we're all very proud of. And Gemma was right. I have so much to look forward to.

Once everyone has begun to disperse, Colin takes me by the wrist and leans in to ask, "Will you meet me at my trailer?"

"When?"

"As soon as you can slip away."

Perhaps he hasn't noticed, but slipping away is my specialty. Unless he's expecting me to do so discreetly. Subtlety is *not* my specialty. Thankfully, the celebratory champagne-popping has already begun, so I'm fairly certain that no one will miss me. That includes Gemma, who has all but wrapped herself around Andrew in the middle of the grand staircase.

"Hey." I hate to interrupt them, but I need to at least tell *someone* that I'll be gone for a little while. It might as well be my fake personal assistant. "I'm running out for just a second. I'll be right back."

Gemma could not care less.

"Okay, bye."

Honestly, what would I do without her?

Stepping into the brisk Scottish evening, I pull my windbreaker tight and scamper behind the castle to the trailer lot. I pass by a few of the extras and crew members, but aside from a quick greeting, no one seems to wonder what I'm doing there. Until, of course, I pass Benjamin.

"And where are you off to, Miss Kimberly?" he teases.

"Forgot something!" I wink.

"Uh-huh. Right. Have fun!"

"I will!" My voice and Benjamin's laughter echo out into the twilight.

By the time I arrive at Colin's trailer, I'm shivering and breathless, but I'm also on a tremendous high.

I knock once before letting myself inside.

"Hey!" He calls to me from the bathroom where he's standing over the sink, splashing some water on his face. He's wearing a thin gray t-shirt and those really sexy jeans that fit him in just the right way. I love those jeans. "You escaped."

"I did."

Hastily, he dries his face with a washcloth and emerges from the bathroom. His hair is disheveled and he smells like fresh soap and winter mint. Without a word, he pulls me into his arms, but to my surprise, he doesn't kiss me. He just holds me. So I close my eyes and savor him.

"I don't want to keep you from the party too long, but I wanted one last chance to be alone with you before..." he trails off, pressing his forehead to mine. But I know what he's trying to say.

He wanted one last chance to tell me goodbye.

"I know," I whisper. "I still can't believe that this is it."

"This isn't it. This is just the beginning," he murmurs, pressing his lips to my temple.

I smile, knowing that what he says is true. This isn't goodbye. It's see you soon. And finally, finally, I lift my head up to look at him. Gazing into those gorgeous dark brown eyes, I think back to the day we met. My first day in Scotland. Back when I still dreamt of nights with Matthew Kent and couldn't begin to even fathom sharing my secrets with anyone. Yet, here we are, living in a beautiful and bizarre twist of fate. And I've never been more in love with life than I am in this moment.

For the record, I've never been more in love with Colin, either.

"Be with me?" I whisper. "One last time."

He responds with a kiss that tells me I didn't have to ask.

Our lovemaking lasts longer than we intended, but not nearly as long as either of us would have preferred. A part of me wishes we didn't have to go back, but I remind myself that Colin deserves this night with his castmates. And I want the opportunity to thank everyone for their hard work, their dedication, and for literally bringing my dreams to life.

We walk, hand in hand, back to the castle, but before we go inside, Colin pulls me into one final embrace. And then we open the door.

The energy in the air is electrifying. Someone has set up a sound system in the great hall and is blasting one of the summer's hottest hits. Chatter and laughter ring out, intermingling with the music, and here and there, I catch a snippet of conversation.

"... not what I was expecting at all..."

"... it's not uncommon, is it? I imagine there are a lot of them..."

"... remarkable. But he's so handsome. Who wouldn't..."

Of course, there's always one voice that rises up above the rest.

"Delaney!" My blood runs cold at the sound of my name. I turn, utterly bewildered, to see Benjamin strolling toward me, swigging beer and smirking. "In a million years, I don't think I ever would have guessed. Delaney Brooks."

"H - How did you...?"

"*There* they are!" Genevieve exclaims, sprinting over to where my feet seem to have permanently planted themselves. "Is it really true? Are you two..." She wiggles her fingers at Colin and me. "You know. *Courting*?"

That's when Benjamin completely loses it. Genevieve giggles as well. They're both tipsy. That's easy to see. But it brings me no comfort, no sense of peace.

And it certainly doesn't answer any of my questions.

"How do you know all this?" My heart is pounding so heavily I can barely get the words out.

"How do you think? Internet," Benjamin answers, holding up his phone. "Lookit. It says right here, *Romantic Revelations: Colin Ward is Dating Delaney -* "

I snatch the phone from his hand before he has the chance to finish.

Romantic Revelations: Colin Ward is Dating Delaney Brooks!

Wait a minute. Who?

Yeah, that's the question we asked ourselves, too.

Who is Delaney Brooks and how did she manage to snag the heart of a terminal bachelor like Colin Ward?

The answer? They met at work. More specifically, they met in Scotland, on the set of the miniseries that her novels inspired. See, reader? You have heard of Delaney Brooks. You've just known her all this time as Lorelei DuBois.

So why the secrecy?

According to unnamed sources, Ms. Brooks worried that a public romance with the much older Mr. Ward might smear her professional image and leave a stain on the public's reception of the new series.

"Even though Colin has cleaned up his act in recent years, he still has something of a reputation. Delaney didn't want to be associated with that, especially at this pivotal point in her career..."

I can't read anymore. My head is spinning. My stomach is turning. I'm feeling suffocated, crushed by the weight of every gaze in the great hall. Colin says something to me, but the rushing in my ears drowns him out. I can't breathe. I can't think. I'm fighting every impulse, every fear, every memory.

And I'm losing.

Liar.

Coward.

Easy.

Weak.

Stupid.

Slut.

And suddenly, my feet are flying before I've even made the decision to run.

Chapter Twenty-Eight

Meghan Shea: *Oh my God, did you guys hear about Delaney Brooks? Is this for real?*

Alyssa Nelson (Taylor): *Which part? The part about her writing dirty books or the part about her and Colin Ward?*

Becky Clark: *There's no way. I mean, I can almost believe the book thing. Everyone has their kinky secrets. But her and Colin Ward? Hell, no.*

Rita Gonzales: *I don't know. She always did set her sights awfully high.*

Alyssa Nelson (Taylor): *Please. She had a one-night stand with Tommy Riggs. So did half the other girls in school.*

Grace Keller: *If anything, I'd say that would indicate a lack of standards.*

Gabe Abrams: *Damn, Grace. That's harsh.*

Lisa Bateman: *I actually really love those books. But it's kind of weird to think about Delaney Brooks writing them.*

Gabe Abrams: *Fifty bucks says my boy* **Tommy Riggs** *inspired them.*

Meghan Shea: *Have you even read them?*

Gabe Abrams: *Hell, no. I don't read trash.*

Tommy Riggs: *I can't believe this is news. You guys seriously have nothing better to talk about?*

Gabe Abrams: *Hey man, you should be honored! You nailed her first. You were like her gateway drug to sex addiction.*

DeeAnna Mars: *Sweet, shy Delaney Brooks. And here I thought she was so wholesome.*

Derek Harkerson: *It's always the nice ones.*

I don't know why I'm doing this to myself. It doesn't make any sense. This is everything that I was hoping to avoid. Gossip. Scandal. Humiliation. Maybe I feel like if I confront it, then it has no power over me. Or maybe this is my own twisted way of torturing myself. Either way, thanks to social media, the entire world now has direct access to what my former classmates and acquaintances are saying about me. The conversation I'm reading now is a public status on Facebook. I'm tempted to leave a comment like, "You know there are ways to make these posts private, right?" But honestly, I'd really rather just go on pretending that I don't exist.

"Delaney? Sweetheart, do you want anything?" my mom asks, peeking her head inside my childhood bedroom.

I've been home for about three days now. And when I say home, I mean my parents' home. It was all my mother's idea. I wanted to go back to my own house and wallow in solitary self-pity, but she took one look at my face the night she picked me up from the airport and decided that I shouldn't be alone. Of course, she'd heard the news by then, as had all of our friends and relatives, who are still calling every other minute to squawk about why they didn't know and how we managed to keep it a secret and if they're invited to the big Hollywood wedding. Not that there's going to be a wedding. Ever.

So, here I am. Curled up in a sad little ball of old comforters and unwashed hair in the same bed where I cried my eyes out after that fateful Monday after Prom. Eleven years later and I've come the full circle. If that isn't a depressing thought, I don't know what is.

And it isn't even just my classmates. I like to think I wouldn't care what they think after more than a decade. But now it seems like the entire world is talking about me, my personal life, and my dirty secrets. There are theories, there are rumors, there are outright lies.

I'm using Colin for fame.

He's using me for headlines.

I'm pregnant.

He's married.

I'm a skank sleeping her way up the Hollywood hierarchy.

He's desperate to clean up his image, so he took me on as a charity case.

I'm a naïve little girl who still believes in fairy tales. I'd have to be... to truly think that I could trust him.

That's what hurts most of all. I *did* trust him. With my whole heart. That night in Scotland, he ran after me, but I never stopped. I ran until Gemma and Andrew came to find me. By then, Colin was already gone.

He's tried calling me at least a dozen times. I have yet to answer. He's texted me, swearing up and down that he never said a word. I can't bring myself to respond. Even if he's telling the truth, there's no way I could face him now. Not after everything that happened.

"I'm okay," I finally answer my mom. She doesn't seem at all convinced.

"You've barely eaten since you've been home."

"I'm not hungry."

"Okay, then." I expect her to turn around and leave. I *want* her to turn around and leave. But she doesn't. She marches right into my room and sits herself down on my bed. "Talk to me."

"There's nothing to - "

"No. I don't want to hear that," she interrupts me. "I know you have your secrets, Delaney. You've always been a private person, even when you were little. I've never told you this, but it actually used to hurt my feelings. You'd never admit it when something was bothering you. You didn't like asking for advice. You never wanted to talk about boys. But I never pushed you, because I wanted you to come to me.

And I always thought that you would, when you really needed me. I know now that I was wrong."

Her words sting. Not because I feel that I'm being picked on or that she's being unfair, but because she's absolutely right.

"I'm sorry," I whisper.

"I don't want you to be sorry. I want you to tell me why you're upset. You have everything going for you. Everything in the world. There's no reason to let a few headlines spoil that for you. Unless there's more to the story, and I think we both know that there is."

"You're going to think I'm being stupid..."

"Stop that. You're my daughter. I would never think that of you."

"I don't even know where to begin."

"You're a storyteller. How about the beginning?"

My story takes well over an hour to tell. By the time I've finished, my mother is looking at me precisely the way I hoped she wouldn't; like I'm a victim. Then again, if it looks like a duck and it quacks like a duck, then it's probably a duck. And right now, in my depressed and disheveled state, I'm looking and acting a lot like a victim. And a metaphorical duck.

"So you think that Colin betrayed you," Mom says.

"I don't know what to think," I admit. "I know it wasn't Gemma. But Colin was the only person I told."

"Is it possible that he told someone by accident? That it may have just slipped out?"

"I don't know."

"Well, here's what I think. And please, don't think I'm saying any of this to be insensitive. But I think you're letting yourself be defeated. Everything that happened was horrible, and I hate that you had to go through it. I hate it even more that you felt like you had to go through it alone. But look at your life now. Look at how far you've come, how much you've accomplished. And now, everybody knows."

"When you put it that way, it sounds like a good thing."

"It *is* a good thing. Let them see the life you've made for yourself. Let them see what a strong, intelligent, beautiful woman you've become. Let them see your success and most importantly, let them see your happiness. Show them that whatever they may have done to you in the past has no power over you now."

"That's a lot easier said than done."

"I know it is. But you've got to try. Otherwise, you're going to let one incident dictate your entire life. And your life, Delaney, is spectacular."

"Thank you, Mom."

She leans forward and kisses me on the forehead, something she hasn't done since I was a small child. Then it's back to business.

"Now, what are you going to do about Colin?"

That's a question with a million possible answers.

"I don't know."

"Well, if my two cents is worth anything at all, I think you owe it to yourself to talk to him. And if everything you've told me about him is true, then you owe it to him, also. Now," she says, rising up off the bed. "How about a pizza?"

"That sounds incredible." It really does. I'd almost forgotten how much I missed fast food.

While my mother steps out to place our order, I reach across my bed for my laptop. I think it's high time I took a break from social media. Before I can log out of my Facebook account, however, a new notification catches my eye; a message request from a Jillian Baxter.

Although her name is unfamiliar, I recognize the woman in the picture immediately. Eleven years hasn't changed her a bit. Of course, when I knew her, her last name wasn't Baxter. It was Seabury. Jillian Seabury. Homecoming queen, class president, captain of the cheerleading squad, and Tommy Riggs' jilted ex-girlfriend.

Hi Delaney,

How are you? I know it's been a while. I'm sorry that you weren't at the reunion last year. I would have loved to have seen you.

I know you have a lot going on right now. I'm not even sure you'll have time to read this. I just wanted to reach out and let you know that I'm sorry for all that you went through in those last few weeks of high school. You were always so sweet and you never did anything to deserve that.

I also need to confess something to you. I was the one who taped all those nasty notes and drawings inside your locker. I have no reason and no excuse, other than that I was bitter and jealous. Tommy and I had just broken up and I was miserable. I wanted you to be miserable too. It was wrong of me, and I had hoped I would have the opportunity to apologize to you in person. I guess this will have to do.

Please know that I wish all the best for you. I think everything you've accomplished is just amazing and I'm proud to have known you. I'm going to go out and buy your books now. I'm afraid I'm not very good at making time for reading, but maybe your books are just what I need to get back in the literary game.

Sincerely,
Jillian Baxter (Seabury)

For a few moments, I sit, blinking back tears, and staring at my computer screen. I don't know how to process what I'm feeling. This letter is the absolute last thing I expected, and frankly, it's everything I never wanted to accept. I've spent the last decade resenting my former classmates and rejecting the notion that anything good could possibly come from further contact with them. Yet now it seems as though a great weight has been lifted, and I'm feeling light-headed, almost giddy, with gratitude, appreciation, and a great sense of humility.

Who'd have thought one message was all it took?

I think I want to write her back. Actually, no. I'm eager to write her back, which is a little strange since I'm never particularly eager to talk to anyone.

Hi Jillian!

How are you? I hope that you're doing well. I see you got married. Congratulations!

Thank you so much for reaching out to me and for your kind words. Everything that you said, well, it was exactly what I needed to hear.

As for the notes, I -

Oh my God.

The note.

The one that I wrote that night in Dunadhar Castle.

I didn't just *tell* Colin my name. I wrote it down for him. And he kept it. At least, I'm pretty sure he did. And if that is, in fact, the case, then that piece of paper could very easily have fallen into the wrong hands. Say, for instance, the sneaky, slimy hands of a sneaky, slimy publicist.

And suddenly, I know. I know that Colin was telling me the truth. That he never said a word. That I *was* right to trust him.

That I was right to love him.

And now, I'm about to ruin everything, if I haven't already.

There's only one way to fix this.

I have to get to Arizona.

Chapter Twenty-Nine

"You know, when I asked for your help, I was thinking maybe you'd be able to get me an address or put me in touch with one of the producers. I didn't mean for you to drop everything and fly down to Arizona with me."

"Dear Kimberly, I think you know me well enough by now to know that I'm always up for an adventure," Benjamin says.

"So, I'm still Kimberly? Even though you know my real name now?"

"Kimberly suits you."

We're about thirty minutes into our two-hour road trip from Phoenix to Sedona and for once, Benjamin is navigating while I drive. He claims that although he's lived in Los Angeles on and off for years now, he can't get used to driving on the "wrong" side of the road.

"So, explain to me again why we're doing this," Benjamin says.

"What are you talking about? You know why."

"I know that you want to talk to him. But why couldn't you just call or drop him a text? You are aware that cellular phones are all the rage now."

"It would be easier," I admit. "But something this important... I don't know. I feel like a phone call wouldn't be enough. I need to see him."

"Ah. Of course. I understand. Just like Cinderella venturing back to the castle to claim her Prince." It's nice to know that even out here on the Arizona Interstate, Benjamin is still the same old Benjamin.

"Sure. Something like that."

"Does that make me your Fairy Godmother?"

"If you were really my Fairy Godmother, you would be driving."

"Hey, I chauffeured you around an entire country."

"Okay, that country isn't even half the size of this one state. This one tiny state!"

"I thought Arizona was one of the larger states."

"Everything is tiny compared to Texas." Except Alaska. But we don't talk about Alaska.

"Admit it. You loved Scotland."

I smile. I couldn't even pretend to deny it.

"With every fiber of my being."

"Think you'll go back one day?"

"Without a single doubt."

Benjamin grins and glances out the open window. Out of the corner of my eye, I notice him squinting in the sunlight and his unruly ginger hair whipping wildly in the wind. I realize he hasn't asked once about Gemma, and I'm hesitant to bring her up. If you can believe it, she's been in constant communication with Andrew since we left Scotland. She's already talking about flying back to visit him next month. Whether or not that will actually happen remains to be seen. I've known Gemma long enough now to know that I'll never be able to predict her next move.

Though to be fair, she probably wouldn't have predicted that I'd make this one.

As though he's read my thoughts, Benjamin asks, "So does Gemma know that we're embarking on this strange and perilous voyage across the Arizonian desert?"

"No, actually."

"Really? I thought you told each other everything."

"We do. I just didn't want to tell too many people about this just in case... Well..."

"In case it doesn't work out?"

"Precisely."

"I don't think you need to worry about that," Benjamin smirks.

"Really?"

"Colin Ward is crazy about you. In fact... No. I shouldn't mention it."

"What?"

"It's nothing."

"Benjamin, we've still got a seventy-five-minute drive ahead of us. Please don't make me torture you."

"Okay, fine." He sighs. Like he wasn't going to tell me anyway. "Colin actually asked me to fly over and find you."

"What?"

"He wanted to come see you himself. He tried to get away from the movie, but he'd already signed the contract. And I don't think I have to explain to you just how binding and soul-sucking those can be." No, he doesn't. "Can't wait to see the look on his face when he realizes I went above and beyond the call of duty and actually delivered you to him."

"Again, if you were the one doing the delivering, you'd be driving."

"Technicalities."

By the time we finally arrive in Sedona, dusk has fallen and the sky is beginning to twinkle with early evening stars.

"All right, according to the schedule, they're filming at the house tonight," Benjamin announces, scrolling through his phone.

"How did you get their filming schedule?"

"I may have dated a girl who knows the location manager."

Of course.

"She isn't holding a Rose-like grudge against you, is she?"

"Not at all. She dumped me for the woman who became her wife."

Oh. Good to know.

I follow Benjamin's directions to a cul-de-sac in a quiet neighborhood of modest houses. It certainly doesn't look like the kind of place you'd expect to find a Hollywood film crew. In fact, if I hadn't known to look for the movie's working trucks, I might have missed them entirely.

We park one street over and walk the short distance to the house, where a small crowd of onlookers has gathered to watch the production, meet with the crew, and perhaps even catch a glimpse of one of the stars. I also notice a police officer standing guard.

And suddenly, I'm thinking this entire journey was a huge waste of time.

"This is crazy. They're not even going to let us get close to him," I mutter.

"Relax, Darling. That's why you've got me."

What does that mean? That he thinks he can just stroll up to the officer, introduce himself, and waltz right on through the blockade? It can't possibly be that easy.

But sure enough, it's entirely that easy. Benjamin strolls up to the officer, introduces himself, and waltzes right on through the blockade. True, he pauses briefly to pose for selfies with fans and to sign the back of one woman's gasoline receipt, but once he's done that, he takes my arm and pulls me past the barricade.

"Come along, Kimberly."

"Is this really how Hollywood works? When you're famous, you can just drop in wherever you want, whenever you want?" I ask him.

"More or less," he answers with a shrug.

Fascinating.

Quietly, we slip into the house, which is crammed with lights, wires, cameras, and so many people, I have to wonder how they expect to shoot a scene without accidentally catching someone's leg or ponytail on film.

Making our way further into the house, passing crew members and producers who greet Benjamin like a long-lost friend, I can feel my heart beginning to race. What if Benjamin was wrong? What if Colin really doesn't want to see me? What do I say to him?

I don't have to wonder very long.

I catch sight of him in the open den, though to be honest, I almost didn't recognize him. He's completely clean-shaven now and his hair is styled to fall across his forehead and into his eyes. He's dressed in brown pants and a pale blue button-down shirt. He's even wearing wire-rimmed glasses.

They're between takes right now. Colin is standing with his hands on his hips, bent over a script and in deep discussion with a man who must be the director. He looks so serious and so handsome. I'm tempted to step back outside so I don't disturb him. I can talk to him once they've wrapped for the night.

But I'm too late. He glances up as soon as he feels my gaze.

At first, he seems too stunned to react. That half a second after our eyes meet lasts an entire lifetime. But then he's stepping away from his director without a word or backward glance. He's crossing the room, maneuvering his way around curious crew members. All the while, he never looks away. Not until the last moment when, in one swift, fluid motion, he sweeps me up in a tender embrace and presses his mouth to mine without the slightest hint of confusion or hesitation or anger.

"I love you," I tell him. "I know this isn't the time or the place, and I know that you're working right now. I just really needed to tell you - "

But Colin cuts me off with another kiss before I get a chance to finish.

Afterwards, he finally turns back to look at his director.

"Hey, Jim? Do you mind if we step outside for a second?"

The director just smiles.

"Yeah, go on. Ten minutes, everyone!"

Colin takes my hand and guides me through the house to the blissfully vacant backyard. Night has finally fallen and a thousand galaxies glitter in the dark sky above us. I see those same stars in Colin's eyes as we stand face to face.

"I hope I didn't just get you in trouble," I tell him.

"Nah. Jim's a good guy. And he knows... well... he knows what's been going on."

"God, Colin, I am so sorry."

"Delaney, why?"

"For everything. For running out on you and for ghosting you and especially for not trusting you. You deserve so much better than that. So much more than that."

"I deserve nothing of the sort. If anything, I'm the one who should apologize for not trusting you."

"What?" That makes no sense at all. "What are you talking about?"

"I thought Benjamin told you. Isn't... Isn't that why you're here?"

"Benjamin never told me anything except that you asked him to find me. He's here, by the way. Somewhere." Probably flirting with one of the tech girls.

"So, you don't know."

"Know what?"

"That you were right about Geoff. He was the one who went to the media. He leaked everything, including your name. I don't know how or when, but he overheard a conversation that you had with Rose. After that, he managed to get ahold of the note you wrote me. The one with your name on it. When I found out, I fired him on the spot. I'm just so sorry that I let him hurt you. Because believe me, Delaney, that is the last thing I ever wanted."

"I know," I assure him, reaching up to stroke his face. "And it's okay. Really. As strange as it seems to say, this has actually been good for me."

"Yeah?"

"Yeah. I'm just sorry that *I* hurt *you* in the process."

"Enough of that. No more apologies. As far as I'm concerned, there is nothing to forgive." And to prove it, he pulls me into a kiss that shatters the remains of my once broken heart and restores it to something strong and brave and beautiful. And loved. So, so very loved.

"I guess I should let you get back to work," I whisper, though that is the exact opposite of what I want to do.

"You'll stick around, won't you? We have one more scene to shoot tonight. I don't know how long it will take, but - "

This time, it's my turn to silence him with a kiss.

"I'm not going anywhere," I promise.

It's a promise I intend to keep. I'm not going anywhere. Not tonight. Not tomorrow. Not for the rest of our lives.

Excerpt from *The Surrogate's Affair*

The night is unforgiving.

The wind howls and tree branches crack and scrape and whip as our carriage hastens through the dark and haunting forest.

All the while, my pains are worsening. I know the sensation all too well. It won't be long now.

"It's all right, my darling. Hold on. Hold on." Tristan tries to soothe me, but to no avail. I stifle a scream as my entire being writhes in excruciating agony.

This cannot be. I cannot have this baby now. Not here. Not in these dreadful woods, in the company of wolves and ruffians and creatures known only to God Himself. This baby deserves so much more. She should have been a Princess, raised in a splendid castle, beloved by her sister and her subjects and most of all, her parents. Her King. And her Queen. Oh, God save her.

Now, who can say what sort of life awaits her as the daughter of runaways? A childhood in the shadows? An education in deceit?

As yet another blinding ache seizes my body, I know I have not the time to mourn for what might be or what might have been. She's coming. Soon, she will be my entire life.

"Pull over!" Tristan yells at our driver. He obeys.

"Tristan... Tristan..." I moan.

"I'm here, Love," he assures me.

"She's... I think... I..."

"Shh. It's okay. I'm going to help you. Don't talk. Just breathe. Just breathe."

And then, in one final burst of unfathomable pain, she's here. My baby is here, alive and healthy. But not a girl. Not a Princess.

A Prince.

Malcolm's son and heir to the throne of a Kingdom that will never know he exists.

"He's beautiful," Tristan whispers, kissing my damp forehead.

He is. Of that, at least, I can be certain. The child in my arms is the most beautiful sight my eyes have ever beheld. And though my mind is still plagued by fear and doubt, this tiny infant fills my heart with a renewed sense of hope. Hope and determination.

I don't know what waits for my son out in the world, but I do know that the world is already a better place because he lives.

Epilogue

Okay, Delaney. You can do this.

Smile. Be confident. And don't trip. For the love of God, please don't trip.

Honestly, if I can make it through today without tripping, it will be a miracle. Especially in these shoes. And this dress.

I don't think I would be quite so nervous if Colin were here with me, but he wanted me to arrive at my first red carpet premiere on my own.

"You need that experience," he insisted to me just last night. "You need to know what it's like to step out onto that carpet and to have every eye on you. To soak up the spotlight. To feel the world spin at your feet."

The idea is rather romantic, or at least he made it seem so in the early hours of the morning as he explained his reasoning to me through a mess of tangled hotel sheets. Of course, anything sounds romantic whispered in the afterglow of amazing sex.

But now, staring out the tinted window of a stretch limousine at the hordes of fans and reporters, waving and cheering and reaching out to the closest stars, I'm beginning to regret everything that has led to this moment. I'm especially regretting these stiletto heels that Gemma picked out for me. I wonder if anyone would notice if I went barefoot...

Just then, the door opens and a middle-aged man in a tuxedo is smiling down at me and holding out his hand.

"Ms. Brooks?"

That's you.

With a deep breath, I take his hand, return his smile, and step out into the afternoon sunlight. The roar of the crowd is deafening and I'm momentarily overwhelmed by the energy and chaos surrounding me. But then, slowly but surely, my senses begin to adjust and the fog begins to lift. Colors take shape to form the faces and figures of people I know and love. Voices blend together to form a chorus of encouragement and enthusiasm. My feet are steady on the ground and ready to move forward.

"Lorelei!"

"Lorelei!"

"Delaney!"

I turn my head at the sound of my name and it's only then that I notice that several of the fans are carrying books. My books.

"Need a pen?" A cheeky voice murmurs in my ear, making me jump. I look up to see Benjamin, dapper and dashing as ever in a dark blue suit, grinning down at me and holding up a fine point Sharpie.

"Thank you, Fairy Godmother," I laugh, taking the pen.

"Don't mention it," he winks.

Colin was right. This is unlike anything I've ever experienced. True, I've had dozens of book signings before, but never in a slinky golden gown, and certainly never on a red carpet surrounded by movie stars.

And never as Delaney Brooks.

I sign as many books as I can reach, and then some. I stop to pose for selfies and to try to answer any questions that the fans may have. It's difficult with so much going on around me, with so many people, with so little time. But I try. And I think, for the most part, I succeed.

Stepping back into the middle of the carpet, I finally see Colin. He's standing a few yards in front of me, posing for a group photo with Matthew, Rose, Genevieve, and Benjamin. My five beautiful leads. My five incredible dream makers.

And then I catch his eye and my dreams come true all over again.

He doesn't say anything as he makes his way over to me. He just slips one casual hand around my waist and pulls me into a kiss that will probably end up on *People.com*.

And you know what? I'm totally okay with that.

"You are radiant," he tells me.

"Thank you," I grin. "You don't look too bad yourself."

Actually, he looks ridiculously sexy in charcoal gray pants and a black button-down shirt. His hair is a bit longer now than when we first met, but he'll be cutting it again soon for a role in a new independent film. We're heading to British Columbia in just a few short days for the shoot and I can hardly wait to put the finishing touches on my new book surrounded by lakes and trees and mountains.

"Delaney! Ms. Brooks! May we have a word?" one reporter calls out to me.

I feel Colin's hand on my back, giving me just the slightest push.

"Come with me?" I ask him. But he shakes his head.

"I wouldn't dream of it. This is your moment." Then he presses his lips to my ear and reminds me yet again, "I love you."

"I love you, too."

And so, with one last smile, one last kiss, one last look at the reassuring smile on his handsome face, I step away from him, out of the shadow of the studio's backdrop, and into the bright and blazing sun.

Acknowledgements

Thank you, as always, to my God, my Lord and my Savior for this life and all its wonders.

Thank you to my parents, David and Susan, who have supported me and believed in me since the very beginning.

Thank you to my sister, KJ, my best friend and my twin soul. Thank you for fangirling with me.

Thank you to my dear and wonderful editor, Hannah, for your constant support and friendship. I don't know what I would do without you.

Thank you to my beloved friends, Jessica, Aïda, Kara, Kat, and Rachel, for putting up with me through thick and thin.

Thank you to the nurses, doctors, and staff of Animal Medical Center for taking such good care of my sweet Midnight.

Thank you to my colleagues, my fellow writers, including but not limited to James William Peercy (*The Wall Outside*) and his amanuensis, Claudette, Miracle Austin (*Boundless*), Terri R. Malek (*My Path to Omega*), Cody Wagner (*The Gay Teen's Guide to Defeating a Siren*), April L. Wood (*Winter's Curse*), Kendra L. Saunders (*Dating an Alien Popstar*), Sarah MacTavish (*Firebrand*), Susie Clevenger (*Where Butterflies Pray*) and her husband, Charlie, and so, so, so many others! Thank you for your guiding light and your love!

And thank you, most especially, to you, the reader. I wish I could adequately express what your love and your friendship mean to me. Thank you to all the friends that I've made, near and far. You all literally mean the world to me.

Image Courtesy of Fervent Images.
https://www.timmalek.com

Jacqueline E. Smith is the author of the *Cemetery Tours* series and the *Boy Band* series. She was born and raised in Dallas, Texas. She attended the University of Texas at Dallas, where she earned her Bachelor's Degree in Art and Performance in 2010. Two years later, she earned her Master's Degree in Humanities. Along with writing and publishing, Jacqueline loves photography, traveling, and nature.

25392301R00226

Made in the USA
Columbia, SC
03 September 2018